Oh my God, was Laurel's only thought as Joe leaned toward her and kissed her.

The contact zinged to every nerve ending in her body, but she gave him what she hoped was a composed look. "What was that for?"

He shook his head when their eyes met. "I'm not sure. I just felt like doing it."

"Uh-huh." She nodded slowly. "I suppose I should be glad you didn't just feel like grabbing my breast."

He laughed. "Maybe I just wanted to see what you'd do."

"*Ha!* I know what you were doing," she said. "You were trying to show me that I'm still susceptible to that kind of thing."

His look was sly. "And were you suscepted?"

She laughed. "That's not even a word. And surely you know me better than that by now."

But he didn't laugh with her. "I'm starting to."

She wondered then, if she'd hurt his feelings somehow. Had the kiss been a real gesture? Had he been . . . hoping for more?

ATTENTION: ORGANIZATIONS AND CORPORATIONS
Most Avon Books paperbacks are available at special quantity discounts for bulk purchases for sales promotions, premiums, or fund-raising. For information, please call or write:

Special Markets Department, HarperCollins Publishers, Inc., 10 East 53rd Street, New York, N.Y. 10022–5299.
Telephone: (212) 207–7528. Fax: (212) 207-7222.

ELAINE FOX

Hot Stuff

AVON BOOKS
An Imprint of HarperCollinsPublishers

This is a work of fiction. Names, characters, places, and incidents are products of the author's imagination or are used fictitiously and are not to be construed as real. Any resemblance to actual events, locales, organizations, or persons, living or dead, is entirely coincidental.

AVON BOOKS
An Imprint of HarperCollins*Publishers*
10 East 53rd Street
New York, New York 10022-5299

Copyright © 2004 by Elaine McShulskis
ISBN: 0-06-051724-7
www.avonromance.com

First Avon Books paperback printing: April 2004

Avon Trademark Reg. U.S. Pat. Off. and in Other Countries, Marca Registrada, Hecho en U.S.A.
HarperCollins® is a registered trademark of HarperCollins Publishers Inc.

Printed in the U.S.A.

10 9 8 7 6 5 4 3 2 1

For Mary McMakin.
Oh, the stories we could tell . . .

One

"*So?*" Laurel Kane's coworker, Angela, looked at her expectantly.

They were standing on the Metro escalator, rising from the warm depths of the Dupont Circle Station into the frigid air of Connecticut Avenue.

A chill wind whipped them both in the face as they emerged. An effective wake-up early on this January morning in downtown Washington, D.C.

" 'So'?" Laurel repeated. "What?"

"So, how did it go this weekend?" Angela flipped the collar of her coat up around her ears, squishing brown, shoulder-length curls against cheeks pink with cold.

Laurel wrapped her gloved fingers around the ChapStick in her coat pocket and squeezed. She had hoped to avoid this topic, at least until she'd gotten into the office and had some coffee, but here she was, not even technically out of the Metro station, having to relive the awful scene. "Not very well."

"You didn't tell him? Or you did and it didn't go well?"

"Oh I told him. And no, it didn't go well." Laurel hunched into her coat as they approached the hot-dog vendor a block away from their office. It was early for hot dogs—just after 8 A.M.—but someone was standing by the cart. Someone with even worse eating habits than Laurel's, apparently.

She pondered how hard it would be to get a hot dog down first thing in the morning.

Angela gasped. "Laurel, look!"

Laurel wheeled to glance at her, then looked where she was pointing, expecting to see an oncoming bus or a mugging, or something other than the hot-dog vendor.

"Coffee!" Angela cried. "It's a coffee cart! I was just thinking I'd *kill* for a cup of coffee."

"Jeez, Angela." Laurel put a hand to her chest as her heart labored to return to its normal rhythm. "I don't even *need* coffee now. You scared me to death. I thought you'd at least spotted Elvis."

But Angela wasn't listening. She was racing down the sidewalk, teetering on the stiletto-heeled pumps she favored, toward what had been, until today, the hot-dog vendor.

Despite being more comfortably shod than her friend (she wore flats with everything, fashion be damned), Laurel arrived a minute or so after her friend, only to see that the greasy, vaguely hostile balding man who sold meat products of questionable origin was now a youngish, rumpled-looking guy of indeterminate age. (Could be twenty. Could be forty. It all depended on what was under that army green ear-flapped hat and maroon scarf. Both of which suggested sixty.)

And it was true, he was selling coffee. The nectar of the gods.

Across the front of his cart was an orange-and-black logo, suggestive of Halloween, that said HOT STUFF.

Laurel had to admit, seeing coffee on this corner after years of smelling grilled fat every time she walked out of her office cheered her. Unbridled coffee consumption was one of her favorite vices.

Angela was ordering a cappuccino when Laurel caught up to her. "Skim milk, vanilla flavoring if you've got it, no sugar and just a single shake of chocolate on the froth." With her cute pixie smile—she was Irish through and through—Angela beamed with open interest at the side of the coffee vendor's face.

"I'll let you shake your own." Without even a glance in her direction, the vendor indicated with a fingerless-gloved hand a line of flavorings, sugars, cream and stirrers along the edge of the cart.

Angela giggled as if he'd said something provocative. Angela would flirt with the Pope if he had more hair.

"God, I *love* this. Don't you, Laurel?" she enthused, her cheeks even pinker than they'd been in the wind. "I'm going to be down here five times a day."

"What happened to Frank?" Laurel asked the vendor.

He didn't look up as he snapped a metal part filled with ground coffee onto the machine. "Who?"

"The hot-dog man. Frank. Who used to be here."

The guy glanced at Laurel. What she could see of his expression—narrowed, lightish eyes—seemed to be lit with amusement. "The hot-dog man's name was *Frank*?"

It took her a moment to realize what he meant, and once she did, she blushed. In the three years she'd worked here, walked by, occasionally bought from and talked to the hot-dog vendor, the irony of his being named Frank had never occurred to her.

She immediately wondered if she'd just assumed his name was Frank because the front of his cart had said FRANK'S. It could easily have meant FRANKS.

See the confusion a misplaced apostrophe can create? she thought.

"I hope he's gone for good," Angela said. "I

hate hot dogs. Please tell me you're a permanent replacement."

"Permanent's a relative thing," Coffee Guy said, Buddha-like.

"God Laurel, think of it." Angela breathed the words like Marilyn Monroe. "Caffeine, just steps away. We'll get so much more done!"

Laurel glanced again at the guy behind the cart. In addition to the hat, his scarf was bunched over the bottom half of his face as he watched the milk steam in the little chrome pot he held, but the outer line of one eyebrow swept the corner of an eye lined with shallow crow's feet. Not old, she thought, but not a college kid.

"So what's your name?" Angela asked.

Though Angela had asked the question, Coffee Guy shot Laurel a sly look. "Joe."

"Well, nice to meet you, Joe." Angela held out her hand.

Laurel scoffed. "His name isn't Joe."

Angela looked at her. "What do you mean? He just said it was."

"Joe" handed Angela her coffee and she took it like a supplicant at the altar of consciousness. "Mmmmm."

"Anything for you?" He lifted a brow. "Laurel?"

It startled her, his knowing her name, but then she quickly realized Angela had just said it several times.

"Yes *Joe*, I'd like a tall latte." She shifted her

gaze to Angela, who cradled her cup and blew on it as if bestowing kisses on a newborn.

"Whole milk, no flavor. Raw sugar. Right?" His voice was low and smooth, like a deep dark cup of espresso.

She turned back to him. He'd gotten it exactly right. She supposed he was trying to make her feel predictable. Unoriginal. And he succeeded. Then she felt spineless for caring at all what the coffee guy thought.

"Yes. Thanks." She picked up a couple bags of raw sugar and a wooden stirrer, shaking the little bags in preparation.

"So you were saying." Angela turned to Laurel, finally finished with her ablutions. "It was awful. Your weekend. Did he cry?"

Laurel winced at the question and turned her eyes to the coffee guy's hands. Clean fingernails, she noted. Another improvement over the hot-dog vendor.

"As a matter of fact," she said with as much detachment as she could muster, "he did cry. That's how awful it was. I felt like the worst sort of shit."

The fingerless gloves manipulated the espresso machine with quick, sharp motions.

"You're joking." Angela lowered the cup from her face and gaped at her.

"I wish I were." Laurel put the sugar down on the edge of the cart and shoved her hands into her pockets, shivering against the cold wind. Her fingers clutched the ChapStick again.

"Lemme get this straight. You made Ethan Connelly cry?"

Laurel glanced uneasily at the two people in line behind Angela. "Keep your voice down. People might know him."

Angela was shaking her head. "I can't believe it. He's just—he seems so in control all the time."

"He *is*." Which was part of the problem. Laurel swallowed over a lump of guilt in her throat. "I guess I just took him by surprise."

"I'll say." Angela sipped her cappuccino. "Wow."

Coffee Guy finished with her drink and Laurel handed him a ten. He pulled a wad of bills from his pocket and dropped some singles and some change in her palm. She looked around.

"What, no tip jar, *Joe*?" She cocked her head at him.

The eyes above the scarf met hers and while she noted they were a lovely shade of light green, she could also swear they were smirking. "Nope."

"Well, here." She held out some change but he shook his head. She laughed. "No tipping? This coffee cart's getting better all the time."

He inclined his head. "We aim to please. Here's a tip for you, though." This time she *knew* the eyes were smirking. "Give up on the sensitive guys."

"I beg your pardon?"

"His name should have been your first clue. *Ethan*? Come on. You should have known he was a crybaby." One corner of his mouth curved upward where his scarf drooped.

"He isn't a *crybaby*. He happens to be a very successful—"

"Yeah, yeah, whatever. Women all *say* they want sensitive men," he continued. "Then when they get one, they can't stand it. He wasn't strong enough. He was too needy." His voice rose to a Minnie-Mouse falsetto, then returned to a cynical bass. "Stick with the macho types, honey. That's my advice."

She gave him a disbelieving laugh. "Thanks, but I wasn't actually looking for advice."

"Don't kid yourself, Laurel. People are always looking for advice." He shrugged. "But you can take it or leave it. Next?" He jutted his chin toward the woman behind Angela. "What can I get you?"

"Think I'll leave it, thanks," Laurel murmured, though he wasn't listening. He was winking at the woman in the fur coat behind them who ordered a triple-shot latte.

She and Angela walked off.

"Can you believe that guy?" Laurel asked.

"That guy?" Angela said. "I can't believe you made *Ethan Connelly* cry."

An hour later Rulinda Mason swept into Laurel's office on a cloud of Chanel No. 5, gauzy skirt flying out behind her slender body like a trail of cosmic dust.

Laurel had smelled her coming. Unfortunately it was too late to run.

Rulinda was Laurel's boss, publisher and founder of *DC Scene*, the weekly tabloid for which she worked. Rulinda was a relentless go-getter who prided herself on actually living the trendy lifestyle their magazine promoted, though none of the staff knew what kind of personal life she had beyond what she chose to brag about—usually an appearance at some theatrical opening or a party at Mr. Very-Important-Senator's house.

The ironic thing was, Rulinda was the polar opposite of most of D.C. society. She was flamboyant and offbeat, believed in astrology, had her tarot cards read weekly, and claimed to be the victim of an overabundance of cosmic energy. She spoke her mind to whomever she was with, and her mind was frequently on a plane—i.e., astral—not often visited by many lawyers, senators, congressmen or lobbyists. The fact that she actually was included in so many upscale social events led Laurel to suspect that she was invited along as an oddity, someone to give the stodgy, conservative, political people something to talk about that wasn't administrative.

According to Rulinda, her parents couldn't decide between the names "Ruth" and "Linda," so she wound up with both. According to her birth certificate—which a disgruntled former assistant had dug up and shared with the rest of the staff—her name had started out as "Ruth Linda Martin," only to morph into "Rulinda Mason" about the time she started the newspaper.

"Laurel, dear," she said in her intermittent British-esque accent, "I've got something I want you to include in the February Two issue. It'll be perfect to coincide with Valentine's Day."

Laurel's brows rose in automatic politeness, while her mind inquired with much less tact, *What the hell is it now? February Two* meant the second week of February in Rulinda's weekly-tabloid-speak.

"But—"

"Dr. Cornelius Nadalov." Rulinda announced the name with arms outstretched and a broad, assured smile.

Laurel worked to find an appropriate expression but, having never heard of Dr. Cornelius Nadalov, she wasn't sure what that might be. She stuck with her raised-brow politeness. "Oh?"

"Author of *Love Is Not the Answer*."

Laurel leaned forward, elbows on her desk, and took a long time shifting in her seat. She gazed at her blotter, pushing aside some papers to see the calendar underneath. "That sounds, ah, good, Rulinda, but actually we've got a Valentine's article. Stephanie Porter is doing one on using the monuments for a romantic outing."

"Can it." Rulinda dropped the accent for this bit of direction.

"Well, but—"

Rulinda waved a hand. "Put it in three."

"Yes, but, we'll have missed Val—"

"I don't care. Save it for next year." She flounced into the chair across the desk from Laurel. "This is big. This is *huge*. You've heard of his book, of course."

"*Love Is Not the Answer*?" Laurel felt stupid even saying the name.

"It's climbing all the bestseller lists, and he's even scheduled for *Oprah*." She said the name reverentially.

Rulinda loved Oprah, whom she claimed was a personal friend, and had been promising the staff an interview with the daytime doyenne for about the last five years. In Laurel's opinion, the chances of that were as slim as the chances of getting an interview with Colin Powell, who was another "close personal friend" of Rulinda's who probably wouldn't be caught dead in a publication with such third-rate circulation.

"What's the book about?" Laurel made a reluctant line through Stephanie Porter's name on her blotter.

Rulinda laughed. "Oh my *dear*! I can't believe you haven't heard of this book. *You* of all people! You have to read it. It's written *especially for* people like you."

Laurel's eyes narrowed. People who hated their jobs? Who didn't respect their bosses? Who wished they were writing for *Time* instead of *DC Scene*?

"People who . . . ?" Laurel prompted.

"Who haven't found Mr. Right. Who've

scoured all of D.C., Virginia and Maryland, and *still* haven't gotten married. Older singles who are wondering what to do with their lives—their *personal* lives," she emphasized, as if anything else might be insulting.

Laurel felt herself flush hot. "I see."

"Wait. Hold on." She leaned across Laurel's desk and picked up the phone, punching four numbers with her index finger, the only one without a carmine-red talon and that only because she'd filed it so hard it broke during yesterday's art/ed meeting.

"Mitchell," she barked into the phone. "Get that book off my desk and bring it to me in Laurel's office." She hesitated, rolled her eyes. "The book about love. It's the only one on the desk."

It was probably the only book in the entire office.

"You can have my copy," Rulinda said. "Read it, Laurel. Seriously. That's an order. It'll do you good. And pick a chapter to excerpt because they've approached us about it and I think it's a *fabulous* idea."

"It doesn't sound very romantic," Laurel hedged. "You know, for Valentine's Day. I mean, *Love Is Not the Answer*, what does that mean? Give up? Look for something else? Grow old alone?"

Rulinda smiled benignly. "Just read it, dear." She was back to her British accent. "It's you. You'll want to live by it. Trust me."

A moment later, Mitchell arrived in Laurel's

office with a book entitled *Your Sexual Sun Sign Planner*, which he claimed was open on her desk. After verbally flogging him for several long minutes—causing the slightly built Mitchell's head to bow lower with every word under Rulinda's superior height, weight and volume—Rulinda stalked back to her office. Moments later a cowering Mitchell returned with the recommended tome.

"Thanks," Laurel said, looking at Mitchell with pity. She wondered why in the world he stayed in his job. He was abused by Rulinda daily, even though everyone in the office knew she would be cosmic energy run amok without his attention to detail and organizational skills.

"No problem," he said. His thin shoulders almost made hanger points in the shoulders of his pale blue shirt. "I don't know why she's so gung-ho on this book. I think it's crap."

Her brows rose. "You've read it?"

He tipped his head. "I glanced through it."

"What's crappy about it?"

"The guy doesn't have a romantic bone in his body." The moment the words were out of his mouth, Laurel noted two bright patches of red on Mitchell's cheeks.

How did this delicate fellow survive in Rulinda's shadow every day?

"Well," Laurel said with a companionable smile, "neither do I."

He was stepping out of her office when she called him back.

"Yes?" Typical of Mitchell, his eyes met hers for a split second, then darted away.

"If you read this book, surely you knew what 'book on love' Rulinda meant when she asked you to bring it."

Mitchell's head was bowed, but his eyes darted back up to hers for a second. Stunned, Laurel saw him smile.

"Well . . . ," he said, scuffing one shy toe on the ground. "I figure if she's going to blow her top at me five times a day, I might as well pick when and what for."

Laurel burst into laughter and Mitchell, with—she could swear—a devilish grin, left her office.

"Listen to this." Laurel stopped at the corner of Connecticut and Q and opened the book in gloved hands. Her breath fogged in the winter air.

Angela turned to look at her, shoving her hands in her coat pockets. Without planning or even thinking much about it, for the last two years Angela and Laurel met nearly every morning at the Metro Center Station and ended up riding in together.

" 'The imperative to 'love,' " Laurel read, "and he has *love* in quotes here. 'Is easily explained by the biological need to procreate. While simple sexual urges might be the only thing needed to compel the male and female to mate, the chemical process we call "love" is required to ensure that any offspring are taken care of. Further proof of this is the average span of the typical "love" relationship—seven years. About the time it would take for a child to be old enough to keep up with the tribe.' "

Laurel raised her eyes to Angela, who was gazing down the street.

"Is that not *incredible*?" Laurel demanded, laughing. "She wants to run this for Valentine's Day. Is she *crazy*?"

Angela looked at Laurel. "The author's a woman?"

"No, Rulinda! She wants to run an excerpt of this in the paper February Two. I mean, for God's sake, have you ever heard anything *less* romantic in your life?" She laughed again, shaking her head. "Though I have to say, the man's got a point or two."

"Maybe she's hoping for a romantic backlash." Angela started walking again.

Laurel followed. "Yeah, right. Well, it's good news for you, Angela. Since you're still in your twenties you're still susceptible to the kind of love that would lead to that coveted seven-year relationship."

Angela's stride was purposeful. "What has age got to do with it?"

"Here, I'll read it to you. Hang on a second."

Angela stopped slowly. "Can't we just make it to the coffee cart? I'm freezing and barely awake."

Laurel looked up. "Oh, sure."

They marched down the last block to the coffee cart, in front of which was a substantial line.

"We're going to be late," Laurel said. "Jim wanted to talk about the restaurant reviews. He says they're the main reason people buy the paper and he wants to put them on the front page. Nothing like making sure people don't look at the rest of the paper."

She flipped through the book, looking for the part that would concern Angela.

"Oh good, he's here." Angela's voice held such a note of relief that Laurel followed her gaze to the figure manning the cart.

Her lips curved slowly and she directed a knowing look at her friend. "Oh, I get it. Got a little crush on the coffee vendor, have we? Well, Dr. Nadalov would say that's just your ovulatory hormones making you think he's virile enough to impregnate you and strong enough to protect you and your young."

Angela glanced back with a coy smile. "He can protect me any day. He's cute. And he's fun to talk to. You should read him some of that book."

Laurel snorted. "He'd probably agree with every word. Nothing pleases men like hearing they're not built to be monogamous."

They got in line. "Does it say *that?*"

"You bet." She opened the book and flipped through the pages once again. "And this is only in the first two chapters."

Angela leaned toward her and spoke in a low voice. "You're in luck. Jim's in line, too."

Laurel looked up, but instead of scanning for

Jim—who was indeed in the middle of the line—her gaze landed on the coffee vendor's and held. His light green eyes didn't waver, despite the movement of his hands on the machinery in front of him and for a second she was unsure what to do. Smile? Nod? Wave? There seemed to be something expectant in his gaze. Or was it that hers seemed to ask something of him?

A split second and the moment passed. The coffee guy's eyes shifted so they were looking at the next person in line, and Laurel had the odd sensation of wondering if they'd ever been looking at her at all.

She glanced down at the open book in her hands.

As females move past their prime childbearing years, the hormones compelling them to seek out and secure a mate diminish. This could be why "falling in love," in the modern sense, is so difficult for women in their thirties and forties. Still in possession of their youthful expectations of romance, older females are far less likely to achieve even the illusion of it. They are destined for disappointment unless they shift their sights from passion to protection, from sexuality to security.

Laurel felt as if a flash of light had momentarily blinded her. "Wow."

"What?" Angela inched forward as the line

moved, grabbing Laurel's sleeve and pulling her with her.

"Listen to this." She read the passage aloud. "You know, if we were to believe this guy, that would explain why all the single women my age are dissatisfied. Why nobody can find the 'man of their dreams.' This is exactly what I've been saying for years, it's—"

"Impossible to fall in love after the age of thirty," Angela finished for her.

Laurel looked up triumphantly. "Exactly."

Angela shook her head. "Except it's a crock. Plenty of people fall in love after thirty."

"No they don't. They only *think* they do." Laurel tipped a gloved finger toward her friend. "What they've fallen in love with is the security and the relief of not being single anymore. You have no idea how many women feel disenfranchised by the whole idea of being 'swept off our feet.' We're not looking for sex three times a day or kisses that make us weak in the knees anymore. We've had that and it led to nothing. What we want now is security. A man who'll stick around for the long haul, be a partner, a father, a friend."

Angela's expression turned to one of pity. "Do you really believe that?"

"You bet I do. God, I can't believe how much sense this makes." She stared back down at the book, paging through it slowly.

"I can't believe how much sense you *think* it makes." Angela sounded appalled.

Laurel sighed. "I would have said the same thing at your age. But trust me, you'll feel different when you're thirty-five."

"I'm going to be *married* when I'm thirty-five," Angela said. After a minute she moved forward a step and broke into a huge smile. "Hi, Joe!"

Laurel raised her head from the book.

The coffee guy looked at Angela, then moved his gaze to Laurel. His mouth curved into a wry smile, exposing deep dimples on either side. "Hello ladies."

"How's it going?" Angela was as perky now as she was appalled thirty seconds ago.

"Joe," Laurel greeted him, her voice heavy with irony.

"What can I get for you?"

"Double cappuccino today, Joe." Angela leaned up against the cart. It shifted slightly and she straightened, giggling as her face turned red.

"Tough day ahead?" His hands moved rapidly over the equipment.

Laurel studied his face, which she could see fully today as the maroon scarf was nowhere in sight. His cheeks were lean and dimples showed sporadically even when he talked. His light eyebrows and ruddy complexion suggested blond hair but it was impossible to tell with the ugly, ear-flapped army hat he wore.

"Yeah, pretty tough." Angela laughed and tossed her head, obviously forgetting that her curls were bound up by her coat collar. "Seems

I'm going to have to listen to depressing excerpts about love from this stupid book Laurel's reading."

Coffee Guy's brows rose. "Oh yeah? You reading a book about love, Laurel?" His smile was positively seductive. No wonder most of the time, 80 percent of the people in line were women.

"Hardly," Angela said.

"It's something we're going to excerpt in the paper." Laurel tucked the book under her arm. "The publisher gave it to me to read. Besides, it's more about biology, or physiology, than love."

Why was she justifying herself to this guy? This opinionated, overconfident guy? She still couldn't get over his calling Ethan a crybaby. He didn't even know the whole story.

"We work for *DC Scene*," Angela explained. "Read him what you just read me, Laurel." She turned to "Joe" with a nod. "Listen to this."

Laurel looked from Angela to "Joe," who glanced up from the milk steamer expectantly.

"Hit me with it," he said. "I could use some philosophy for the day."

She glanced at the line of people behind them. She would read him a short excerpt, just long enough for him to make coffees for her and Angela.

"All right." She took a deep breath and opened the book. It took her a moment to find the passage, during which time "Joe" handed Angela her cappuccino. She paused. "First, though, you need to tell me your real name."

Without missing a beat, he started another coffee. "Why do you want to know?"

She folded her arms across her chest, one finger in the book in her left hand. "Because I feel like a jerk calling you Joe."

Angela stopped blowing on her coffee to ask, "Why?"

Laurel gave her a patient look. "Because it's not his name."

The coffee guy laughed. "Honey, you can call me anything you want." He winked at Angela.

Laurel narrowed her eyes. "Trust me, you don't want to know what I want to call you."

Coffee Guy raised his brows at Angela. "Is she always this feisty in the morning?"

"Only when she's uncaffeinated," Laurel answered.

Angela laughed. "Quick, throw her a coffee bean."

Coffee Guy feigned intimidation and pulled out a fresh cup. "Yes ma'am. Help is on the way."

"So I'm going to have to settle for 'Joe,' is that what you're telling me?" Laurel put a hand on her hip. God, he was stubborn.

"*I've* had to, for years. Now read."

"Fine." Laurel yanked the book from under her arm and opened it. " 'As females move past their prime childbearing years, the hormones compelling them to seek out and secure a mate diminish . . . ' "

She finished the passage and looked defiantly back up at him. "So the older women get, the less they need men. Makes sense to me."

"It does, huh?" The dimples showed, though he didn't look up. His hands were busy, pouring another carafe of steamed milk into a cup.

"Yes, actually it does." She raised her chin. She was sure this was something *this* guy, more than most, needed to hear. "Women's priorities change as they get older. They're more practical, less prone to the vagaries of love, the insincere promises of passion. Men can no longer take advantage of women's youthful desire for infatuation because the women have grown smarter, choosier, harder to blind with false emotion."

Joe's face was thoughtful as he finished preparing the drink in front of him. He even picked up a couple of raw sugar packets and dumped them in before snapping the plastic lid on the cup. Laurel was sure he was buying time to think of a response, stumped by the unarguable logic of what she'd just read.

Finally, he picked up the cup, handed her the latte she hadn't even ordered yet, just the way she liked it, and looked her dead in the eye.

"If all that's true," he said, his eyes, she was suddenly sure, laughing at her, "how come you dumped the crybaby?"

Laurel was appalled that he remembered.

"He wasn't a crybaby," she said. She hoped he at least didn't remember Ethan's name.

"Then why'd you dump him?" He wiped coffee grounds out of a piece of machinery with a cloth.

"It wasn't because he was a crybaby. It was . . . I just don't think that's any of your business. It's not even relevant." Laurel looked at Angela, hoping for a commiserative look in return.

Joe asked, "So whattya need?"

"And what on earth does *that* mean?" Her head whipped back and the words were out before she realized he was talking to the customer behind them.

Joe turned a slow look on her. It was the kind of look men give women they suddenly realize are insane.

"Large coffee," the guy behind them said. "Black. None of that fancy shit."

"No fancy shit, comin' up." Joe's entire being focused on the espresso machine.

Laurel pressed two fingers to her forehead and turned away.

"God, that was embarrassing," Angela said.

"Thanks. Yeah, I wasn't sure."

They stepped away from the cart. Laurel shifted the book under her arm and held the warm cup in both hands.

"You know, I'm not sure this coffee-on-the-corner thing is going to work out for me," she said.

"What do you mean?" Angela glanced behind her toward Joe. She smiled slightly and gave a little wave.

Laurel sighed. "I mean, I think I'd do much better talking to that guy *after* I've had coffee, not before."

Two

"Laurel, I think you've lost your mind." Carole, Laurel's sister, had made a rare appearance at Laurel's apartment to drop off a dress Laurel's mother had bought for her. Or rather, had bought for herself and had decided was too young. "In fact, I should probably confiscate this book."

She sat on Laurel's couch, flipping through *Love Is Not the Answer* and shaking her head.

Laurel didn't expect her sister to agree with her. The two rarely saw things the same way and in fact lived completely different lives. Carole was in the suburbs, with three children, a husband who worked for the navy and a whole host of duties from being president of the Junior

League to shuttling her kids from piano lessons to baseball games to ballet classes.

Still, Laurel occasionally liked to run an idea by her sister, if only to understand a side of the issue she might not have anticipated.

"I think it makes a lot of sense," Laurel said, pulling the dress from the paper Talbot's bag. As if anything from Talbot's could be "too young" for anyone.

As she suspected, the style, the length, the little round collar, were not the kind of thing she would ever wear. She lay it over the arm of the sofa to give to Women In Transition. Most of the clothes her mother gave her ended up there, which made her feel better about them than wearing them would have anyway.

"A lot more sense," she continued, "than, 'When it's right, you'll know it.' Or, 'It'll happen when you least expect it.'"

Carole grimaced. "Oh God, have I said that?"

Laurel waved a hand and sat on the couch. "Everyone's said it. *I've* probably said it. It's what we say when people feel alone, or break up, or get broken up with. We're all looking for a reason why we haven't found *that special someone*." She rolled her eyes with the words and put her feet up on the coffee table. What the hell, it was hers and it was junk. Once she made editor at *DC Scene* she would get some real furniture.

"Oh Laurel." Carole looked at her sadly. A look that for a second was too much like the one Laurel's mother wore around her when this subject came up. "Aren't *you* looking for *that special someone?*"

Laurel thought a moment. "No. Actually, I'm not. Not anymore. I'm tired of thinking something magical should happen, that fate should step in. Everyone wants to feel as if something is destined, but what if it's not? What if you just have to work to get what you want? Isn't that, in a way, better?"

Carole's expression was skeptical. "Why would that be better?"

"Because we have control. We just have to *figure out* what we want and go get it. No magic. No fate. No chorus of angels singing when he walks through the door." Laurel stood and walked toward the kitchen. "Do you want some tea?"

"Sure." Carole got up from the couch and followed her into the kitchen.

On the way, Laurel picked up the dress to hang in her bedroom closet. "You didn't want this?" she asked with a sly smile.

Carole's expression was wry. "I was blessed by its being the wrong size."

Laurel laughed. "So how come Mother didn't drop this by on her way to bridge with Mrs. Bigby? She's not, by any stroke of luck, avoiding me, is she?"

"Have you forgotten?" Carole's face was filled with glee. "She and Dad are at the Greenbrier for two weeks."

"Oh my God. I *did* forget. No wonder she hasn't ambushed me lately."

Carole sighed. "Lucky you. She got me right before they left. Spent an hour and a half telling me how to strip the wax off my kitchen floor. All as I was trying to clean up the breakfast dishes, help Seth get out the door with the dry cleaning and three bags of clothing for the Salvation Army, and get the kids dressed and ready so I could take them to their annual screaming trip to the dentist."

Laurel shook her head in commiseration. She and her sister had often compared notes on the impeccable timing their mother had for her unannounced visits. It was like a sixth sense; she always picked the *worst* possible time.

"So what were you doing in town today?" Laurel asked.

"I had to pick up Penny's portrait proofs down on K." Penny was Carole's daughter. "So, are you saying you're not looking to get married? Have you told Mother?"

Laurel tossed a smile over her shoulder. "Do I look crazy?"

Carole pulled a chair out from the kitchen table and sat. "There is *some* sense in what you say, I suppose. Telling people something's just going to happen magically really does take away any responsibility for them going out and making something happen."

Laurel filled the kettle with water and put it on the front burner. "Exactly. But even aside from people's responsibility to make things happen for themselves, it just makes good sense. I'd actually like to get married." She paused, feeling the oddness of the statement on her tongue.

"You would?" Carole's tone was almost offensive in its surprise.

"Of course. I want that partnership. I want to find someone I can respect and admire. I'd like to have that someone here at the end of the day, someone to share life with. I've lived alone for five years, and believe me, it's not all it's cracked up to be."

"Wow," Carole said softly, looking at her.

"I'd also like a child," Laurel continued, warming to her subject. "Time's running out, and I don't want to do it on my own. So why can't I make a rational, logical, calculated decision to find a respectable, admirable guy and build the life I want?"

Carole leaned back and crossed her legs, looking at her consideringly. "But . . ." She took a deep breath. "What about love?"

Laurel turned from the stove and leaned back against the counter. "I've done a lot of research lately. A lot of it on arranged marriages. And *all* the research, literally everything I could find about it, said that love grows in those unions from respect and admiration. But it's not the love that's important anyway. Love comes and goes, we all know that. It's the *commitment* that matters. Did you know that arranged marriages are statistically far more successful than love marriages?"

"Laurel." Carole sat forward on the chair.

"You're not thinking of making an arranged marriage, are you? Good God, what would you do? Hire somebody? A—what's it called—a yenta? A yentyl? No wait, that was a Streisand movie. Anyway a matchmaker, or someone like that?"

As if in horrified agreement the tea kettle whistled shrilly.

Laurel took the pot off the stove and poured boiling water over bags of tea in two large mugs. She loved these mugs. She'd bought them years ago in a home store in Georgetown that had them set up in the middle of a fake log-cabin scene, complete with roaring gas fireplace. At the time, she'd pictured herself cozying up to a flannel-clad Mr. Right in front of a crackling log fire with a steaming mug of apple cider on a crisp fall evening. They would talk about things . . . intelligent, interesting conversations that would have them both thinking in ways they always knew they were capable of but couldn't achieve alone.

How young and naïve she'd been then.

"No. I'm going to arrange my own marriage. I'm going to formulate a plan, seek out and interview candidates, and then make a decision." Laurel handed her sister a mug. "Careful, it's hot. Besides, I wouldn't be surprised to discover that finding the right guy this way, with a goal and a plan, is much easier than anyone's willing to admit."

Carole stirred cream into her tea. Her chestnut

hair, the same color as Laurel's, was cut short
and layered, her previously long, shiny locks the
victim, as Ethan used to say, of motherhood.
Why did women who had children always cut
off all their hair? he would complain. To signal
that they were off the market?

Laurel would say it was so their babies
wouldn't grab hold and not let go, but that theory didn't work in Carole's case, because her
daughter was seven and her sons ten and twelve.
Sometimes style was just a decision.

Maybe sometimes love was too.

"Okay," Carole said slowly. "Maybe you're
right. Maybe that can work. It just . . . it just
seems a shame."

"What does?" Laurel sat down in the chair
across from her.

"That you won't know love."

"No, I just said—"

"I mean *real* love." Carole looked at her
firmly. "Spontaneous love. Mutual, lightning-
struck, walking-on-air love. How can you give
that up? How can you believe you really won't
miss that? I'm sorry, honey, but I think you're
kidding yourself here."

Stung, Laurel raised a cynical brow. "Is that
what *you* have? You came in here today bitching
about Seth's smelly feet. About how he leaves his
shoes all over the place and couldn't be paid to
wash his own socks. In fact, you said he probably hadn't done laundry since the day you got
married. As I recall you were also recently an-

noyed with him for leaving great gobs of toothpaste in the sink. Seems to me you said something at the time about wanting to live alone."

Laurel's heart was racing. For some reason she
felt a need to prove her point, to believe that
even her sister's marriage was little more than
luck and stamina.

Carole looked startled. "Well, yes, I did say all
that. And, in a way, I meant it. In the same way
people mean it when they say they could kill
someone." A soft smile touched her lips and she
looked at her hands on the table. She glanced
back up at her sister. "But there is no question in
my mind that Seth and I were meant to be together. And I don't know if you remember,
though you *should* because I talked your head
off about it, but I was cloud-walking for months
after he finally asked me out. And for months
more after the first time he said he loved me."

Laurel's heart softened. She did remember
how over the moon Carole was about Seth. But
she also remembered that at the same time she
herself was crazy about a guy in her calculus
class. She and Carole had even spent an evening
speculating about a double wedding.

"I was that way about Johnny Mulroney, remember?" Laurel pulled the tea bag out of her
mug and let it fall onto her saucer with a *splat*,
an apt commentary on what had happened to
her and Johnny Mulroney. "I was also crazy
about Don Kennedy for a while. And countless
others. It always wore off. So what did any of

those infatuations get me, except another opportunity to hurt someone else and feel bad about myself?"

Carole moved the spoon in slow circles in her mug. "Well, it didn't wear off for me and Seth. I can . . ." She paused and looked up at Laurel through her lashes. "Don't laugh."

Laurel leaned back. "Of course I won't laugh."

"I can . . ." She sighed. "I can still get nervous talking to him."

Despite herself, Laurel laughed. Not with mirth, more with incredulity. "Sorry. That wasn't a laugh. I just . . . you get *nervous*?"

Carole put her spoon down. "Yes. You know, that kind of flirty-nervous. Or, okay, not nervous. Excited. Sometimes he can still seem . . . I don't know, *new* to me. My heart can flutter when he walks in a room."

Laurel swallowed over an unexpected lump in her throat.

"That's all," Carole concluded with a shrug. She sipped her tea. "But okay. Maybe that can develop, over time. Or something like it. Maybe I was just lucky. Or maybe . . ." She set her cup down and raised a finger. "And this is probably it, maybe I'm just *the type* to feel like that."

"The type . . ."

"Right. I'm more romantic, more emotional than you are, so I'm more likely to get all wound up over a man."

"So . . . I'm just not the type," Laurel said.

The idea had the ring of truth to it, and she wondered how she'd gotten that way.

"Yeah, you're not." Carole was matter-of-fact. "It's just not in you."

Laurel knew her sister didn't intend to hurt her feelings, but for some reason she did.

Carole stood up and put her mug in the sink. "You've always been more analytical than I ever was. More methodical. Maybe this is the perfect thing for you to do, the perfect way for you to go about it."

"Maybe . . . Or maybe some Kane women just aren't meant to have love. Remember Grandma Twila? Whose one true love died in the Great War?"

Carole snorted. "That was just her excuse for not liking Granddad."

"I still have that charm her lover gave her," Laurel said, thinking of the little metal four-leafed clover she carried in her purse. Her grandmother had treasured it, though it was not anything close to fine jewelry.

"Listen." Carole clapped her hands together and held them. "I know a guy, from Seth's work, you might like. He's in the computer department, head of data processing or something like that. He's really stable, got a good future at the company, and making good money, I'm sure."

Laurel wondered if she should ask for a résumé. "Is he new?"

"Oh no. No, Seth's known him awhile. I wouldn't have thought of him for you before, but maybe he's what you're looking for."

Laurel took a sip of tea. "Why wouldn't you have thought of him for me before?"

Carole tipped her head and looked off into the middle distance. "I guess I would have thought he was . . . maybe too stable. A little . . ." She laughed. " 'Square,' to borrow an old expression."

Laurel felt a refusal creep into her throat but squelched it. If she believed what she'd been saying—and she did—she was going to have to get rid of her adolescent reactions to certain kinds of men. Specifically, the stable, responsible, "boring" ones. "Okay. What's his name?"

"Larry Lutzki."

A laugh burst from Laurel. "*What*?"

Carole frowned at her. "On second thought, maybe that's why I never mentioned him before."

"No, no. It sounds good. I mean, the introduction, the fix-up, whatever, sounds good. Not the name." She laughed again. "Laurel Lutzki."

Carole tried to keep a straight face, but after a second a giggle escaped.

"Okay, fine," Laurel said. "Set me up. But make it someplace neutral." She drummed her fingers on the table a minute. "Like Café Quiz."

"That place next to your office?"

"Yeah. I don't want him thinking he has to show up at the door with flowers or anything."

Carole gave an exaggerated grimace. "God forbid."

"That's right. This is more like an interview

than a date. You might want to mention that."
Laurel grabbed a napkin from the pile at the end
of the table and mopped up tea dregs that had
dripped from the bag on her saucer.

"Sure, that ought to make it sound fun."

"Hey, the guy's in data processing, how much
fun could he stand?" She wadded the napkin to
toss it into the trash.

"Laurel?"

She stopped, arm raised. "What?"

"If you're looking for responsible, respectable,
all that—if you're not so concerned with love,
why did you break up with Ethan?"

Laurel tossed the napkin. It glanced off the
side of the can and landed on the floor. "Why
does everyone ask me that?"

"Because it seems to me your only problem
with him is that you weren't in love with him."
Carole moved toward the napkin and picked it
up, dropped it neatly in the can.

Laurel shrugged, suddenly uncomfortable. "I
wasn't. He just—he just wasn't right. And no, I
wasn't in love with him. I'm not even sure he was
in love with me—"

"But he was so upset when you broke up with
him!" Carole objected.

Laurel shook her head. "Maybe. But maybe it
was just the shock. He was upset about the rou-
tine he was going to miss. In any case, I couldn't
have done the arranged-marriage thing with him
because he never would have gone for it. He
liked the fiction that we were in love. And you

can't have one person thinking the marriage is arranged and the other person thinking it's not. Just because you give up on love in a marriage doesn't mean you give up on honesty."

Carole nodded but looked unconvinced. "Uh-huh."

Laurel looked at her, wheels she didn't want spinning beginning to move in her head. She *wasn't* in love with Ethan, but that wasn't the point. The point was the relationship wasn't working. And it never *was* going to work. If she could trust her feelings on anything, she could trust them on that.

Carole looked at her watch. "I've gotta go. Penny's at soccer practice and she'll be furious with me if I'm late again."

Laurel walked her to the door, reluctantly letting her sister leave her alone with her thoughts. She *did* believe she could arrange her own marriage. She knew she wasn't the type to lose her head over a man. She'd thought she was once, but that had been a long, long time ago. She'd grown up and grown practical.

The air felt like glass. Cold and crisp and crystal clear in the winter night's darkness. There were even a few bright stars visible in the city sky, Laurel noted as she walked briskly from the Metro toward Café Quiz.

Across the street Kramerbooks was packed, the windows steamy and the interior moving with bodies like a kaleidoscope. She was headed to the corner of Connecticut and Dupont Circle, her hands shoved deep in her pockets and her head tucked into her collar for warmth. She hadn't worn a hat for fear of "hat head." Despite the fact that tonight was more of an interview than a date, as she'd told Carole, she didn't need Larry Lutzki thinking she didn't care about her appearance. After all, she expected him to care about his.

She stopped for the light at Q Street, stepping softly from foot to foot to keep warm as traffic moved through the intersection, when she saw a familiar ear-flapped hat up ahead. Coffee-cart guy "Joe" was standing at a street vendor's table, apparently buying a pair of gloves.

Well, she thought, *that explains where he got the hat.*

The light changed and the Walk sign flashed, but Laurel didn't move. She wasn't sure she wanted to talk to him, though she was tempted to ask him why he was here on a weekend. Surely he didn't work every day of the week.

After a second he completed his transaction and moved down the block away from her. She crossed Q Street, staying a safe distance behind him, but noticed that he didn't put the gloves on, despite bare hands.

She studied his back. His gait was unhurried though purposeful. She liked the way he moved, his legs agile and limber in his jeans. And she had to admit he had a great ass.

She arrived at the door to Café Quiz, grasped the metal door handle, but hesitated before opening it. Joe continued down the sidewalk, turning right at the corner.

After a second's thought, Laurel followed him. She was a little early anyway—on purpose, so that she could see Larry Lutzki before he saw her—but Joe seemed to be up to something. She would never have been able to explain how she knew that, but she did.

She reached the corner at the circle and turned right, stopping dead in her tracks as Joe was not ten feet away. Leaning against a wall in front of him was what looked like a pile of discarded clothing and blankets. Laurel had been a Washington resident too long not to know that the pile undoubtedly held a homeless person.

Joe was bent at the waist with one hand on the gloves he'd bought and just placed on top of the person's blanket. Laurel looked close—it appeared to be a man, but could have been a woman. The face was weathered and lined, the head concealed by a tight hood.

Just as she was concluding that since the face was stubble-free it must be a woman, Joe straightened and stepped toward her.

She jerked to attention, but it was too late to look as if she hadn't been watching him.

He seemed to recognize her instantly. She could tell by the slight hitch in his step as he came toward her.

She smiled. "Aren't you the Good Samaritan?"

He didn't look pleased to have been caught. As he moved closer his face got clearer in the light of the streetlamp behind her. "What do you mean?"

"I watched you buy those gloves and give them to that person. Is it someone you know?"

His lips moved upward just enough to make the dimples show. "Would you be less impressed if I said yes?"

The question was obviously contentious. "Did I say I was impressed?"

He laughed, deepening the dimples and exposing white, even teeth. It was a fabulous smile, she noted objectively, the kind that felt like a prize to the one who received it.

"Excuse my arrogance." His eyes settled more appreciatively upon her now. She found herself feeling glad she was dressed to go out—hair curled, makeup subtle yet sultry, she'd even worn lipstick.

"Do you ever take that hat off?" She tilted her head to get a better look at the thing.

He scanned her face. "Sometimes."

Something about the way he said it made her think of sex, and that bothered her.

"Well, I wouldn't," she said, turning back toward her original destination. "It suits you."

"Hey."

She stopped, debated briefly whether to turn back to that curt command, then decided since she'd already stopped she might as well, and turned.

"Hey?" she repeated, brows raised.

"Laurel," he amended, with a reduced-wattage

version of the smile. "What are you doing down here on a Saturday night? Not working overtime, are you?"

"No, I'm not working. Do I look like I'm going to work?" She stretched her arms to her sides. "I do happen to have a social life, you know."

"Really?" His tone was surprised.

She put her hands on her hips. "I have a date waiting for me right now, as a matter of fact." She glanced at her watch. *Damn*, now she was late. She hated being late.

"Great. Let's go." He started walking, passed her and turned the corner onto Connecticut again.

" 'Let's go?' *Excuse me.*" She trotted to catch up with him. " 'Let's go'? You can't come with me. You know that, right? Tell me I've misunderstood you."

He kept walking. "Boyfriend the jealous type?"

"He's not my boyfriend." She had to walk fast to keep up with him. Suddenly the night was not so cold.

He stopped abruptly. She pulled herself up sharply to keep from running into him.

"First date?" He looked delighted.

She blushed, thankful it was nighttime.

"Look, I've got to go." She pushed the sleeve of her coat back and looked at her watch again. She forged ahead toward Café Quiz.

"Where'd you meet this guy?" he asked, stepping neatly beside her.

She stopped in front of the café. He peered in the foggy window.

"Which one is he?"

She looked in the window too, wishing she knew. "Look, it's none of your business."

"My glove mission was none of *your* business," he pointed out.

She lowered her head. "Okay, sorry about that. I was just curious."

"About me?" He looked delighted again, though this time she felt the look was tinged with sarcasm.

"I've got to go." She turned to the door.

"Hey, does he know you're past your prime childbearing age and therefore not susceptible to hormonal manipulation?" He put his hands in his pockets and looked at her. Light from the café made his pale eyes glitter.

"I'm sure that's obvious," she said wryly, suddenly wishing she'd never followed him around the corner.

He waited a beat, his gaze steady on her, then said, "Trust me. It's not."

She flushed hotly, crimson to her hairline. "Okay. Well, I've really got to go. See you." She turned quickly away, back to the café door.

"I won't wait up for you," he called from behind her, laughing.

Three

Joe walked away from her, back toward the Explorer, and perfunctorily checked the lock on the back of the white trailer it towed. Inside, the coffee cart was strapped to the back wall with bungee cords, which he briefly considered checking as well. He knew it would be a waste of time, however. A mere delaying tactic for the purpose of being nearby in case Laurel and her date left Café Quiz.

Abandoning the idea, he moved around the back of the trailer to the side of the SUV and leaned against the shiny black passenger door. He looked down the street toward Café Quiz.

His breath fogged in front of him and he crossed his arms, slapping his shoulders for warmth.

He was curious about her, he had to admit that much. What kind of guy would she date? What would he have to offer to make her say yes?

What could a woman reading a book about how love wasn't real possibly want in a man?

Money was one obvious answer, but she seemed as if she was doing well enough on her own. Besides, she didn't seem the dependent type.

Security? Companionship? Intellectual stimulation?

Sex?

He pushed himself off the side of the Explorer and sauntered back down Connecticut Avenue to Café Quiz. He stood outside the window and looked in. The window was still fogged and the street outside had enough passers-by that he was certain she wouldn't notice him. In fact, he was fairly certain she would never have noticed him in the first place if he hadn't been wielding caffeine almost directly in front of her office building on a daily basis.

A man in a trenchcoat elbowed by him and Joe stepped closer to the window. That's when he saw her, sitting on a barstool, scrunched up in a corner, a tall, graying, bespectacled man in a wrinkled suit leaning over her.

She had to bend her neck at an awkward angle to look up at him and keep her distance at the same time.

Joe took in the man's face. It was weary-looking, in the way that people's faces and eyes dulled after spending too much time on their income taxes. Then Joe noted a corner of the man's not-quite-white shirttail was sticking out of the top of his fly.

Laurel looked away from the guy as he spoke and took a sip of her drink, still keeping her head angled away from him, her shoulders canted forty-five degrees over the bar.

To Joe, it didn't look as if her date was offering much in the way of intellectual stimulation. Security, on the other hand, he might have in abundance. This guy looked nothing if not stable. Or maybe *stagnant* was a better word. The man's entire demeanor screamed Dead End.

Sex? Joe hoped not. Though he didn't make a habit of envisioning virtual strangers having sex, something about the idea of Laurel and this man in bed sent a shudder through him.

Laurel, serious and opinionated as she was, glowed with life and beauty; while this man looked as if he'd been dragged, musty and cobwebbed, from someone's attic.

Joe tried to imagine the moment the man had asked her out. How had he done it? Had they been engaged in some witty, enjoyable banter at some party? Did they know each other from work, find themselves sharing personal tidbits from their weekends by the copy machine? Could they possibly have met on the street, and something about him impressed her enough to say yes? What could she have been thinking?

Hell, she could have been thinking anything.

She could be attracted to this man. For all Joe knew, he could be exactly her type. Joe barely knew the woman, but he certainly wouldn't have picked this guy out of a lineup to have been Laurel's date for the night.

He shook his head and turned back to the Explorer.

She was an interesting one, all right. He'd thought he'd had her pegged that first day he'd heard about her dumping the weeping Ethan. But then she'd surprised him with that insane book she'd read him a portion of. And she'd surprised him again tonight.

Yep, he thought, casting a glance back at the café as an older couple came out, *this one bears watching*. And fortunately he was in the perfect spot to do just that, on a daily basis.

Larry Lutzki was *not bad*, Laurel told herself firmly. Okay, so maybe he seemed boring. She probably did too. That's what happened on blind dates. You had to search around for things you had in common, and until you found those things, conversation could seem a little dull.

"I used to build airplanes," Larry said.

"*Really.*" Now here was something unusual.

A man who built airplanes probably knew how to fly airplanes. And a man who knew how to fly, probably liked to travel. And a man who liked to travel, who could fly his own airplane, had probably been to many an exotic locale.

"Model planes," he amended. "I was in a club."

Laurel discreetly massaged one temple. If she had to swallow one more yawn, she was afraid her head would explode.

Aside from having a stiff neck from trying to keep away from Larry's coffee breath, she was having trouble coming up with anything at all to say in response to Larry's remarks.

To his credit, however, he kept trying.

"But lately I've gotten into computer games. Some of them are quite sophisticated, you know."

Laurel nodded and conversation faded. "And do you . . ." She wracked her brain. "Do you belong to a club for that too?"

Lame, she thought. Thank God she wasn't attracted to this guy or she'd be kicking herself for being such a dud.

Not that attraction was the point.

The point, she reminded herself, straightening, was to consider compatibility. Shared goals, shared visions for the future, shared desire for family, companionship, teamwork.

"Oh yes," he said, nodding seriously. "We meet once a week. Usually on Fridays."

Larry hadn't cracked a smile since he'd gotten here, even when they'd first met. Laurel had beamed at him, held out her hand and said how *nice* it was to meet him, she'd heard *such* good things. She'd even made a joke about the weather, laughing to cue him that it was a joke, and he had taken it all in without a twitch of the lips, like a therapist looking for clues about her psyche. For a second Laurel wondered if he had teeth.

"I have a 2001 Lincoln Town Car at home," Larry was saying.

How on earth had they gotten onto the subject of cars? Laurel straightened again and resolved to pay better attention.

"Oh?"

"Yes, that's my one indulgence, I guess you could say. I bought it because I know the Impala's going to die one of these days and the Town Car was a good deal."

"So you drive an Impala, but the Town Car's at home?" Laurel asked, if only to prove she was following the conversation.

She could ignore the coffee breath, she thought, and could possibly get beyond the boring conversation eventually, but she wished he'd either find a barstool or notice that his shirt was caught in his zipper because with him standing right beside her she couldn't avoid seeing that little finger of shirttail sticking out.

"Yes, I don't like to drive it much, considering it's new."

"So you have a new car at home, but you don't drive it because it's new?"

He nodded. "That's right. I don't want to put mileage on it."

"Why not?"

He looked at her as if he hadn't quite understood the question. "It's bad for the resale value."

She paused. Was she being dense? "But you're driving your old one until it dies?"

Larry nodded.

"And you probably plan to drive the new one until it dies too, right?"

He nodded again. His head reminded her of a horse's head, the way it hung down from between his shoulders. Everything about him, in fact, was kind of horselike. Not in the sleek thoroughbred sense. More in the swaybacked drafthorse-in-the-yard sense.

"So Larry," she continued abruptly, afraid he was about to describe the way vehicle depreciation worked. "Tell me about your family. Did you grow up around here? Have any brothers and sisters?"

He didn't look surprised at this sudden change in topic. Indeed, he looked as if he were used to having someone tug on his reins and steer him in a new direction at unexpected moments.

"No, I grew up in upstate New York. I have a sister. Leslie."

"Leslie Lutzki?" Laurel said, before she could stop herself. What was with all the l's?

"That's right." He moved his horse head again.

"So what does she do, Leslie? Do you talk to her very often?"

"We're not close." His tone was deadpan, and

Laurel knew at once that there was nothing like an exciting family rift or sibling feud in the Lutzki family. They just had the sense not to waste long-distance money to talk about the Town Car in the garage.

"Excuse me a moment, will you, Larry?" Laurel got up from her stool and squeezed away from the bar toward the ladies' room.

She glanced at her watch. God, she'd only been here forty-five minutes. How long did she need to put in before calling it quits for the night? Was Larry expecting dinner? She had the sense that she should have made up a list of "interview" questions before arriving. Who knew conversation could be so difficult?

She passed an enormous ficus tree and turned down the hall that led to the phones and the bathrooms.

A tall guy with short blond hair leaned next to one of the wall phones, his back to her, the receiver cradled between his ear and shoulder. He had long legs leading up to a broad back, and something about his posture was arresting.

She turned to look at him as she pushed on the ladies' room door.

Heat ran from her chest into all her extremities as her eyes met Joe's.

"What are you doing here?" she asked, one palm still on the bathroom door.

He looked different without the awful hat. Better. A *lot* better. The blond hair worked on him without making him look soft.

He held a finger up, his hand holding a pen, then lowered it to write in a small, spiral-bound pad.

"Yep. Yeah. Got it. At one. Will Ginny be there? Okay, good. Gotta go. Yeah. See you."

He hung up the phone and turned back to her, eyes dancing. In the dark light they looked greener than they did outside, a very light gray green, to go with that Scandinavian blond hair.

He patted his chest where a pocket might have been hidden inside his coat.

"Cellphone died," he said with a rueful look.

She nodded slowly, sure he had followed her in here for some other reason but not wanting to accuse him of it for fear of being too convincingly contradicted.

"So how's the date going?" He continued to lean next to the phone, looking considerably more comfortable than she felt.

"Fine."

He just looked at her.

A slight heat rose to her face. "All right, so it's a little . . . slow."

"*It's* slow? Or *he* is?"

"It's just tough getting to know people." Why was she explaining this to him? Maybe coffee-cart guys were like bartenders, people automatically opened up to them.

"Laurel, the guy looks like one of the undead. Like it would take a bolt of lightning to wake him up."

"What do you mean? You think I'm boring him?"

"No," he said slowly, watching her like a teacher trying to make a point, "I think he's boring you. In fact, I think he's got you thinking about how nice Saturday nights are at home. About that video you've been wanting to watch. About that crossword puzzle you haven't finished yet."

Laurel put her hands on her hips. "Well, my goodness, aren't we sure we've got everybody pegged?"

He gave her a cheeky smile.

"So you just back here talking to your stockbroker?" She moved her head in the direction of the phone. It was a nasty remark. The guy obviously didn't have a stockbroker. She felt immediately ashamed of herself.

He laughed softly. "He doesn't work weekends."

The ladies' room door opened and Laurel stepped back to let the woman exit. It was a girl, really, dressed to kill on her Saturday night out. Short skirt, high heels, skillfully applied makeup and carefully vamped hair.

While Laurel would not have wanted to look like her, she suddenly felt old and dowdy.

Joe winked at the girl as she passed.

Laurel shook her head. What was she doing talking to this guy? Men like him were always on the make. Was it just because they were good-looking? Or were they all brought up in barns?

In any case, men like Joe managed to make men like Larry Lutzki look good.

"What?" he asked, looking at her.

She started. "Nothing. What?"

"What was that look you just gave me?"

"I didn't give you a look."

"Yes, you did. Just now, when that girl passed by. You gave me a look."

"You're the one giving looks, Winky." She tossed her head in what she hoped was a nonchalant manner.

" 'Winky'?" He gave her an incredulous look. "Did you just call me 'Winky'?"

"Did you not just wink at that girl?"

He laughed. "I don't know."

She glared at him. "You don't know? What, are you just perpetually on automatic flirt?"

He tilted his head, his eyes devilish. "She smiled at me first."

"I'll just bet she did." Laurel wondered what on earth she was doing. This was a conversation more suited for people who were involved with each other. Not two strangers. One of whom had a date waiting for her.

"I've got to go," she said, and started to move past him back toward the bar.

He stopped her with a light touch to her arm. "But . . . ah . . . I thought you had to go." He tipped his head toward the bathroom.

She sighed, tired of the whole evening. Apparently men like Joe couldn't make men like Larry look good for long. "No, I was just taking a breather from my date. The undead can be exhausting."

Joe laughed, this time with a low warmth that made Laurel want to stay in this back hall until Larry Lutzki gave up on her and went home.

"Well, good luck with that. But remember, just because you're not looking for love doesn't mean you have to resign yourself to being bored for the rest of your life."

The comment hit her with the clarity of a butter knife on crystal.

"You know what? You're right. I've been sitting there thinking there's something wrong with my plan, that I've got to give this guy a chance, but you're right. I ought to at least be able to expect a decent conversation."

"At least. Though there still could be something wrong with your 'plan.' What is it you're looking for, exactly?"

"Things you'd probably barely understand, Winky." She softened the words with a smile.

"I don't suppose you'd tell me what this plan of yours is."

For a moment, she was tempted. In the same way that she liked to hear Carole's point of view, different from her own, she would have enjoyed hearing what Joe had to say about her plan to arrange her own marriage.

"Not tonight," she said instead. "Though I'm pretty sure it's a good deal different from any plan you'd ever make."

"What sort of plan do you think I'd make?"

She let her gaze drift out toward the bar. "I think . . . I think your plan would go as far as picking up Miss Vampy Hair over there, and devil take the conversation."

His eyes lowered to half-mast, amused. "I can converse with anyone."

Laurel ignored the warmth his gaze ignited in her. "Sure, but for how long? You take that girl home and you'd be done with her by morning, wouldn't you? And I mean done with her forever. Beyond, 'Let me give you cab fare,' you probably wouldn't have two more words to say to her."

He considered. "Maybe not."

"So I wouldn't call *that* 'looking for love' either."

"Then again I might have a lot to say to her. Seems to me picking someone I'm at least attracted to is a smarter way to find love than picking up some corpse in a bad suit."

She sighed. "He came highly recommended."

"By four out of five dentists?"

She looked at her watch. She'd been gone almost ten minutes. "Listen, I really have to go."

"Sure. Sorry to hold you up." He gave her a closed-mouth smile that still managed to produce those dimples and give his eyes that devious look.

"No. Actually, I'm glad I ran into you. If nothing else, I'll have gotten at least one interesting conversation out of the evening."

"I'm sure you'll have the choice of something else. After all, the guy's not actually dead." He waited a beat. "Is he?"

She rolled her eyes. "Have a good night." She started to pass again, then turned back to him with a devious smile of her own. "Oh, and if you do pick up Miss Vampy Hair, tell me how it went on Monday, okay?"

He raised a brow. "You want details?"

Laurel laughed. "God no. I just want to know if it turns out to be true love."

He nodded his head once. "You got it."

Four

Laurel liked doing laundry. She thought about this fact as she folded shirts from the dryer and wondered what the coffee guy was doing that night. Probably out with some gorgeous bimbo. Laurel rolled two socks together.

No, that wasn't fair. Just because a girl is young, pretty and dressed stylishly doesn't make her a bimbo. But that girl at the bar last night hadn't been particularly stylish. More trendy. Or trashy. Which, Laurel decided, made her a more valid candidate for bimbo-dom.

Besides, Laurel thought as she gathered up several pairs of underwear, folded them and put them in the "clean" basket, she really did like doing laundry. Didn't mind at all that she was spending her Saturday night with Whirlpool instead of the dating pool.

There was something so orderly about cleaning clothes. Taking the pile of dirty stuff, sorting it by color and fabric, washing each set, then folding it all for neat replacement in the closet. It was a kind of alchemy, changing a wadded-up mess into functional order. It was a peaceful activity. One she would much rather be doing than sitting in some trendy bar, her elbows in somebody else's ribcage or someone's in hers, shouting a conversation over deafening music to a companion who would probably be assessing her for post-date privileges.

She thought about shouting a conversation to Joe. Granted, he would be enjoyable to look at. She liked his combination of light coloring and rock-edged features. The combination of ruggedness with the offhand wattage of that smile.

But hell, he'd probably be scanning the crowd around her for someone with better post-date potential. It was obvious she wasn't his type. And he wasn't hers. The last thing she needed was a good-looking guy just out for a good time. She needed someone serious. Someone interested in the future, in children, in forging a *bond*, not a chemically combustible sex life.

Still, he was interesting. Intelligent, she thought, which made him better than the average commitment-phobic manchild. And considerate. She thought of the homeless person he gave the gloves to. But her favorite thing about Joe was the fact that he seemed to be paying attention. He *listened*. She could say anything—challenge him—and he would take her ideas and use them when he answered her. So much different from most men—most people—who tended to fall back on well-rehearsed speeches when talking to someone new.

She wondered if that made it harder for him to stand the bimbos, even for a night, and figured it did. Then she wondered if he knew it, and figured he didn't. Why else would he continue to be partial to them?

She folded the last pair of pants from the dryer and lifted the basket as the phone rang.

She set the basket on the back of the couch and picked up the phone to look at the Caller ID. Sue, her best friend, who had married and moved to California two years ago.

She answered the phone.

"This book you sent me is amazing," Sue said without preamble.

"Which one? Dr. Nadalov's?"

"This *Love Is Not the Answer* book. It's *so* on-target I can't believe it."

"*Thank* you." Laurel rounded the arm of the couch to plop onto its cushions. The laundry basket teetered on the back. She pulled it down and set it on the floor. "I've been in more conversations with people lately who've thought I was nuts," Laurel continued, wishing for the thousandth time that Sue hadn't felt the need to bolt out of Washington. Then again, Laurel felt that need to bolt every couple of months and probably would have acted on it if she'd found a guy as perfect for her as Kevin was for Sue.

Sue snorted. "No doubt from people who either got married at eighteen or haven't had a date in a decade. That infatuation crap is for the birds."

Laurel thought of Joe. Neither of those things, she was certain, applied to him. "For the most part. But there's one guy—well, it's not important. The important thing is, I know what the book says is true and I'm going to be smart enough to act on it."

"Act on it? What do you mean? Oh jeez, Laurel, you're not giving up, are you? I mean, the author's got some good points, but I don't think even *he's* advocating a life alone."

"No, I don't either. What I mean is"—Laurel put her feet up on the coffee table—"I'm forming a plan of action. I'm not going to spend my life alone, but I'm not going to wait for the white knight on the silver steed to find me and give my life meaning."

"I think it's the steed that's white, and the knight's in silver armor. Or shining . . . Isn't it shining armor?"

"Whatever. I'm going to find myself a man, a life partner, a companion, who suits me and my life. And I'm going to do it methodically, intelligently and successfully."

"What about a husband?" Sue's voice was wry.

"That's what I said." Laurel laid her head

back on the couch. Had she gotten so boring on this topic no one even listened anymore?

"Actually, no, that's not what you said. You said *companion, life partner*, something else I forget. But it's a husband you want, right, Laurel? A *husband*?"

"What's with the third degree? Sure, okay, husband." Laurel sat up straight and reached for the laundry basket. "But not because I'm a desperate thirty-something woman with a ticking biological clock."

"I know, I know." Laurel pictured Sue throwing up her hands in mock surrender. "All I'm saying is that until you can say the word, you're not going to get what you want."

Laurel stood up. "I can say the word." She put the basket on the couch and a hand on one hip.

"Then say it. Say, 'I want a husband'."

Laurel's hand moved from her hip to her front pocket, where she fingered a nickel she'd found in the dryer earlier. "This is stupid, Sue. I just told you—"

"Say it."

"Fine. I'll say it."

"Go ahead."

"I want a husband." Despite herself, the words emerged weakly. She continued in a stronger voice, "But not because I can't make it alone. I'm not one of those women who believe they're not good enough without a man."

She picked up the laundry and stalked into the bedroom.

"I know."

And Sue did know. Laurel knew she knew. So why did she feel such an intense need to explain?

"I just don't want that sentence hanging out there in the cosmos, drawing bad, desperate, pathetic energy to me instead of the proactive, precise determination I need for finding a person who will enhance my life. And I his," she added as an afterthought.

Sue was laughing. "Hon, you've got issues."

"Issues?" She picked up a bunch of rolled socks and moved to the dresser.

"Yes, you can't even say what you want without tripping all over yourself to qualify what it is you *don't* want. It's like golf."

Laurel dumped the socks in the sock drawer and gave the phone receiver a skeptical look. "Golf?"

"Yeah. If you stand at the tee and say, okay, I'm not going to hit it in the trees, not the trees, anywhere but the trees. All your mind hears is 'trees.' And where does the shot go?"

"I don't play golf."

"In the trees!"

"Sue . . ."

"My point is, you have to think about what you *want* in order to get it."

"I know that."

"And to think about what you want, you have to be able to actually *say* what you want."

"Sue." She gathered the folded underwear from the basket and put it in the top drawer.

"So what do you want, Laurel?"

Laurel sighed and sat down on the bed, one hand clutching a pair of Victoria's Secret bikinis. She looked at them, she'd been the only person to lay eyes on these since she'd bought them, and she'd had them quite a while. "A husband."

Sue laughed again. "Congratulations, Miss Kane. You are now well on your way to getting what you want."

Angela met Laurel at the Metro, full of stories about her weekend. Laurel wasn't completely paying attention, but there were parties, alcohol and at least one guy named Philip involved. In fact, Angela said Philip's name so quickly and so many times that after a while Laurel could only think of him as "Flip."

"And how was *your* weekend?" Angela asked, as they rode the interminable escalator up once again from the depths of the Dupont Circle station.

"Fine. I got a lot done." She thought about the laundry, about how it was the most satisfying thing she'd done all weekend.

"Did you go out?"

Laurel nearly winced. "Yeah. Friday. But it was kind of a nightmare."

"Really, why?" Angela looked at her as if shocked that Laurel might have an interesting weekend story.

Of course, it would have been shocking, Laurel had to admit. "No real reason. Just a dull date."

"Philip says all encounters are important, even dull ones I guess, because they get you where you're supposed to go. Philip thinks we're all just pinballs bouncing off each other on our journeys through life."

"And we're going downhill fast."

They crossed Q Street and Laurel's eyes immediately found the cloud of steam that was the Hot Stuff cart. She remembered the surprise of Joe's blond hair when she caught sight of his ear-flapped hat and thought, laundry wasn't the most interesting thing she'd done this weekend. Then she laughed, thinking how flattered Joe would be to know he'd beaten out laundry on her Top Ten Encounters Over the Weekend list.

"What's funny?" Angela asked, shooting her a glance. "You're not still reading that book, are you?"

"No, I finished it. You should read it," Laurel said, as they got in line for their morning coffees. "Flip should read it."

Angela eyed her. "Philip."

"That's what I said. I'd be interested to hear a male perspective on it."

As she said the words, Laurel's eyes met Joe's. He winked.

She should get *his* perspective, she thought suddenly. He'd have a lot to say about Dr. Nadalov's theories, she was sure. After all, he had something to say about everything else. She could even write a column on it. On their divergent points of view. Male vs. female. For vs.

against. Conservative vs. slutty. Can a man be a slut?

"Tall latte this morning, ma'am?" Joe asked her with a couple watts' worth of smile. His hands, she noticed, never stopped moving. "Or was your weekend such that you need something a little stronger to wake you up? Double espresso, maybe?"

"Are you implying that my weekend was so dull I'd have trouble waking up from it?"

He laughed and shook his head. "No, but that answers my question. Tall latte it is."

Laurel's brow lowered. "What do you mean by that?"

"I mean, a latte's enough to wake you up from a dull weekend. The double espresso's more for the wild ones. So the Gray Ghost didn't improve with alcohol, eh?"

"The Gray Ghost?" Angela repeated.

"I didn't stick around to find out," Laurel said. "Most things that improve with alcohol become disastrous with the light of day."

He shot her a knowing look. "Most, but not all."

Laurel smirked. "Which brings us to Miss Vampy Hair."

"Miss *Vampy Hair*?" Angela's head swiveled from Joe to Laurel.

Joe smiled, but not at Laurel. He was looking down, pouring steamed milk into her cup, and smiling a satisfied smile that did not include her.

She felt a blush hit her cheeks. For what, she couldn't imagine.

"So Miss Vamp . . . ?"

"Did not disappoint." He handed her the cup and looked her dead in the eye. "Which proves my theory."

Laurel looked down at the sugar bags, plucked one out, shook it, then ripped it open with such force it sprayed all over the coffee cart. Without missing a beat, she picked up another, ripped it open, and directed its contents into her cup.

"Your theory?" she asked mildly.

"Actually, it disproves yours. What can I get you?"

She glanced up as Angela answered with a proud smile. "I think I'm going to need one of those espressos you mentioned."

He grinned. "Wild one, eh?"

"You bet." She giggled. "So what are you guys talking about?"

Laurel glanced at her. "I ran into Joe at Café Quiz Friday night."

"During your dull date?" Angela asked her.

Joe chuckled.

"He was just . . . older," Laurel said.

"Thank God," Joe added.

"Very funny." Laurel stirred her coffee. "Anyway, I fail to see how your getting lucky with Miss Tramp disproves my theory."

"I thought it was Miss Vamp."

"Same thing."

He gave her a sidelong glance as his hands manipulated the machine in front of him. "Uh-huh."

"My theory?" Laurel prompted.

"Well, you went the practical route. The, shall we say, head over heart route, and had, by your own admission, a terrible time. I went with my gut, and have a Monday-morning smile to show for it."

Laurel studied him a long moment. "I hardly think it was your *gut* you were going with. And I wonder if Miss Vamp—do you even know her name?"

He gave her an offended look that was pure exaggeration. "Carla."

"Carla, then."

His brows furrowed. "Or Carol."

She put a hand on her hip. "Oh my God."

He laughed. "I'm kidding, it's Carla."

"Well, I just wonder if Carla's feeling the same this Monday morning."

"Sure she is."

"You know this for a fact? You've talked to her? You *called* her?"

"No, but she was happy yesterday morning. Why should anything be different today?"

Laurel smiled. "Nothing, I'm sure you're right. Next Monday, on the other hand, will probably be a different story."

Joe handed Angela her coffee and asked the next woman in line what she'd like.

"Double espresso," the woman said.

Joe sent Laurel a grin. "Looks like you weren't part of this weekend's trend."

"You should get Joe to read that book," Angela said. "You said you wanted a male perspective."

"What book?" Joe asked.

"That love book she was reading," Angela said. "She just told me she'd like a male perspective, and yours is certainly male."

Joe gave a one-shouldered shrug and winked at Angela. "Can't help what I am."

Laurel laughed cynically. "That's for sure, Winky."

At that Angela made a noise and sprayed coffee all over the sleeve of Laurel's coat.

"Angela! What—"

"I'm sorry!" Angela was laughing and looking at her as if she'd just whipped off her own head. "What did you just call him?"

"What?" Laurel brushed the arm of her coat and looked from Angela to Joe, who was smiling in a way that confirmed she'd said something stupid. She tried to run back over her last words. "I didn't call him anything. What?"

"You called him . . ."—Angela darted a glance around her and said in a lowered voice— "Winky. Didn't you?"

Laurel relaxed. "Yeah, because he winks at everyone. Surely you've noticed that."

But Angela was in hysterics again. Sincere, red-faced, eye-watering hysterics.

Laurel glanced again at Joe, who was chuckling as he worked on another coffee. Even his cheeks looked a little pinker than normal.

"It's just that—well, a lot of people refer to the male . . . uh"—Angela paused to giggle some more—"*you know*, as Winky. It's kind of a nickname. A kind of universal nickname."

Laurel felt her face flame. "Are you talking about a penis, Angela?" she asked, thinking bluntness might make her look slightly less stupid. "People call penises 'Winky'? Is that what you're saying?"

Angela laughed so hard she bent over at the waist, carefully holding her coffee level in front of her.

Laurel glared at Joe.

He shrugged. "That's not what I call mine."

"Oh my God," she muttered, putting her forehead in one hand. "I'm surrounded by philistines."

"Oh, get off your high horse, Socrates." Joe chuckled again. "And give me the damn book, if you're so hot for a male perspective."

She tried to look haughty. "Would you even read it?"

"Sure." His light eyes skewered her where she stood. "What, you think I can't read?"

"Of course not. I just think you probably don't. Well, maybe the sports page." She tried to calm the blush on her face by willing it away, but she was afraid she might be red for life.

"Oh my," he said mildly, "aren't we superior this morning?"

"Are you saying I'm wrong?" She arched a brow, still feeling the best defense was a good offense. And she was being as offensive as she'd ever been.

"Bring me the book."

"I've got it right here." She pulled it from her shoulder bag and handed it to him.

He gave the woman in line her double espresso, then took the book from Laurel, tucking it into a compartment in the bottom of the cart.

"Would you like a written report, or just an opinion?"

"Just an opinion. I don't want to take more time from you and your budding relationship with Carla than is necessary."

His lips curved but his eyes were serious as he said, "We'll talk tomorrow." His gazed shifted to the next in line. "What can I get for you?"

"This is a load of crap," he said the next morning, handing the book back to her. In fact it had been all he could do to get through the damn thing. The author had obviously never been laid in his life.

"You read it?" She gaped at him, which he found amusing.

"Last night."

"All of it?" She was incredulous.

He shot her a glance. "All except the big words."

She pursed her lips in the know-it-all way she had. "That's not what I meant."

"Yes, *all* of it. And it's *all* a load of crap. Where's Angela? She'll back me up on this."

"I don't know. She must be running late today."

She watched as he prepared her latte. He liked that she wanted the same thing every morning. He liked her consistency. It made her seem . . . dependable. Yeah, that was it.

"Well, thank you for that in-depth literary criticism," she said finally.

"Hey, you said you didn't need a report, just an opinion. That's my opinion."

He watched her pick up two bags of raw sugar and start to shake them by one end. Slowly, thoughtfully. She turned her eyes to his and he dipped his gaze down to pour some milk into the metal carafe.

"So you're saying you think it's a load of crap," she said, studying him.

He grinned at her. She cracked him up. So serious, all the time, but underneath it all he had the feeling she was really funny. She just refused to let it out. "Yeah, I think that's a fair assessment. Crap, garbage, trash." He thought a moment. "Bullshit."

She nodded. He steamed the milk.

"Would you be willing to go on record with that?"

He looked mock-intimidated. "You got a Bible you want me to swear on?"

"I mean, can I quote you? In my column. I'm thinking of writing about us."

His brows rose quickly, automatically, and he shot her an ironic glance that he had no control over, one that appeared anytime someone said the word *us* to him.

She blushed. Or he thought she did.

"Our divergent points of view," she clarified. "I even thought we could exchange dating stories. Or, well, not stories. Techniques. *Philosophies*," she said, finally satisfied with the word.

He handed her the latte. "In print."

"Yes, in my column."

"What can I get for you?"

It was the surly woman from the office building on the corner. The one with the hard face and strangely graceful hands. She came out at least seven times a day, looking more unhappy as the day went on. He knew not to keep her waiting.

"Triple espresso." She had her money out, as usual.

He glanced at Laurel, who was delicately sipping at the hot coffee. Had the surly woman not been in front of him he'd have liked to spend more than a split second watching the way Laurel's dark lashes lowered as she brought the steaming cup to her face.

"Let's talk about this later," he said to Laurel, taking the surly woman's money and rapidly giving her change.

"Okay, I'll be back tomorrow morning."

"No. Not here." His eyes trailed to the long line of people behind Ms. Surly. He was good at serving and chatting, but what Laurel had proposed deserved more than the one-fifth allotment of attention he could give it while working.

He glanced at Laurel again. Her eyes, as usual, were frank, candid. "Where, then?"

He looked down the street, past the line of people. "I don't know. Someplace I could get a bite to eat, maybe."

"Not Café Quiz," she said, a sour look on her face.

He laughed and turned to look the other direction, past Laurel, then let his eyes drop to her. "Bad memories of the Gray Ghost?"

She shook her head. "Too loud."

"Vespucci's." He jutted his chin up Connecticut Avenue toward the small Italian restaurant between Hillyer Place and R Street. "They've got a great osso bucco."

She arched her brows. "A gourmet. All right, when? Tonight?"

He nearly smiled again. The woman had no pretensions. She would no more fake being busy than she'd pretend to be stupid. "Six thirty. I'll meet you out front."

"Done," she said, and gave him a beaming smile.

Before he could think, it brought an answering smile to his face.

"Can I have my goddamn espresso, please?"

The surly woman's voice could have chilled ice.

Joe handed her the cup and she swore again under her breath.

"Have a nice day," he said as she marched away. He turned back to Laurel, but she too had left. He just saw the back of her coat as it disappeared into the revolving door of her building. Even that made him smile.

He had a date with her. He was pretty sure she wouldn't characterize it that way, but *he* would. If only to needle her.

And that made him smile even more.

Five

A cold snap blew in on an afternoon wind, making Laurel clutch her arms and stamp her feet where she stood outside of Vespucci's. With one gloved hand she pushed the sleeve of her coat back to look at her watch. Six forty-five. He was fifteen minutes late.

She stamped her feet again and blew her breath out in a cloud of quickly dispersing fog. A couple hurried down the sidewalk toward her, the man's arm around the woman, holding her close to his side. They were laughing as he opened the door to Vespucci's.

Laurel watched them dispassionately. Once upon a time she would have felt sick with longing to be part of such a scene. Now she watched them with a sad but informed omniscience. She *had* been part of such a scene, many times, and it didn't last.

Dr. Nadalov said if you cling to someone because of how they make you feel, you're eventually going to be disappointed. Because eventually they're going to make you feel bad. Maybe not forever, maybe not even for long. But once they've made you feel bad, your reason for being with them is compromised. And you'll forever wonder when they're going to make you feel bad again.

Not so with someone you're with for other reasons. A companion of the intellect, for example.

Dr. Nadalov also said that emotions are always children. So if you get together with a man because your emotional children get along with his, you're going to have to face the fact that eventually you're going to end up fighting over the cookies.

Two men emerged from the restaurant and got into a car parked directly in front. As they pulled out of the spot, a black Explorer pulled in, managing the tight space efficiently despite the SUV's size. A moment later, Joe emerged from around the hood.

He looked good, as he was no doubt aware. The ear-flapped hat was gone and his short blond hair lay in stylish disarray. He wore a black leather jacket with black jeans and a dark shirt open at the neck, and walked as if he'd just stepped out of an ad for the vehicle from which he'd emerged.

The whole presentation was calculated. He was just too cool for school, she thought, following that with the realization that even her disparaging phrases were unfashionable.

The moment he saw her, he grinned.

She smiled back, momentarily forgetting the cold. Then, remembering that she'd been left waiting, she shot her arm out of her sleeve and glared at her watch.

"Have you got any idea how cold it is out here?" she asked.

His grin turned sardonic and he directed his gaze at her wrist. "Are you wearing a thermometer?"

"It's nearly six fifty." She shoved her hands in her pocket and let him open the door to the restaurant for her. "You're late."

"I know. Why didn't you wait inside?"

She hesitated. Why hadn't she? She had no idea. "Why didn't you arrive on time?"

"I stopped by my office after dropping off the cart and got ambushed by a phone call. Sorry about that."

"You have an office?"

They stopped in front of the maître d' podium and he sent a sidelong glance down at her. "And a telephone, too," he said. "If I'd known how to reach you I'd have called."

"I guess I should have gotten the number of the pay phone on the corner," she joked. She thought about pointing out that he could easily have called the *DC Scene* office, but she didn't need to be sounding like a shrew to this guy, who probably liked nothing better than to divide women into the categories "shrews" and "bimbos."

Besides, it didn't matter. This wasn't a date.

He opened his mouth to say something, but the maître d' appeared. A tuxedoed man with a pencil-thin moustache, he was vaguely reminiscent of Pee Wee Herman. "Have you got a reservation?"

Laurel glanced into the dining room. Plenty of empty tables with stark white tablecloths glowed in the dim lighting.

"No," she said, ready to follow up with an indignant "Do we need one?" when Joe spoke.

"Something near the fireplace would be good. Is Arturo in the kitchen tonight?"

PeeWee's brows rose. "Indeed, sir. Shall I tell him who is asking?"

Joe's face was amused. "Just tell him to fire up the osso bucco, he'll know."

"Yes sir. One moment." Joe glanced down at Laurel, who had expected him at any moment to pass a twenty in a covert palm to the pretentious man. She'd have been mortified if he had.

"He must be new." Joe shrugged.

Laurel nodded, wondering if there was any chance he was trying to impress her. It seemed as doubtful as it was certain that they would soon be seated near the door to the kitchen, the spot reserved for the unreserved and grasping.

A second later, however, a tall man, made even

taller by a chef's hat, in a white food-stained jacket came through the kitchen doors, wiping his hands on a towel.

"Welcome, welcome," the man said, beaming, his arms aloft in, well, welcome.

Laurel looked up at Joe, who was smiling back at the chef, apparently not concerned at all with whether or not she was impressed. She took a deep breath. She really had to get off her high horse. She may be able to see right through Joe's *type*; still, he was a nice guy and should be treated like one.

"Hey Arturo. How's the veal tonight?" He shook the chef's hand.

"Excellent, as usual. Where have you been? We haven't seen you for weeks."

Joe made a dismissive gesture. "Busy. Too busy. But it should be temporary. Arturo, this is Laurel. Laurel, Arturo."

"Busy, indeed," Arturo said, with a smile at Laurel as he took her hand. "Nice to meet you, Laurel. Come, let me seat you. It's a nasty night, no?"

"Yes, awful," she said. Joe's hand was on the small of her back as they threaded their way through the cozy room. The touch was light, but enough to spread heat up and down her spine.

"Cold weather's good for business, though," Joe said. Arturo laughed.

"Always thinking of business, Joseph. Be careful, it will make you a very dull dining companion."

Laurel shot a quick look back at Joe, whose name, it seemed, really *was* Joe, unless he'd taken the coffee marketing thing way too far.

"But no matter," Arturo continued, "we will find you a nice romantic table to take your mind off work."

"That's all right," Laurel inserted. "We're here to talk business."

Arturo turned a surprised look to her. "Ah, I see. Here we are."

The chef stopped by a table just to the side of the fireplace and next to the exposed brick wall. The spot was intimate, and Laurel wondered if it was somehow reserved for Joe and whatever romantic peccadillo he happened to be embroiled in that week.

Too bad it was all being wasted on her.

They sat and Arturo graciously excused himself to get back to work. Not even a moment later, a waiter appeared with a bottle of red wine and two glasses.

Joe gave her a politely inquiring look. "Do you want some wine? Or would that interfere too much with business?"

She couldn't tell if his smile was teasing or polite, but his eyes were warm. The waiter hovered as if on tiptoe, ready to retreat if his offering turned out to be unwanted.

"No, wine is fine," she said. After all, she didn't want to offend the waiter, or whoever had sent the wine. This was a nice restaurant. One she hadn't tried yet, though she and Ethan had had plans to come here.

She looked at the man across from her as the waiter uncorked the bottle.

Joe, the coffee guy, she reminded herself, though that was hard to remember when he wasn't wearing his ugly hat and army coat. Without those things, he was a handsome blond man in black who obviously knew his way around a bottle of wine.

The waiter had poured a dram into Joe's wine glass and stepped back as if awaiting a royal pronouncement.

For a moment Laurel was transfixed, imagining herself in some sort of play, or old black-and-white movie, where the debonair hero is really a prince who rescues the scrappy American girl from a life of subways and diners.

Joe lifted the glass, tilted his head to see light through the color of it, took a sip, then nodded at the waiter.

"That's the stuff," he said.

Laurel's image of the secret prince disappeared with a nearly audible *pop!*

"What?" Joe looked at her as the waiter poured their glasses, then drifted away.

"Nothing," she said. "I just think you should stop with the gourmet nonsense. You're ruining my impression of you as a regular guy."

He laughed, those long dimples creasing his face, and she thought he ought to stop doing that too, for the same reason. There was something about that smile that got to her, and she'd bet her last dollar he knew it.

"Why's it so important that I be a 'regular' guy?"

"Because if you're not, you won't work at all as my point-counterpoint guy." She sipped the wine. It was good. Really good.

"Your *what*?"

She reached one arm around the back of her chair and unhooked her purse. Bringing it forward, she reached in and pulled out a steno pad.

"My point-counterpoint guy. You said you'd be willing to give me your opinions for my column." She flipped the cover of the pad back and clicked her penpoint out.

He leaned back in the chair. "And I have to be a regular guy to do that?"

"Yeah. Someone our readers can relate to. Now, I don't need a whole lot of personal information, but I need to know a few things, just to give you some background."

His eyes narrowed. "I'm not sure I'm ready to agree to this."

She paused, pen poised over the paper. "Why not?"

He tipped his chair back slightly, his hands on the arms. Her eyes were drawn to the open neck of his shirt and the column of his throat. He was so . . . masculine, she thought. Like one of those guys in *National Geographic's Adventure* magazine—the kind you think is rugged and tough and impossible to date because you'd never be able to keep up with him. The kind who looked good in an L. L. Bean ad, but whom you knew would not be happy by that log-cabin fire all the time. The kind you'd have to rappel down a mountainside for.

"For one thing," he said, bringing his chair back to all fours, "I'm not a publicity hound. I don't like the idea of my private life being made public."

"It'd be really good for business," she said. "Imagine all the women who'd come check out the Hot Stuff coffee cart to see who this guy is."

If she included a picture he'd probably be able to retire, and the paper would sell like hotcakes. Or beefcakes.

"But wouldn't that skew your results?" he asked.

"What do you mean?"

"I mean, if you're thinking we're going to compare dating strategies, how fair of a result would it be if I've got women coming to my cart because of the article? It's not as if you've got a public place to be checked out."

Laurel paused. "You've got a point." She tapped her pen on the pad. "We could do it anonymously. In fact, it would be a lot better for me if my part in it was concealed too."

"I could just be Regular Joe," he suggested. "And you could be Plain Jane."

Her eyes darted to his.

"No one will ever know it's us," he grinned.

She let out a long breath. Well, no one would know it was *him*, anyway.

"Okay," she said, taking another fortifying sip of wine. "We'll be anonymous. I'll have to run it by Rulinda, but I'm sure she'll understand the need for it."

"Rulinda?" he repeated.

"My boss. She's the one who had me read the book. She said it was written specifically for people like me, and I'm starting to think she was right."

Joe leaned forward, his forearms on the table, his hands—hands whose shape and dexterity she'd grown quite familiar with at the coffee cart—circling the bottom of his wineglass.

His eyes were crinkled slightly at the corners as if he were smiling, though his lips weren't. "What do you mean, 'people like you'?"

Laurel took another sip of wine, then realized her glass was nearly empty, while his had barely been sampled. She pushed hers away. She needed to keep her wits about her.

"Well . . . never mind," she said. The last thing she needed was this guy thinking she was a spinster, not that anybody else on the planet still used that word.

He looked at her skeptically.

She decided it was a look she liked receiving from him. It meant he was paying attention, that she was not being predictable.

"Okay, so Regular Joe and Plain Jane," she said, writing the words down on her pad. "I'll still need some background, just reference points, you know?"

He raised a brow and finally took a sip of his wine. "All right. Like what?"

"How old are you?" She gave him her best journalistic look.

The eyes smiled again. "Forty."

Objectivity be damned. Her mouth dropped open. "No way."

He laughed. "Thank you." Then frowned. "Unless . . . did you think I was older?"

He looked so sure it was possible that she had to smile. "No. I thought you might be thirty, maybe thirty-five. Not that I think forty is old or anything."

The corners of his mouth tipped up. "How old are you?"

She hesitated. She wanted to tell him to guess, but she hated it when people did that to her. Plus, she'd be devastated if he guessed too old.

"Come on," he coaxed, with a look she was sure many a young girl in his high school days had succumbed to. "I'm going to find out when I read the article, anyway, right?"

She sipped her wine and took a fortifying breath. "Thirty-five."

This time it was his turn to look shocked, and he did it well. "I really *don't* believe that," he said.

She tried to stop her smile by tucking her chin down and looking at her steno pad. "Thanks but it's true. So, forty." She wrote it down, ridiculously pleased that he was older than she was. "That's good. We're close enough that it'll be an even playing field."

Yeah, right, she thought. *Beauty and the beast. Or rather, the beautiful beast and Laurel.*

"Ever been married?" she asked.

He sat back, hesitated only slightly, then answered with a cool look. "Yes. Once."

Her brows rose again in surprise, though she couldn't figure out which of the many questions that popped into her head to ask first.

"I'm divorced," he supplied.

"Children?" She suddenly pictured those dexterous hands tying a small shoelace and tousling a small head of hair.

He shook his head. "No, thank God."

" 'Thank God'?" Despite her noninvolvement with the man, that statement had her awash in disappointment in him.

"It would have made the divorce that much harder. Not to mention ill advised."

He looked up as the waiter arrived again.

Ill advised? Joe went through a divorce that was hard? He was hurt by a woman? Had he not wanted it to end, and she had? Did she cheat on him? Did he cheat on her? Did they fight? She couldn't imagine him fighting . . .

These questions and more assailed her, but much to Laurel's annoyance the waiter was placing a huge tray filled with ice and raw oysters in the middle of their table, so she couldn't ask.

She glanced again at the tray, registering again

what it was filled with. *Oysters!* She looked at the slimy creatures in disgust, sure now that Joe had some sort of arrangement with the restaurant. *He shows up with a woman, is seated at the coziest table, brought the best bottle of wine and served oysters . . . lots of oysters.*

"Arturo's pretty optimistic about your evening," Laurel said.

Joe laughed. "Why Laurel, are you suggesting something?"

She looked pointedly at the oysters. "Are *you*?"

He laughed again. "I always order them, or at least I used to. Now they just bring them. Help yourself."

She made a face. "No, thank you."

"Ah." He looked at her, his head cocked, his expression only half-teasing. "You disappoint me. I thought you'd be more adventurous."

Her spine straightened and she reminded herself she was *not* on a date. She didn't have to rappel down a mountain, and she didn't have to eat an oyster to impress this guy.

"I fail to see," she said, "how ingesting uncooked invertebrates with the consistency of slugs would make me adventurous."

Joe picked up one of the tiny forks, speared an oyster, dipped it in the cocktail sauce and slid it into his mouth.

Good God, she had to admit there *was* something sensual about them.

His expression was thoughtful. "They're more the consistency of jellyfish. Slugs are . . . chewier."

"You *know* how slugs are?"

"No, but I imagine they aren't very different from snails. Which are chewier."

Laurel sighed and looked down at her paper again. "So, this marriage," she said, angling her pen officially, "how long did it last?"

He didn't answer right away and she looked up.

"Do you want to know for the article or for yourself?"

She hated herself for it but she blushed. "For the article. I think it's relevant how long the relationship was."

"Ten years."

Surprised again, she wrote it down.

"Have *you* been married before?" he asked. "And if so, for how long?"

She kept writing—or rather, surreptitiously doodling—as she said, "Nope. Never been married."

"Then what's your longest relationship?"

She was glad he hadn't expressed surprise. "Four years."

"Live together?"

She looked up. He was studying her, but not in anything but a curious way.

She shook her head.

He nodded. She thought his expression was kind, maybe pitying. Like she was a failed adult. She was thirty-five and hadn't even had a relationship serious enough to live with a man.

She picked up her wineglass—mysteriously refilled—and took a gulp.

"How long have you been at your job?" she asked, professionally.

"About eight years. No, nine." He thought. "Between eight and nine."

"Really? How come I've never seen you before?"

He smiled—God, there was something about that smile, even the closed-mouth version—and looked amused. "You haven't? Well, I haven't been on that corner very long."

"You must be doing . . . pretty well?" She hoped she wasn't being too obvious, but she wanted to know what he made. For the article.

His amused look remained. "I get by."

"More than that, I'd say, judging by your car. Or rather, your environmentally incorrect SUV." She kept her voice light to show she was mostly joking.

"It's a company car. Gotta tow the cart, you know."

She nodded, wondering what coffee-cart company gave its employees cars. She'd never heard of *Hot Stuff* coffee before it showed up on her corner.

"Would you classify yourself as a yuppie?" she asked, with a hint of a smile. It was just the sort of question that would bug him, she was sure.

He got that cool look again. "I don't like to classify myself at all."

"Naturally not." She laughed. "Yuppie" would never go with the image he was trying to project.

"But since we're making you 'Regular Joe' in the article, I think we should figure out how to classify you just the same."

"I have to confess I don't know how to do that."

"All right." She leaned her elbows on the table, sliding her pad next to the oyster tray. "Have you got a nice stereo?"

His lips curved. "Yes."

"You obviously like to eat out at nice places." She made a brief gesture encompassing the room.

"Yes."

"You drive a nice car. *Company* car, sure," she added as he was about to interject, "but a nice one just the same. You dress nicely."

He inclined his head in thanks.

"Where do you live?"

His eyes smiled. "You want an address?"

"Give me a quadrant." She picked up her pen. "Or suburb, though you don't strike me as a suburb type."

He sighed, still looking amused. "Northwest."

She smiled triumphantly. "Yuppie," she pronounced.

He shook his head, picked up the little fork and downed another oyster.

"And you?" he asked after sipping his wine.

She shrugged. "Yuppie, I guess, though my car isn't nearly as nice as yours."

"Is the term *yuppie* really still being used?"

She wrote a few more notes. "It will be. Now, do you date much?"

"This is getting awfully personal."

"It is for Regular Joe, maybe, but nobody's going to know who you are." She paused. "Unless . . . are you embarrassed to tell *me*?"

He inhaled and exhaled deliberately. "I'll tell you if you eat an oyster."

"What?"

"Come on, just one. Broaden your horizons." He held out the other little fork to her.

She leaned back. "My horizons are broad enough, thank you."

"Have you *ever* tried one?"

She paused. "I could never get past their appearance. Or rather, their appearance could never get past my lips."

He speared one with the little fork and leaned toward her. The thing quivered on the end like an unsettled amoeba.

"If you let me get this past your lips I'll answer anything you want," he said, his voice low, his eyes hot.

Her heart crawled into her throat. She laughed to tamp it down. "How many times have I heard *that* line?"

This time he laughed, that smile warming his face in the way that made her feel as if she'd just received a bouquet of roses.

"Come on, I'll even put some cocktail sauce on it." He dipped the thing in the sauce. To his credit, he'd chosen a small one.

"Just one?" She couldn't believe she was considering acquiescing to his disgusting demand.

He tilted his head down and back. "Just one."

She opened her mouth and, her eyes on his, his eyes on hers, he slid the thing past her lips. She felt her body tingle as his hand lingered momentarily near her face.

Then she began to chew, first noting the strange texture, then the cocktail sauce—something hot, like horseradish, invaded her sinuses—and finally, the oyster. Her brows drew together thoughtfully as she swallowed. It . . . it . . . wasn't bad.

"It tastes like the ocean," she said finally.

He beamed. Another prize for her, she thought, wishing he'd lean toward her again, thinking it might even be worth downing another oyster.

"Exactly." He nodded. "What could be better than that?"

She laughed and shrugged evasively. She didn't want to puncture his delight in her.

After a second, the silence seemed awkward and she worried he might feel compelled to say what might be better than that.

"So, listen," she said, pulling a sheet of paper from her bag and leaning forward onto the table a little. "Here's what I want to do."

She pushed the paper toward him and he picked it up.

" 'Short Stops, Inc., a speed-dating service,' " he read. " 'An evening of brief encounters with members of the opposite sex. For just thirty-five dollars meet up to fifteen potential dates. Call 202-555-DATE for more information.'" He looked up at her, his face as serious as it had been all evening. "You're joking, right?"

"No." She shook her head. "Between ten and fifteen men and women get together and rotate every six minutes. So you get six minutes to give someone your spiel, see how they look, get a feel for their personality, and then afterward you tell the coordinator who you'd like to see again. If they say they want to see you again, then you get phone numbers, e-mail, whatever. I figure we both go, I talk to them about looking for a partner with shared values and goals, and you talk to them about, I don't know, exchanging body fluids, and we see what happens. Then I'll record the results for my column."

Joe had been watching her with his mouth partly agape for the first part of this speech, then with an incredulous smile for the last, but when she finished he didn't say anything.

The waiter came and cleared the oyster plate away. He took a moment to brush away crumbs, during which time Joe and Laurel were silent, then he disappeared.

"So what do you think?" She folded her hands in front of her on the now clean tablecloth.

She could picture him, looking as he did now, with fifteen women standing in line waiting to talk to him—well, fourteen, because she'd be there too—while fourteen men sat glaring in angry loneliness.

"I think I need to revise my opinion about your adventurousness," he said finally.

"What do you mean?"

"I mean, doing something like this is . . . well, it's certainly unusual." He gazed at the paper thoughtfully. "I guess it'll at least be interesting."

She brightened. "So you'll do it?"

He raised his shoulders, taking a deep breath. "Why not?"

She could think of dozens of reasons why he wouldn't—not needing such a scheme to secure a date being the most obvious one—but she wasn't about to point them out to him.

"Great! I'll call the number and let you know what we have to do. Are you free that night?"

He read the paper in front of him again, still looking a little shell-shocked, and nodded. "That's next Friday, right? Yeah, okay."

She smiled as two plates of something that smelled heavenly were placed before them.

"But we didn't even order!" she said, *sotto voce*, once the waiter had left.

He looked immediately concerned. "I'm sorry. Arturo probably assumed we both wanted the osso bucco. Do you want to order something different?"

"No, no, this is fine. I was just surprised, that's all." She leaned into the heavenly aroma coming off the plate. "It smells incredible."

"It tastes incredible too. Trust me." He

started to cut his up, then paused, picked up his wineglass and raised it to her. "To adventures in dating."

She smiled into his eyes, picked up her glass and said, "Adventures in dating."

Six

"You're doing what?" Bennett Bridges, Joe's accountant, gaped at him from across his desk. Bennett was a big man with coffee-dark skin whose voice boomed whether he was commenting on the weather or chastising a subordinate.

Joe chuckled and put his feet up next to Bennett's overflowing IN box. "I'm going to a speed-dating, uh, *encounter*, is what they call it."

"Speed dating. What the hell is that?"

"I'm not exactly sure how they do it, but it's a series of six- or eight-minute dates all in the same room. You talk to a set number of women or men as the case may be, see if you've got anything in common, and if you do, they hook you up."

Bennett put his elbows on the arms of his chair

and tented his fingers in front of him. "And you need to do this because . . . ?"

Joe gazed at the wall of diplomas and pictures on the wall next to Bennett's desk. "Because I'm helping out a friend."

"By speed dating."

Joe nodded. Bennett's three children beamed out of a framed shot of a collapsed kid-pyramid on Bennett's desk. "She's writing a column—"

"Aha!" Bennett's smile was wide. "A woman, you're doing this for a woman. I get it. Okay, go ahead."

Joe cocked a partial smile. "She wanted to do it as an experiment, and since she and I see the whole dating thing differently, she wanted to get my take on it. And what the hell, it's not as if I've been involved in any great relationships since my split with Renee. Couldn't hurt."

"Are you kidding?" Bennett laughed. "You've been in some *great* relationships since then. Hot, heavy and here today, gone tomorrow. What could be better?"

Joe eyed him skeptically. "Tell me something, when happily married people pretend they miss dating, is it to make single people feel better, or is it a form of condescension?"

Bennett nodded. "It's condescension, mostly."

"I thought so."

"So who's the girl?" Bennett asked.

Joe studied his friend a moment, knowing there wasn't much he could get by him. "She works in a building near the cart and writes for *DC Scene*. I took her out for dinner the other night."

Bennett's eyebrows rose. "Really."

"Really." Joe smiled placidly.

Bennett nodded, obviously choosing his next question. Joe bet himself it would be something about her looks.

Bennett eyed him. "She hot?"

Joe laughed. He could make millions on Bennett if he could find anyone to bet against him.

"She's tough," Joe said, "that's what I like about her. She says what she means."

Bennett frowned. "So she's ugly."

Joe shook his head, thinking of Laurel's dark eyes and the way they didn't miss a thing. "Not by a long shot."

His friend perked up. "She's good-looking?"

"She's a beaut. But one, she doesn't know it. And two, she wouldn't care if she did."

Bennett scoffed. "Yeah, right."

"And three, she doesn't pull any punches. If she's got something to say, she says it. You always know where you stand with Laurel."

Bennett nodded slowly, a knowing smile on his lips. "Unlike Renee."

Joe's foot, which he'd been jiggling on the desk, suddenly stopped. "What do you mean?"

"I mean, Renee was as sweet as the day is long. Wouldn't fight with you to save her life, you said once. And then . . ." Bennett shrugged.

"And then she left me in a cloud of dust," Joe finished for him.

Maybe that *was* why he liked Laurel's straight talk so much. Maybe it was the reason her contentiousness didn't bother him. But he was pretty sure he wasn't just reacting to his ex-wife's behavior. For one thing, he was far too attracted to Laurel to give his ex-wife much thought at all.

"Hey, listen, I'm sorry I brought that up," Bennett said.

Joe held up a hand. "Forget it."

"No, really—"

Joe took his feet down from the desk and prepared to stand. "Listen, I need you to run some numbers for me on the Dupont Circle location. I'm talking to the owner of that building Monday and want to know where we stand."

"No problem." Bennett leaned forward and moved some papers around. "I think your projections were right on the money this time around. The cart's numbers from just the last two weeks support the move."

"Great. Keep me posted." Joe stood and headed for the door.

"Hey, Joe?"

Joe turned with a laugh. "Bennett, I can handle the mention of my ex-wife's name. Don't worry about it."

"I'm *not* worried about it. I was going to say, you keep *me* posted," Bennett said. "I want to know exactly what this speed dating favor gets you."

Joe gave him a sly look. "If nothing else, I figure it gets me a favor in return."

Bennett's laugh followed Joe out the door.

Don't be late, she'd told him. Speed dating wasn't the sort of thing that could start at anyone's leisure. It was a tight schedule and depended on everyone who'd made a reservation showing up on time.

Laurel looked at her watch as she waited in the lobby of the Washington Hilton. At least she wasn't standing out in the cold this time. He was four minutes late. Good thing she'd built in a cushion of thirty minutes.

Ten minutes later Joe came sauntering through the revolving glass doors. He was wearing the black leather jacket again, this time with blue jeans, hiking boots and a white sweater. With his slightly windblown hair and his rugged cheeks reddened by cold, he looked like he'd just come into a lodge for an apres-ski drink.

Laurel studied his athletic walk. The women at this thing were going to fall all over themselves to get to him. Which was good, because it would leave all the other guys to her.

"Hey." He smiled, perhaps thirty-five of the full hundred watts. "Been waiting long?"

"About twelve minutes," she said. "It's twelve minutes past seven."

He looked amused. "Right around that, yeah.

I called and they told me it didn't start until seven thirty, so I made a stop on the way over."

Laurel decided not to say anything about how he'd agreed to meet her at seven. Instead she thanked God she wasn't dating the guy. That kind of thing would drive her to distraction and before either of them knew it she'd be fulfilling all his expectations of a ball and chain.

They started walking toward Ballroom C, which Laurel had already scoped out since she'd arrived twenty minutes earlier.

"I left a message on the cell number you gave me," he added.

"Really?" She reached for her cellphone in the side pocket of her purse, saw the little voicemail symbol and cursed the thing. For some reason, half the time the phone didn't ring, just took messages and showed missed calls, as if arbitrarily deciding which calls she could have.

Well, at least he'd called. That was something.

"Yeah, I was starving, so I stopped and got a bite to eat. The drive-thru at McDonald's was slower than usual."

Laurel looked up at him, skimming her eyes first along his trim torso. "I don't know why you don't weigh a thousand pounds."

"Hey, you drink whole-milk lattes every morning."

Laurel laughed incredulously, smug all over again that she wasn't dating him. "Thanks a lot, Prince Charming. Are you calling me fat?"

Joe tilted his head toward her. "I did not call

you fat. I meant that I eat McDonald's hamburgers and you drink whole-milk lattes and neither one of us weighs a thousand pounds." A step later he stopped and settled his full attention on her. "Are you nervous?"

In the spotlight of his attention, Laurel suddenly felt tongue-tied. There was something about his gaze that—when he wanted it to be—was intense enough to make intelligent thoughts fly from her head.

Laurel made great work of putting her cell-phone back into her purse, rearranging the pens and mints and lip balm that vied for space to shove it deeply into the pocket. "Yeah. I guess. A little. How about you?"

Joe's expression was instantly kind. "Sure, who wouldn't be? This is a really weird thing to do."

She gave an acknowledging laugh. "I guess so. But then, when you want something to change, you have to try new things, don't you think?"

His gaze left her and scanned the lobby. "That's what they say."

Once more off his radar, she started walking again, but he took her by the elbow and steered her past the Ballroom C, SHORT STOPS, INC., slide-on-letter sign.

She pointed in the direction of the sign. "But— wait. Where are you—?"

"Oh, cool your jets, Miss Punctuality," he said with a dry laugh.

" 'Cool your jets'? You *are* forty, aren't you?"

He shot her a disgruntled look, belied by the

smile in his eyes, and dragged her into a bar just off the lobby. He pulled out one of the tall bar chairs. "Sit," he commanded.

She raised her brows and sat.

A bartender with close-cropped hair and pinched, discreet-looking features drew up to idle in front of them.

"Two kamikazes." Joe sat in the tall chair next to Laurel's.

"Are you nuts?" Laurel objected. "I can't do *shots*—"

"Just one. It'll take the edge off."

She rolled her eyes, smiling. "That sounds like classic frat-boy philosophy, Joe, but I'd rather be coherent tonight, thank you very much."

He leaned on one hip to pull his wallet from his back pocket and looked back at her over his canted shoulder. "Much as I would like to see you incoherent, I don't think one shot'll do it. In fact, in your case I think we'd have to be here quite a while before you lost your composure."

Laurel sat back, unsure whether he'd just complimented her or not. She decided he had.

The bartender, all too quickly, returned to pour the shots from a metal cocktail shaker. The little glasses looked so innocent, like elaborate paper cups filled with lemonade. Joe passed him a twenty.

"You don't have to drink the whole thing." Joe picked one of the shots up. "Just a nip to show we're not taking ourselves too seriously.

Come on." He held the thick, heavy glass aloft. "Adventures in dating," he toasted.

She smiled ruefully and put her fingers on the other shotglass.

"Oh, what the hell," she said. "As my former professor at Columbia always said, 'Alcohol is one of the grand traditions of journalism.'" She picked up the glass, smelled it tentatively, then downed it, wincing as the tart flavor hit the back of her throat.

Joe grinned, passed her the bowl of goldfish crackers by his elbow and they each popped a couple into their mouths. For a second, she was consumed by a feeling of camaraderie she hadn't known since college.

They sat recovering for a moment, wiping their hands on napkins and getting the goldfish salt off their lips. Laurel had to admit, she felt braced.

Joe slapped a palm down on the bar and stood up. "Let's go."

"Into the lion's den," she said, the warmth of the alcohol spreading pleasantly through her chest. Maybe taking the edge off *was* a necessity for something like this. And kamikaze was certainly the right attitude to have.

Ballroom C was huge, too huge, for the twenty-five or so people loitering about the one long table set up in the middle of it. Off to the side a small clutch of people appeared to be registering with a man wearing a red tie, a plastic nametag and a red baseball cap.

Joe and Laurel approached the group and weren't ten feet away when a brightly smiling woman of indeterminate middle age approached them with a canvas bag in each hand. She too wore a red baseball cap, with SHORT STOPS written in old-time baseball lettering above the brim. She also had a whistle around her neck.

"Hi! Here for Short Stops?" she asked, her eyes drifting curiously from Laurel to Joe, apparently wondering why a couple had come. The woman's cap perched delicately atop coiffed hair.

"Yes," Laurel answered. "That is, *I* am. I can't speak for this gentleman." She took a step sideways and looked impersonally up at him.

Joe offered the woman a good 75 watts of smile and said, "You bet. What do I do?"

"Great." She beamed back at him. "My name's Cindy and I'm the coordinator. Now, you all have missed the introduction, but I can fill you in."

Laurel shot Joe a mildly reproving glance as Cindy handed each of them a canvas bag. They'd missed the introduction. She hated missing introductions.

"If you have any questions at any time, feel free to ask. In each of these bags you'll find paper, pen, stick-on nametag and a few other extras thrown in by some of our sponsors. There's also a coupon in there for ten percent off your next Short Stops encounter. Please put your nametag on before we begin, which will be shortly."

Laurel peered into her bag, hoping a next Short Stops encounter would not be necessary.

Cindy leaned toward her, a pen angled on a clipboard held in front of her. "What's your name, dear? I just need to check you off on my list."

"Laurel. Laurel Kane."

"Wonderful. Laurel, you can have a seat there at the end of the table." She looked down the list on the clipboard. "And you must be . . . Joe."

"That's right," he said.

"Joe. Great. Nice to meet you." She beamed again. "You'll start by taking a number from that gentleman over there in the red tie. Whatever number you choose, you start with that woman. All the women will be seated at the table, one through ten. If you start with five, for example, when time is up you will move to six, then seven, then eight, until you finish with ten. Then you'll start with one. Are we clear?"

"Got it," Joe said, already scoping out the women.

"So the women stay seated and the men move?" Laurel asked. This was good. That meant there wouldn't be a line a mile long in front of Joe. It also guaranteed she wouldn't be standing there like the last girl to get picked for kickball in elementary school.

"That's right," Cindy said. "As soon as I blow this whistle, the eight minutes are up and the men have one minute to move on to the next person. Please do not go over the allotted time."

This last she said in such a strict tone that Laurel wondered if her day job was teaching grade school to a particularly recalcitrant class.

Laurel whispered a quick "Good luck" to Joe, seated herself in her assigned spot and took the paper, pen and nametag out of her canvas bag. First she put on the nametag, then jotted a few notes about the room, Cindy, the setup and the fact that Joe, she noted surreptitiously from her seat, was commanding the attention of every woman in the room as he got a number from the man in the red tie.

She let her gaze turn to the other men loitering uncomfortably across from the table. They were an eclectic crew, some wearing suits, some jeans, some gray-haired and one in a turban. They ranged in age from thirty-five to fifty, according to the brochure she'd gotten in advance, and they looked it. She was reminded of junior-high-school dances she'd been to, where the boys and girls stood on opposite sides of the room, posturing and gazing at each other until someone had the courage to venture into the chasm between.

In this case, the chasm was breached by Cindy and her whistle. Smiling broadly, she said, "Gentlemen, please go to the woman whose number you drew from the hat. In eight minutes you'll hear this sound"—she blew sharply into the whistle three short times, then cocked her head at the sound like a small dog—"at which time you will proceed to the next woman. Gentlemen . . ."

She invited them to the women's table with a game-show flip of her hand.

"Start your engines," the woman next to Laurel muttered as the men shuffled toward them.

Laurel glanced over at her and they shared a smile. She was probably about Laurel's age, maybe a couple of years older, was nicely dressed and certainly attractive.

Joe, Laurel noted, was starting somewhere around four. She herself was ten. Across from her a fiftyish man was seating himself with a smile.

She smiled back, noting his loosened tie and wrinkled suit jacket. He had obviously just come from work.

"Hello," he said. His voice was deep and she liked that he said 'hello' instead of 'hi'. "My name's Stan."

"Laurel." She held out a hand.

He paused, then laughed. "You're joking."

She hesitated a moment, then got the joke and laughed with him. "Wow. That has to be a good sign, doesn't it?"

Joe's ear was caught by the sound of Laurel's laughter. He glanced over in time to see her touch the arm of the man across from her. It was a gesture of hers he recognized, having had his arm touched several times the other night at dinner. She tended to do it when someone made her laugh unexpectedly. At the time he'd thought it charming. Tonight it looked a little insincere.

He turned his attention back to the woman across from him. She was probably thirty, a little plain, but with a determined look in her deep brown eyes.

"Do you like cats?" she was asking.

He smiled. "Sure. I grew up with a couple cats. Heckle and Jeckle."

"I've got seven." She stated it like a challenge, as if he might actually say, "No you don't."

"Seven," he repeated. "That's a lot of cats."

"Do you have any pets?"

He paused. He was probably thirty seconds into it and knew this match wasn't going to work for him. Maybe there *was* something to this speed dating.

"I have . . . iguanas," he said slowly. "Ten of them." As her face registered this oddity, he added, "And four parakeets. Twenty-five gold-fish, a gerbil, six mice and a boa constrictor. No wait, five mice."

The woman—Julie, according to her nametag— sat stunned for a moment, then let out a piercing giggle. "Oh, you're *kidding*!"

Laurel saw the woman Joe was with throw back her head in apparent ecstasy and laugh.

She jotted a note. *Regular Joe is a regular card*.

"What do you do for a living?" she asked Stan, who was leaning on his elbows toward her.

"I'm a consultant," he said. "Management consultant."

"Uh-huh," she said, writing down *manage-*

ment consultant without a clue as to what that actually meant. "I'm not sure I know just what a consultant does."

He chuckled. "We're the guys you hire to tell you what time it is with your own watch."

She laughed politely. He had an eyeglass case in his breast pocket. She pictured him wearing them, sitting in an armchair by a fire, reading some large, nonfiction book—on the Roman Empire or some other brainy subject she would never get through herself. It was a comfortable vision.

"So what do you do?" he asked, glancing furtively at her notes.

She put her pen down. "Listen, Stan. I'm going to be totally up-front with you."

His brows rose and he looked at her as if she might be about to tell him she was an undercover cop or a prostitute.

"I'm not looking for my soul mate, or true love, or that 'indefinable chemistry' that so many people—and personal ads, if I can be so candid—talk about. I don't believe in any of that stuff." She leaned her forearms on the table between them and looked at him earnestly. "You seem like an intelligent, sensible guy who might appreciate my approach. I'm not looking for fireworks, but I am looking for something special. I'm looking for someone who shares my values and goals, who's stable and mature, who wants the security and enrichment that marriage can offer without the fairy-tale illusions and emotional claptrap."

She looked at him expectantly.

He was leaning back in his chair now. His brows drew together. "So you're, uh . . . you're . . ."

She nodded. "That's right. I'm essentially looking for an arranged marriage, but one arranged by us. Or, you know, the 'us' who agree on this. So what do you think?"

His expression went from nonplussed to alarmed. "You want to get married?"

"Yes. Well, you know, after talking about the terms and arrangements and making sure we suit."

He laughed nervously and looked sideways along the line of women next to her. He looked down at his hands, then back at her. "Does this mean I'd get, like, some kind of dowry if it worked out?"

She laughed, hoping he was kidding, and wrote *sense of humor?* next to his name. "I guess we could talk about that."

"Look, honey." He leaned forward again, then dropped his head and shook it. "Sorry, sorry. I didn't mean to call you honey. I get into trouble with that all the time."

"It's all right." She touched him lightly on the arm. In truth, the kindly way he said it went perfectly with her vision of him bespectacled by the fire.

He brought his head back up. To her, his eyes suddenly looked tired. "I think I understand what you're trying to do. And as someone who's a little bit older than you, let me just say it's not as bad as it seems out here."

"Out here?" she repeated.

"I don't know what your circumstances are, maybe you're fresh out of a failed relationship or a divorce or something that's made you want to give up. But dating isn't all bad. And the right guy could be just around the corner. You just have to keep plugging away at it."

She sat up straight. "I'm not—"

The whistle blew.

"All right everyone!" Cindy's voice rang out. "Move to the woman on your right!"

The tone of her voice said *Drop your pencils and turn over your tests!* All the men immediately stood up.

"Wait," Laurel said as Stan rose with the rest of them. "I'm not—"

"Good luck, honey." He leaned down to shake her hand, then smacked his forehead. "Darn, did it again." He smiled, turned and walked briskly alongside the table toward Woman #1.

"I believe in romance," Laurel heard Joe tell Woman #9, next to her. "I think dating is a go-with-your-gut kind of thing."

"I do *too!*" Woman #9 gushed back at him.

"Isn't it sad how cynical everyone's become about finding their soul mate?"

Laurel revised her opinion of the woman. She'd thought her mature and self-possessed until Joe had sat down across from her.

Laurel dragged her attention back to the man across from her. Vince, his nametag said.

"I think romance is overrated," Laurel said. "I'm not looking for an accelerated heartbeat or sweaty palms. I don't need flowers and chocolate. What I want is much more substantial. Do you know what I mean, Vince?"

Vince didn't know what she meant. Vince was looking at her breasts and scratching the side of his neck with three stubby fingers.

"Yeah, yeah, sure. I'm not really a flowers-and-chocolate kinda guy anyway." He laughed what could only be characterized as a Beavis-and-Butthead laugh. "I don't like sweaty palms either, you know. Especially 'cause, you know, I work with my hands and all."

"Oh? What is it you do?" She made some doodles on the pad in front of her. She was pretty sure Vince wasn't going to make her list.

"Well, I work as a beer distributor, and you don't want to be dropping any cases of beer on yourself, lemme tell you. But in my spare time I work on Harleys. You know, the big hogs?"

"Oh?" she said again, trying to infuse the word with a tone of interest, and wrote *Mechanic. Handy?*

"Yeah, you ever ridden one?"

"I don't think so," she said.

"If you did, you'd know it, Laura. Once you wrap your legs around a Harley you don't ever forget it." He brought his eyes up from her breasts just long enough to see how she liked his joke, then let them drop again.

Four interminable minutes later, Joe was in front of her.

"They could have at least had some music on," Joe said as he sat down across from Laurel. It was a relief to get to her, frankly. If he had to listen to one more live-action personal ad he was going to resort to belching and farting and generally making an asshole of himself.

She was finishing up writing some notes and asked, "Why?" before looking back up at him.

"Because this is so damn dry we might as well be interviewing each other for household help. Oh wait, I forgot—that's what you're doing."

She grinned. "That's right. And there are some really good prospects here. I'm actually getting excited."

"Oh yeah?" He sat back in the chair and folded his arms across his chest. "These guys are responding to your spiel?"

"As a matter of fact, they are." She crossed her arms over her chest too. Pointedly. But she couldn't keep it up. She leaned forward and put her hands on the table. "In fact, one of them, Vijay, thinks he's going to do that same thing." She nodded her head once. *So there.*

"Is that so?"

"Yes. And another guy, Edward, told me he thinks I'll find my mate in no time."

"Well," he said, thinking if he'd said that to a woman he'd have meant it as a kiss-off more than a vote of confidence. "Good for you."

She leaned her cheek on one hand and Shakespeare's line *O! that I were a glove upon that hand* sprang inexplicably to his mind.

"So how's it going for you?" she asked with a gentle smile.

She was positively glowing with success.

He forced a smile. "Great. Everyone seems really nice." Which was true, he thought. So why did it all seem so depressing to him?

Her gaze skewered him. "You're going to have to be more honest than that when we talk afterward."

He spread his hands out to the sides. "What do you mean? I'm always honest."

"I mean, you don't have to sugarcoat your reactions. You're not doing this for my benefit. Or even yours, really. It's for the article, right?"

Her rich dark eyes were perfectly candid, and he had a hard time not interrupting her to say that in that case he was ready to leave.

"So we both need to be completely honest for this to work," she continued. "I think our degrees of satisfaction and success will be interesting to people reading the column, but only if they ring true."

"Hey, I was just trying to be a good sport."

"Don't think I don't appreciate it." She gave him another glowy smile. "But I want to know what you really think. Maybe you should take some notes."

He looked down at the scrawl-filled pad in front of her, several of its pages folded over the back.

"Don't worry about that," he said. "I think the details of this evening are going to be with me for a long time."

Seven

They agreed to meet afterward at Clyde's in Georgetown. Even though it was a Friday night, the bar was pretty subdued. This time, it was Laurel who was late.

"What took you so long?" Joe asked. "It's twelve minutes after nine."

She looked at her watch, clueless that he was echoing her earlier reprimand to him for being late. "No it's not. It's nine thirty. Besides, I stopped to interview a couple of the women who were there, just to get some more perspective for the piece."

Joe picked up his beer. "Just women? Or did you and Vijay get a moment to talk about how many cows he'd get if he agreed to marry you?"

"Glass of white wine," Laurel said to the bartender, then turned on the barstool to rest her feet on the bottom rung of his. "No, just the women. I didn't want to skew any results by talking further to any of the men. Besides, I didn't get the impression the Short Stops organizers were encouraging that. They seemed to be hustling us out of there pretty quickly."

"Probably had to clear the room for Round Two. Pit Stops. Portable John convention." He took a long swallow of beer.

She was silent a moment. Then: "You're in a bad mood."

"No, I'm not."

"What, did the kamikaze wear off?"

He turned to look at her. She was smiling. She looked really pretty. What the hell was she doing, arranging her own marriage? Maybe she was crazy, maybe that's why she'd never found anyone. Maybe she had some hidden personality defect that chased off anyone who showed an interest. Maybe she was one of those women for whom nothing was good enough.

"As a matter of fact, I think it did." He raised a hand to the bartender, who was unloading a plastic tray full of clean pint glasses. "Hey Lou! Two kamikazes."

"Comin' right up." Lou abandoned his task to take up two shot glasses.

"No way," Laurel said. "I've got to work tomorrow."

"Me too, and a helluva lot earlier than you do."

She reached into her giant tote bag and pulled

from it the pad of paper supplied by Short Stops.

"So tell me what you thought. Just off the top of your head. First reaction to the evening." She laid the pad on her knees.

She was close to him, with her feet on the rungs of his barstool, and he could smell her light perfume. Her hands, one on the pad, one holding the pen, were pale and graceful, the nails cut short, but shiny. He liked hands, always noticed them, and hers reminded him of birds.

"Honestly," he said, looking her in the eye, "I found it depressing."

"Really." She looked at him intently. "Why?"

He took a deep breath. "All those people—seemingly good people, people who shouldn't have trouble finding someone to date—putting themselves through the awkwardness of a night like this . . ." He paused, shook his head at the effort of trying to put into words the nature of his discouragement. "It was like a violation, like a small-talk mugging."

She was writing furiously. "A small-talk mugging, that's *great*. Go on."

He looked at the top of her head, her hair shining in the dim light of the bar.

"It's everything that's wrong with modern life," he said, wondering if she were actually listening to his words or just writing them down. "We look for instant gratification in everything. Communication has to be instantaneous, and accessible no matter where we are. We need to be entertained constantly. Not a moment can go by that we don't have a television or a radio or a cell phone nearby so that we don't have to be alone with our own thoughts. We're assaulted nearly every second of every day by some form of advertising—hit-and-run contact that makes us evaluate who we are for a split second so we never actually stop and look outside ourselves. And now we've got speed dating. Cut to the chase. Make your decision in eight minutes or less. Knock up to ten people off your list in one efficient evening."

He sat back and took a deep breath. The bartender had put the shots in front of them and disappeared at some point during this diatribe; suddenly, they didn't look nearly large enough to Joe.

"Wow," she said quietly.

He looked over at her. Her eyes were on him, but she seemed not to be seeing him.

"That's really true," she said thoughtfully. "But why do you think so many people feel the need to do it, then? Do you think the speed of our culture is making people feel they need to hook up faster? That by taking the time to be sure one thing's right means they'll miss out on the next thing?"

Joe picked up a shot glass. "Laurel."

Her eyes focused on him. He held up the glass.

She shook her head. "I shouldn't. That first one was plenty for me."

"Well, cheers then." He downed the shot.

For some reason, Laurel gave a short laugh and reached for one of the glasses. "All right. I guess I can't let a depressed man drink alone."

"I'm not depressed," Joe said. He watched her wince as she swallowed the kamikaze and he couldn't help smiling. "I'm discouraged. For those people. For mankind in general."

Her eyes watered from the shot and she dabbed at their corners with a napkin. She swiped the napkin across her lips and chuckled. "That's big of you."

"Well, someone's got to keep an eye on these things."

She thought for a moment. "But . . ."

He could practically see the wheels turning in her dark eyes. "But what?"

"Well, isn't dating by attraction—which is your preferred method—isn't that just another form of instant gratification? We want to be pleased right off the bat, just by looking at someone, before they even open their mouth. That feeds right into all that you just said is wrong with the world. While my method, on the other hand, takes more time, more thought, more conscious effort to discover not just who we are, but who our partner *should* be."

Joe suddenly felt tired. She had a point. A point he wasn't sure how to contest. "It's still gratification."

"Sure, but it's not instant. It's not that shallow, insincere, here-today-gone-tomorrow kind of gratification that disappears so easily."

"Well, okay. But still." He sipped his beer, wondering if the kamikaze had short-circuited his brain or if her theory really was starting to make sense.

"My method," she pressed, "by being more of a contract between two people, is more equitable from the outset. You have to think about both people before the arrangement is made. It's not a matter of me finding someone to make me happy, and the second they don't I bail," she said. "So in a sense, it could be a kind of antidote for an increasingly self-obsessed world. Don't you think?"

He let his eyes rest on her a minute, the details of her argument swirling in his head. "Has it really never worked out for you, Laurel? The attraction thing?"

She'd been leaning slightly toward him, but at that she sat up straight. "What do you mean?"

"I mean you must have followed your heart before, been attracted to someone and gotten carried away in a relationship." He shifted so he looked at her more directly, more intently. "You've felt that, that incomparable thing that's bigger than you are, bigger than you've ever been, that thing that grabs you by the throat—*by the heart*—and doesn't let you go. Haven't you?"

She laughed tightly. "Of course! Why do you think I'm so sure it doesn't work?"

He opened his mouth to ask how, having felt it, she could possibly consider doing without it, but she held up a hand.

"Before you say anything about my just being jaded, let me add that I know that it can be fun and exciting—exhilarating, even—but it doesn't work, not long term. It's just infatuation. If you go into a relationship because of the excitement and fun and everything, then you're screwed when all that goes away."

He tilted his head, scanning her face, the guarded expression of her eyes. She hadn't felt it. She couldn't have. "Why does it have to go away?"

She looked at him as if he were the most naïve person on earth and spread her hands out helplessly. "Because it does."

He laughed. "Pretty compelling argument."

"Have you ever been in a relationship where it didn't?" she countered, leaning forward again.

"Of course." He answered automatically, and took another sip of his beer.

"Then why did it end?"

He started to answer blithely that there were plenty of other problems that could destroy a relationship, when something in his gut shifted. He pictured Renee telling him she was moving out, that their problems weren't fixable. He remembered at the time thinking she was right, that their issues were too complex, their disagreements too ingrained and habitual to be changed. But when he'd discovered shortly thereafter that she was living with another man, he'd known. It wasn't their problems that had split them up, it was that the excitement, the fun, the exhilaration, had left their marriage *for her.*

"Listen," Laurel said, twirling the base of her glass on the high polish of the bar, "I was in a relationship once with a guy I thought might be it. He was perfect for me. We never fought. In fact we got along famously. Then it just sort of . . . went away. For me and for him. And after a while it became obvious to both of us that we were staying together just because we were used to it."

She shrugged. He watched her sip her white wine. The glass looked wrong in her hand, too bland. She should be drinking a rich dark red, and smiling that rich unfettered smile he'd seen only once or twice.

Sitting here dissecting an old relationship with the emotional investment of an eighth-grader poking a dead frog in biology class was dispassion on a criminal scale. She couldn't possibly be that unfeeling. Could she?

He motioned to the bartender for another beer. "Mind if I ask who the guy was?"

Her expression turned wary. "Why?"

"I'm just wondering if it was the guy you made cry, the one your friend was talking about that first day I met you."

She looked at him a long moment, then nodded. "Ethan, yes."

He let out a slow breath, looking at her assessingly. Maybe this was her flaw. Maybe she genuinely had no feelings. Maybe she couldn't even *understand* feelings. "Then surely you see the fallacy in your thinking."

Her brows drew together. "What do you mean?"

"I mean, if Ethan was crying when you split up,

then he wasn't staying in it because he was used to it. And he wasn't getting out because it was over. He was getting out because it was over *for you*."

She looked down, thoughtful, spinning the base of her glass on the bar again.

"The trick for him now is to find a woman whose emotions stick around as long as his do," he added. Better advice he couldn't give to himself.

"And for me?" She looked at him with a slight smile. "What's the trick for me now?"

"For you, I'd say the trick is to find a man who compels your feelings to stick around." He watched as she took this thought, rolled it over and discarded it.

"Or maybe . . ." She cocked her head and looked him confidently in the eye. "Maybe the trick is for me to realize that feelings *don't* stick around, and to find a partnership based on something else."

She picked up her wineglass and took another sip. He studied the side of her face, the way her burnished hair curled around one ear to her chin, the way her lashes made her eyes look lined. She couldn't look so passionate and be so cold. She just couldn't.

"Laurel." He said it on impulse, to feel the word on his tongue, then wasn't sure what to say. She was wrong, he knew it with every fiber of his being. He just didn't know how to explain to her *why* she was wrong.

She turned toward him, her eyes dark and unfathomable. Maybe it was her questioning expression, maybe it was the slight flush of her cheeks, maybe it was the warm flush in his gut, but he leaned toward her and planted a kiss on her startled, parted lips.

Oh my God, was her only thought as Joe leaned toward her and she realized he was going to kiss her.

The movement was swift, the kiss tender, and for the brief second it lasted the bar seemed to go silent and the world to stop breathing.

The contact zinged to every nerve ending in her body.

He sat back, his light eyes on her face and his lips in a slight smile.

She didn't know what to do with her expression, and had the feeling she might look angry, which wasn't the case. One of her hands started to rise to touch her lips, which felt hot at the point of contact, but she thought better of it and reached for her wine.

She gulped the last three sips down and gave him what she hoped was a composed look. "What was that for?"

He shook his head when their eyes met. "I'm not sure."

"You're not sure."

"No. I just felt like doing it."

"Uh-huh." She nodded slowly. "I suppose I should be glad you didn't just feel like grabbing my breast."

He laughed. "Maybe I just wanted to see what you'd do."

She crossed her arms over her chest and raised her brows. "I haven't done anything, so what does that tell you?"

"That's not true. You looked surprised, you polished off your wine, you took a moment to collect yourself, then you asked what I did it for. You did a lot, actually."

"Okay, and what did that tell you?"

He smiled. "That you were surprised, thirsty, confused, and curious."

She looked at him. "Well. That's just fascinating."

"Hey, I participated in your experiment. This one was mine. Besides, I don't have to give away all my results right away, do I?"

"*Ha!* I know what you were doing," she said with a smile of her own, though truth be told she wasn't all that pleased to have figured it out. "You were trying to pull me in to some romantic moment to show me that no matter what I say I'm still susceptible to that kind of thing."

She watched his face for a telltale blush or a look of chagrin, something to show her she'd guessed the truth, but he was poker faced.

"That's what you think, huh?" he said.

"That's what I think."

His look was sly. "And were you suscepted?"

She laughed, a tremulous, defiant thing, and said, "That's not even a word. And surely you know me better than that by now."

But he didn't laugh with her. Instead, he watched his fingers turn the base of his beer glass around and around on the cocktail napkin in front of him. "I'm starting to."

She wondered then, if she'd hurt his feelings somehow. Had the kiss been a real gesture? Had he been . . . hoping for more?

"Joe," she began, trying to still a vague fluttering around her solar plexus, "you're not—"

"I guess you just seem really normal." He sat up straight and looked at her frankly again. "You know, after the group of crazies I just spent the evening talking to."

"Group of crazies?"

He looked at the pad of paper on her lap. "Shouldn't you be writing that down?"

She glanced at the paper, then back at him. "Did you think they were crazy?"

He shrugged and picked up his beer. "Maybe not crazy. Just weird. For being there. For being so *serious* about being there."

"*I* was serious," she said.

"Yeah, but you were serious about the article. The experiment. That's different."

She wasn't sure he was right. Not about it being different, but about her being serious only about the article. She felt good about her prospects. For the first time since coming up with the scheme to arrange her own marriage, she felt like it might really be *possible*. That there might actually be a way to circumvent all the hoopla and hassle and heartbreak of trying to fall in love.

"So that was a thank-you kiss?" she asked. "For being normal? Because if that's the case, then you should probably be kissing everyone here."

He glanced at her out of the corner of his eye. "No thanks. And since you dragged me to that dating fiasco, I guess you can't be considered completely normal either. So . . ." He hesitated, then shook his head, dismissive. "It was just an impulse."

Laurel tried to keep her mind on the article after that. She took notes on his comments, made notes on her reactions to his comments, then told him she had to get home and get to bed.

But that night, lying in the darkness of her room, her fingers traced her lips. And she stretched that brief moment of contact out in her memory to decipher just what, exactly, her feelings about it had been.

Not that her feelings about it mattered. That was the whole point. She could do this without feelings; she could control her whole life with her head and never have to worry about her heart again.

The fact that Joe's kiss, brief as it had been, had awakened parts of her body she'd nearly forgotten about meant nothing. Nothing! She knew where those kinds of responses led—to complicated mistakes that took a long time to recover from. She wasn't going to be fooled by a bunch of hormones, or pheromones or whatever chemical components were kicking up their heels over Joe. Those things meant nothing, and frankly it was liberating to know that and be able to act on it with perfect confidence.

The fact was, her life was improving daily. The column was going to be great. Rulinda was going to love it, and that, along with the book review she was doing on *Love Is Not the Answer*, was going to make her look really good when promotion time came along.

Plus, she was well on her way to finding her life partner, and she was ready to make that choice. She was confident, she was successful, and she was controlling her destiny.

Essentially, she told herself, sliding one finger along her lower lip, she'd figured life out. If you put your feelings aside, it just wasn't that hard.

It was Thursday before she made a point of seeing Joe again. She hadn't gotten coffee in the mornings that week because she'd been getting to work early to write the column and polish up the book review while still getting her other editing done.

But she had it marked down on her calendar to talk to him on Thursday. She needed the results of his evening to put the finishing touches on the column.

She'd heard nothing from Short Stops, Inc., and when she'd called them that morning to find out when she would get responses from the men she'd met, she was told that everyone had been notified of them on Tuesday.

"No one called me," Laurel said, unimpressed by their organizational skills. "I called

Monday morning with *my* list well before the noon deadline."

She'd put down five of the men she'd met as those she'd like to see again, which meant that those five men would be informed of her interest and supplied with her phone number and e-mail address. So it wasn't as if she'd indicated she wasn't interested in knowing who'd wanted to see her again.

"Hold on," the girl on the other end of the line said wearily.

Minutes passed and the girl came back on the line. "Okay, I've got your night here. What was your name again?"

"Laurel Kane. K-A-N-E."

More shuffling of papers. After a minute, the shuffling stopped and there was a brief silence.

"Uh . . ." the girl said.

"Yes?" Laurel was all politeness. How hard could this be? You make a list of everyone she wanted to see and everyone who wanted to see her and then you share that. Could the girl not just read her the list?

"Hang on a second," the girl said.

Laurel sighed heavily, but she was already on hold.

A moment later a perkier voice came on. "Hi, this is Cindy! How may I help you?"

"Hi, Cindy. This is Laurel Kane. I was calling for my responses to last Friday's Short Stops meeting?"

"Oh yes," she said briskly. There was a brief

pause. Then, "I'm sorry. This meeting didn't produce any good leads for you, but we've got another event scheduled for a week from next Friday. Would you care to sign up for that one? If you've got your coupon from the last event, the next one will only cost thirty-one fifty."

Laurel's brows drew together and she hunkered down over her desk, the receiver very close to her mouth and ear. "I'm sorry, what do you mean it didn't produce any good leads for me? Shouldn't I be the judge of that?"

Cindy cleared her throat. "Of course. And yes, I see here that you indicated *you'd* be interested in seeing some of our participants again. But I'm afraid you had a zero response quotient."

Laurel paused. "A what?"

"A *zero response quotient.*" Cindy said the words slowly as if English were not Laurel's first language. "In other words, we received no responses for you."

For a second the statement hung in the air, much like the coyote before he realized he'd run off the cliff.

"A lot of times it takes several tries to find someone suitable," Cindy continued perkily. "And it may sound silly, but there are many, many fish in the sea! Can I schedule you for our next event? As I said, it's a week from next Friday and it's a whole new set of faces. Do you have the coupon from your goodie bag?"

Laurel's cheeks were starting to burn as the coyote began to fall. "Cindy, let's be blunt here.

Are you telling me that no one, not one of those . . ." she wanted to say *losers* ". . . men said they wanted to see me again?"

There was a long pause.

"I'm sorry, hon. But again, sometimes it takes—"

"Not even when they were notified that I was interested in seeing them?"

Cindy cleared her throat again. "You know, I think that evening we had an unusual group. Everyone seemed to have someone very specific on their minds. There were no overwhelming responses to anyone, male or female. Sometimes it just happens like that. You know how it is. Chemistry is so unpredictable, and if you happen to have a group of men who are . . . maybe less than open-minded . . . ?"

Laurel was having difficulty drawing breath. Anger, mortification, and most of all an intense hatred for Cindy were constricting her airway.

"So can I sign you up for next time?" Cindy's voice suddenly sounded very small.

Laurel's, however, was not. "No. Thank you," she said coldly, and hung up the phone.

None of those guys—not even Stan, with whom she'd shared a very genuine laugh—had wanted to see her again. *None.* Her mouth went dry with indignation. How could none of them have wanted to see her? Vijay! He'd said he was thinking about doing the same thing she was. Why hadn't *he* at least put her on his list?

What was it with those losers? Even back in

college, when she'd had a steady boyfriend, other guys would still try to date her. They'd even ask her out as "just friends," then try to get her into bed anyway. So she knew it wasn't as if men were notoriously good at listening to and respecting what a woman said about her dating intentions. These guys just hadn't wanted to see her. Ever again.

Then it hit her. Even *Joe* hadn't put her on his list.

She stood up with the force of a geyser jetting from the ground. The backs of her knees hit her chair and sent it careening into the bookcase behind her. She stalked around the desk, grabbed her coat and headed for the coffee cart.

There was only one person waiting at the Hot Stuff cart when she emerged from her building. An old, white-haired man wearing a hat and a black wool coat over his stooped shoulders.

Joe looked up as she neared and flashed her a smile. She felt her cheeks burn all over again.

"So how come you didn't put me on your list of people to see again?" she demanded as soon as she was close enough.

Joe handed the old man a small coffee cup and waited patiently while the gentleman counted out change and lint from his pocket with gnarled hands.

"That wasn't the point, was it?" The air was warm for a winter day, so the ear-flapped hat and army coat were abandoned for a blue UVA sweatshirt and jeans. "Besides, you didn't put me on your list, either."

The old man counted fifty-three cents into Joe's palm. "Thanks a lot," Joe said and the old man waved one hand vaguely as he turned away.

"You actually sell something here as cheap as fifty-three cents?" She watched the old man's retreating back as he headed for Dupont Circle. She wondered if he was one of the old people who sat on the benches there and fed the birds.

Joe wiped a cloth over the top of the cart. "Senior-citizen discount."

She glanced at Joe, then back at the man inching down the sidewalk, and knew, somehow, that Joe made that discount up for that man.

She drew herself back to the matter at hand. "How do you know I didn't put you on my list?"

"Because . . ." He looked at her as if she were dense. "You weren't on my list."

A rushing sound started in her ears. "You got a list?"

Of course he'd gotten a list. There was no way in hell a guy like Joe would get a zero response quotient.

"Sure. Tuesday afternoon. Haven't you gotten yours?"

She swallowed hard. "Yeah. Just now." It wasn't really a lie. "How many responses did you get?"

His cheeks seemed to go a little red and for a second she felt relief. Maybe everyone there was deranged and he hadn't gotten any responses either.

"Nine," he said.

"*Nine?*"

He nodded and continued wiping down the cart, giving it much more attention than she figured it needed.

"Nine of the women wanted to see you again," she stated, just to be clear.

"That's right."

"In other words, all of them. All of them wanted to see you again."

He gave her a sidelong look. "All except you."

"Which hardly counts." She threw one hand out with the words, then folded her arms across her chest and gazed down the street. *There were no overwhelming responses to anyone, male or female*, Cindy had said. If *nine* wasn't overwhelming, Laurel sure as hell wanted to know what was.

Joe straightened and looked at her with interest. "Why? How many did you get?"

She ignored his question. "How many did you say *you* wanted to see again?"

He hesitated.

"Come on," she said, "how many?"

He looked sheepish. "Promise you won't get mad."

"For what?"

"For being a bad sport?"

She just looked at him, indignation still quivering along her nerves. *Zero response quotient.*

"None," he said. "I didn't want to see any of those people again."

She slowly digested this information. "So you gave them no names, and they gave you nine."

He nodded, studying her. "And how many did you say you got?"

"What did you say to them? The women, that is? That night. Did you tell them you wanted to see them? Did you lead them on somehow?"

"No." He looked insulted. "I was just trying to be nice."

"Oh come on, I heard you tell the woman next to me that you *believe in romance*." She fluttered her hands out sarcastically with the words.

"I do."

She planted her hands on her hips. "And did you happen to mention to any of them your romantic love-'em-and-leave-'em philosophy of dating?"

He squinted his eyes as if trying to think. "I wouldn't call that a philosophy. More of a bad habit, really."

She blew air out of her cheeks and looked at the sky. It was cloudy, for all of its being warm, and she suddenly wished it were pouring. This was humiliating. Beyond humiliating. But then, trying something new was always difficult at first. Her problem was, she was thinking about her feelings, and her feelings didn't matter.

"Look," she said, pulling herself together, "we need to get together so I can take some final notes. The column's due Monday, so do you have any time tonight or tomorrow when we can talk?"

"Tonight's better."

For some reason, she felt her dander go up again. "Hot date tomorrow?"

One shoulder lifted. "We'll see."

She brushed her hand back through her hair, forgetting she'd pulled it back that morning, and had to disentangle her fingers, dislodging the French knot she'd worked so hard on.

"Okay, how's tonight?" she asked, working to undo the knot, now that it was half in her face anyway.

He watched her with a small smile. "Great."

"Great." Her voice was considerably less enthusiastic. "How about five thirty, Café Quiz."

"Fine."

She turned away.

"Laurel?" he said after she'd gone just a couple of paces.

She turned around, locating the last of the bobby pins in her hair, and let her hands drop to her sides.

"Are you okay?"

"Of course!" she said, but the words were a little shrill even to her ears. She took a deep breath and an explanation tumbled out with her exhale. "But just to let you know, since it'll be in the column anyway, I wasn't on anyone's list. *No one's*. Not one of the guys in that room wanted to see me again."

He shook his head, his expression painfully

kind. "Not one of the guys in that room was good enough for you, Laurel."

She had to work to keep a lump from growing in her throat. "Thank you, Joe, but I think it's me. Well, that and they're still deluded by the idea of falling in love. If I could send each of them a copy of Dr. Nadalov's book, I would."

Joe chuckled. "I'm sure Dr. Nadalov would appreciate that."

Laurel turned toward her building, then stopped and turned back. "Can I ask you something?"

"Of course." He stopped wiping down the cart, his hand resting on the balled-up rag, and looked at her.

She wanted to ask why he was so nice to her all the time, when she was such a pain, but she couldn't figure out a way to phrase the question so that it didn't sound self-pitying. He was probably just nice to everyone, out of habit, as part of his business sense.

"Laurel?" He prompted with a smile.

She shook her head. "Never mind. Just, uh . . . just thanks."

He looked at her a long moment, then said, "You're welcome."

Eight

Joe stood in front of Café Quiz, enjoying the last strangely balmy breaths of the unseasonably warm day.

He pictured Laurel's hair as it had looked that afternoon, after she'd wrestled it out of that prim little bun she'd been wearing, and wondered if he should tell her how sexy she'd looked with it all tumbling around her shoulders in disarray. If she'd looked like that last Friday night at the speed dating thing, she'd have been on every guy's list. Including his.

But then she'd apparently wanted to convey, in words as well as looks, her austere approach to dating. To life. He didn't know why, but he couldn't shake the feeling she was forcing herself into the role. She was decisively squelching something innately opposed to the task she'd set for herself. He found it intriguing, and challenging. Every time he got her to laugh it felt like a triumph, like one small brick knocked out of the wall. And if he knocked enough small bricks out, the whole wall could come tumbling down. Then they'd see what she was made of.

He leaned back against the wall next to Café Quiz's front window and rested one foot flat against the brick. Arms crossed over his chest, he watched men and women in varying states of business attire leave their buildings and head toward the Metro.

A dreadlocked twenty-something in a tie-dyed shirt went into Kramerbooks, and a gray-suited woman came out. On the corner a grizzled homeless man leaned against a mailbox, eating an onion like an apple and staring past the world with rheumy eyes. On the opposite corner, a young man played a violin. He was neatly dressed in a collared shirt and jeans. He might have been a college student. Certainly he had some talent, his violin case was rapidly gathering bills from passersby.

It was a breath of spring in January and everyone, it seemed, was out. Even the Childe Harold restaurant down the block had its outdoor tables set up.

Joe saw Laurel emerge from her building, hoisting her purse up onto her shoulder along with an overstuffed tote bag. She looked as focused and businesslike as the others who had passed him by, each seamlessly metamorphosing into the next.

Behind *her* no-nonsense exterior, however, Joe again thought he could see a woman of passion. A woman of passion who was struggling to deny it, he corrected.

Of course, he could be making that up to suit his own idea of what she should be. Then again, maybe every single person who passed him had that in common with her. Maybe he was an arrogant jerk for even wondering if she, and everyone like her, was hiding some inner depth or covering for the lack of one.

In any case, she was walking down the street with the same inward focus as all the other people leaving their offices, seemingly encased in their own circumstances and not trying terribly hard to see past them.

Her eyes found his and he smiled. It was easy to smile at her, she always seemed to need one.

She gave him a tight smile in return, then looked at the ground as she approached. Still smarting over the speed-dating results, he guessed. Taking it personally despite having gone out of her way to make it impersonal to everyone else.

"Hey," she said as she got close. "You could have waited inside."

"I thought we could take a walk." His eyes took in her creamy skin and the deep, rich brown of her eyes. Could a person's looks have anything to do with what was inside? Was that what kept him wondering about her? "We should take advantage of this weather," he added.

She looked up at the sky automatically, as people do when you mention the weather, and hefted the tote bag a little higher on her shoulder.

"I'll take that." He took the heavy bag from her and turned down the sidewalk. "Come on. It'll do you good. You don't get enough sunshine."

She laughed at that. "It's going to be dark in ten minutes."

"Fresh air, then."

She walked briskly beside him, her heels clicking on the pavement. They walked down to the circle and crossed into its center, walking around instead of straight through.

"When I was a kid my dad would come here to play chess," Joe said. "I used to come and watch, amazed that some of these ragged old guys could beat the pants off him in minutes."

"They could?"

"Yeah. I mean, Dad would beat a lot of them, but there were some, the real regulars who always had a crowd watching them, who knew the game inside and out."

"Did you ever play?" she asked.

He shook his head. "Nah. My dad and I never shared the same kind of logic. I'm sure a psychologist would have a field day with our relationship—that he was a linear thinker and I'm an instinct kind of guy. Really, I think it was more of a generational thing."

"You're of a generation with a shorter attention span," she said with a smile.

"That's right. It's kind of a problem." It was a conclusion he'd only recently made about himself, and he wondered why he was telling her about it.

"I know what you mean," she said, surprising him. "I battle it all the time. I feel like it's both inherent and self-indulgent to be so mood driven, but I am."

Well, that explained something, he thought, glancing down at her as they stopped at the crosswalk on the other side of the circle. Traffic moved past slowly, like a herd of large, heavy-breathing beasts.

"I don't fight it." He watched a stray breeze pick up a lock of her hair and lay it against her cheek. "I try to use it, keep moving, you know?"

"A rolling stone gathers no moss?" she teased.

"More like leave no stone unturned. I like to see the whole picture, or as much of the picture as I can. You can't do that by standing still."

They crossed the street and strolled past shops closing down and restaurants gearing up. It felt good to be moving so slowly while everyone around them hustled from work to buses, cars and metros, to happy hours and restaurant reservations.

"How long have you been divorced?" she asked.

The question surprised him. Or maybe it was her tone of voice, which was friendly but impersonal. Too impersonal for the question, he thought. She had on her journalism hat.

He looked down at her, but her eyes were focused ahead of them. "Two years. Almost. In March."

She nodded slowly. He could sense her desire to have pen and paper in hand.

"Why?" he asked.

"Just . . . that sounds like the philosophy of a recently divorced man."

He raised his brows. "Two years is not recent. Besides, I was thinking of that more in terms of business. Though I guess I've applied some of it to dating."

"I'd say."

They passed a waiter setting tables on the sidewalk, napkins fluttering from his back pocket in the breeze.

"Would you, now?" Joe shoved his hands in his jacket pockets. "And how much do you think you know about my dating life? You've seen me with one woman. That's not even true. You would never have known about Carla if I hadn't told you."

She put her hands in her pockets too and looked up at him, her cheeks lightly pink. "That's true. I guess I'm just making assumptions because, well, you know." She fluttered a hand out beside her as a substitute for elaboration.

He mimicked her gesture. "Actually, I don't know."

She looked up at him again, this time coyly,

through her lashes. "Why Joe, are you fishing for compliments?"

He wished he were, if it would keep that look on her face. If she ever had a mind to, she could devastate a guy with that coquette act. "Compliments?" he repeated. "It's a compliment to be considered a womanizer?"

She laughed. "Did I call you that?"

"Just about."

"Look, all I'm saying is that when you meet a good-looking guy who's comfortable with women, who has no trouble talking to, picking up and dating women, and he's not in a relationship, you assume he's a playboy."

Joe scoffed. "A playboy. Laurel, I'm a humble coffee vendor. I'm divorced—recently, according to you—and I have professed to believing in love. Whereas you, my judgmental friend, have professed the opposite. How do you figure *I'm* the one who's not sincere?"

"I didn't say you were insincere."

"Right. And playboys are so trustworthy."

Laurel laughed and touched him lightly on the arm. "Joe, I'm just kidding. I mean, I thought you were the run-around type when I first met you—probably because you're good-looking enough to get any girl you want—but I'm revising that opinion. Slowly." She gave him a teasing smile.

He shot her a skeptical look and she laughed again.

"Really," she said. "I want to know the truth. And I'm not going to pre-judge."

"Anymore," he added.

She grinned. "Anymore. Promise."

He chuckled as she held up one hand and crossed her heart with the other.

They reached Farragut Square and took one of the diagonal sidewalks across it. The grass smelled moist in the declining daylight.

"Let's sit down, okay?" Laurel said. "I want to take a few notes, if you don't mind." She stopped, reached for her purse and dug a hand into it. "I've got to finish this thing up tonight. I'm swamped at work."

She pulled out a pen and they turned to one of the park benches. Joe sat down without a thought, but Laurel brushed a small area off with her hand first. She sat and, as she reached for it, Joe turned over her bag. She pulled out a pad of paper. After folding several used sheets over the back of the pad, she angled herself toward him on the bench.

"Tell me, Joe, what *is* your philosophy of dating? Now that I know it's not just love 'em and leave 'em, what is it you're looking for?"

"Are you looking for a list?" He looked at her with amusement.

"Of course not. But you're rather freshly back in the dating pool; surely you've thought about how you want to go about dating after such a prolonged period of monogamy."

He thought back to his first date after Renee

had left him, how strange and awful and ill fitting it had felt to him. Like putting back on a wet bathing suit.

He'd decided then that he would make no promises, forge no commitments, take each event as it came and judge it on face value alone. He was not going to risk feeling anything.

It was only recently he'd discovered how unsatisfying that tactic was. How essentially boring. If your feelings weren't engaged in some way, the whole exercise felt pointless.

Except for sex. Sometimes sex called for compromises.

"You're having to think awfully hard there, Joe."

He looked into her laughing eyes. "It's a tough question. Could *you* answer it?"

"We're doing you now."

"Then let me know when we get to you, because I want to take some notes. And maybe indulge some misconceptions. Can I think of you as a playgirl for a while?"

"Hey, I believe I already apologized for that. Besides, I didn't really think you were a playboy. I was just feeling . . . well, it's not important. I've got to stop acting on feelings, is all. So." She donned a businesslike expression again. "What is your outlook on intimacy? Are you looking for another long-term relationship? Or are you just ready to do some dating after being married for so long?"

Joe studied her a long moment. He knew she was asking for the article, but wondered if she had any curiosity about him herself.

He laid an elbow on the back of the bench between them. "I want to be clear, you're not using my actual name in this column, are you?"

She tucked a lock of hair behind one ear with the hand holding the pen. "Of course not."

"Good." He nodded once.

"Well . . ."

He'd been about to go on, but stopped. " 'Well,' what?"

"Well, nothing really. I was going to call you 'Regular Joe' and me 'Plain Jane,' as *you* suggested, but even though Joe *is* your real name 'Regular Joe' isn't, don't you think? In fact, I don't even know your real name. What is your last name?"

He paused. " 'Regular Joe' is fine."

Her brows rose. "You're not going to tell me your last name? What, are you wanted for something somewhere?"

He laughed. "Not by the law. At least I don't think so."

"Well, that inspires confidence. But I do need to know who my source is, so what is it? If you don't mind."

"You're not going to use it?"

"I'm not going to call you 'Mr. Whatever-it-is,' if that's what you mean."

He laughed. "I meant in the column."

"No. You're going to be Regular Joe, like I said. If you like, I'll refer to you as Deep Throat to my associates."

He donned a kid-in-a-candy-shop expression. "*That* would be *great*."

She gave him a look.

"Fine. It's Squires. Joe Squires."

She let out an exaggerated breath and held her hand out with a smile. "All right then, nice to meet you, Joe Squires."

He took her hand and smiled back. "Nice to meet you too, Laurel Kane."

Night was falling rapidly, and after a few more minutes of talk, Laurel could no longer see her notepad.

"Do you mind if we go somewhere? I can't see to write anymore, and I have a few more questions to ask." She folded her pad back up and reached for her tote.

"*More?*" he complained, but she could see he was joking.

"I want to be sure I'm representing you accurately. We can get dinner somewhere. It'll be on *DC Scene*."

He cocked his head. "Do you like shrimp?"

"Sure. You know a good shrimp place? I'll take you anywhere you want to go. The world's your oyster, Joe Squires."

He laughed. "Mighty generous of you."

"It's easy to be generous with other people's

money." She stood up and held out a hand to help him.

He took it, his palm warm and dry against hers. She indulged a momentary fantasy of tucking it into her jacket pocket with her hand but let it slip away. His touch may feel as good as he looks, she thought, but that was all just outer packaging, and therefore irrelevant.

"I was thinking about my place." He cast a sidelong glance at her as they headed back toward K Street, past the statue of David Farragut forever holding his spyglass. "I live pretty near here, and I've got some shrimp that won't last if I don't cook them soon. Plus, I make an excellent scampi, if I do say so myself."

Despite herself, she was impressed. And curious. Would it be a mistake to go to his house? Too personal? She glanced at the statue of Farragut again, remembered someone once telling her that he'd coined the phrase "Full speed ahead."

"My goodness," she said, "a man who cooks. I hope you put that in your verbal résumé the other night. Not that it apparently mattered if you didn't."

With that, the thing she'd been trying to forget —rejection by ten men in one evening—came rushing back to her. She'd felt bad about it all day, even though she knew she shouldn't. They had rejected her idea, she told herself, not *her*. Besides, it didn't matter. If she was honest with herself she had to admit there weren't any great prospects in that bunch anyway.

"As a matter of fact I did slip that in here and there," Joe said. "So what do you say? We can catch a cab and be there in three minutes."

"You think you can catch a cab in three minutes?" She gestured toward the street. "Have at it. If you're willing to cook, I'm more than willing to eat."

Full speed ahead. Besides, she thought, she could see how he lived, whether he was a slob or a neatnik, an expensive-stereo-and-cheap-furniture kind of guy, or one of those who believe you should be able to fit all your belongings in the trunk of your car.

Joe flagged a cab in about twelve seconds flat. As they got into the backseat she heard him say, "Hillyer Place."

"Hillyer Place?" she repeated.

That was a nice address, and about half a block from her office. Houses on that street went for the upper hundreds of thousands, if not millions. But then there were some basement apartments too, like hers on the much less affluent Fourth Street near Capitol Hill. Well, hopefully not *too* much like hers. She wouldn't mind spending an evening in a place that did not smell of mildew and wet cement.

He turned his face toward hers. "You know it?"

"Of course, it's about ten seconds from my office. And two blocks from your cart."

"Oh yeah." He leaned back in the seat with a smug kind of look.

The cab's backseat seemed to sag in the middle, so she kept her muscles tensed to keep from leaning into him. As it was, on the occasional bump their knees touched, sending off currents of alarm within her. She didn't need to be getting chummy with this guy. If there was one thing she was learning from all their encounters, it was that he was dangerous. Dangerous to her peace of mind, dangerous to her resolve and dangerous to her mission, with his cocky grin and physical charm.

The last thing she needed was to have this guy thinking *she* was after him. How professional would that look? Not to mention that it would be a complete misunderstanding. She might be able to see he was attractive and appreciate what other women saw in him, but she was far too experienced to believe that that held any promise for her. She'd had flings with pretty boys before.

The cab pulled up in front of a tall blue row house on Hillyer Place, and before Laurel could get her wallet from her purse Joe had paid the man.

"*DC Scene* would get that," she protested, but he just shot her a sardonic look. "Look, I know it's not much money," she continued, sliding out of the car and dragging her purse and tote bag with her. "But I'd rather you let me pay, just to keep this all on the professional up-and-up."

He started up the main staircase to the wide double front doors of the house. Laurel looked down at the curving slate stairs to the basement apartment, the ones disappearing from view as Joe took out a set of keys and opened the front door.

"You want to pay me for the shrimp?" His lips were curved as he pushed the door wide with one arm and stepped back to allow her to enter before him.

Such gentlemanly gestures from him always surprised her. And, it seemed, they were always popping up. Someone raised him right, she thought, entering a hardwood-floored foyer that smelled lightly of wax. Her mother would definitely approve.

Joe entered behind her and flipped on the light. A chandelier that looked more like modern art than household furnishing let off a pleasantly diffused glow. On the walls were several paintings, abstracts, framed simply and elegantly. She was only in the front hall and already she could tell that the place was owned by someone with taste. Or rather, Taste, with a capital T. Was it the ex-wife? Or was it Joe?

She turned her eyes to him as he took off his jacket and held his hand out for hers. She dropped her bags on the floor and handed him her coat.

"The kitchen's straight back," he said, hanging the coats in a closet by the door. "Here, follow me."

He strode down the hall in front of her and she took the opportunity to gaze into the darkened living room. A metal sculpture she couldn't define in the dark stood just inside the archway, and a large painting in a gold frame that glinted in the hall light was above the mantelpiece. Other pictures lined the wall but as far as furniture went, he could well be a belongings-in-the-trunk kind of guy. From what she could see only two armchairs graced the room. The dining room, just before the kitchen on the right, was similarly bereft of furniture, though an abstract marble sculpture sat on the floor in a corner.

"This is your house?" She reached the enormous kitchen to find it replete with every appliance known to culinary man, including a Sub-Zero refrigerator, dual ovens, a professional-grade stove and miles of counter space.

He laughed and turned around to look at her. His smile seemed easier, somehow, his posture more relaxed, now that he was in his own home. She noticed that with people a lot, that other parts of their personalities emerged when you saw them in their own living spaces.

"You think I just let myself into someone else's house?" The crow's feet crinkled with amusement, and she had the thought that he was probably even more handsome now than he had been as a younger man.

She smiled slightly, aware that she was having to erase and rewrite large portions of his identity that she had previously extrapolated from his smart-aleck mouth and coffee-cart employment. The ear-flapped hat hadn't exactly prepared her for this house either.

There might not be much furniture, but the beauty of the house and his obviously sophisticated taste in art said some very interesting things about him.

"Have a seat." He gestured toward a couple of stools on the other side of the island that held the professional-grade cooktop.

She sat and let her eyes trail about the room again. "The coffee vending business must be pretty damn good."

He gave her a sidelong look. "It is."

He was hiding something, she thought. As a journalist, it was her job to get it out of him. "You must work that thing seven days a week to afford a place like this."

He paused and gave her a quizzical look. "You didn't think I owned just the one cart, did you?"

Laurel opened her mouth to speak, but jumbled it, because of course that was exactly what she'd thought. "I—of course—well . . . So, how many do you own?"

He laughed and pulled a bottle of wine from a rack on one counter. "Just the one cart. But three coffee shops. And counting." He rummaged in a drawer, presumably for a corkscrew.

"Three *shops*? Where?"

"In town. But they're not called Hot Stuff. That's just the cart."

Three coffee shops? An actual chain? She must have heard of them. "What are they called?"

He moved to another drawer. "I know I have a corkscrew . . ."

She waited.

He found one in the dishwasher and turned back to her. A second later it hit her.

"Oh my God. You own Hot & Sweet." Another second and another revelation hit her. "You're J. P. Squires." An incredulous laugh burst from her.

J. P. Squires was one of Washington's up-and-coming entrepreneurs. He'd been mentioned in an article in *Washingtonian Magazine* just two or three months ago because his shop on Capitol Hill was a favorite of Senator Cummings, one of the more flamboyant personalities in Congress. She remembered the article because Rulinda had talked about possibly interviewing him, then had dropped that to pursue Senator Cummings.

"Oh my God, Joe, I can't believe you never told me that."

He shrugged and peeled the foil from the top of the wine bottle.

"J. P. Squires." She shook her head. "What an idiot I've been. Rulinda would just die if she knew."

He shot her a glance. "Does it matter?"

"No. No, it doesn't matter. But it makes sense now why you're so anxious to be anonymous."

J. P. Squires, she thought again. She'd actually

heard of him, for pity's sake. Though for some reason she'd thought he'd be an older man.

"So how come the cart's not called Hot and Sweet?" she asked.

"Because I'm trying to be anonymous there, too, so I'd appreciate it if you kept this to yourself."

"Of course, but why—?"

"I'm just doing a little market research, that's all. There's no other coffee shop near there, so I'm checking out the location."

Laurel nodded. That made sense. She'd love it if a Hot & Sweet went in so close to work. Not that Joe would be working there, she knew, but he definitely made some of the best coffee in town, and the Hot & Sweet cafés carried the most wonderful baked goods too. Even *Washingtonian* had said as much. And wouldn't an actual coffee *shop* be better than a cart? Even a Joe-himself-manned cart?

She decided not to think about that.

"You know, Joe, maybe you shouldn't be anonymous for the column. I mean, think about it. Women might come into your shops in droves hoping to catch a glimpse of Regular Joe after the column comes out," she teased. As if droves of women actually read *DC Scene*. "Could help business."

He laughed. "I don't need that kind of help."

"Hm. No. From what I hear, you don't need any kind of help." She chuckled once more to herself and looked around the kitchen. "That explains the house. How long have you lived here?"

"About five years."

So, she thought, before the ex was an ex. She looked more closely as if there might be some trace of her dwelling in an overlooked corner.

She looked back at him consideringly. "You're quite the art collector too."

He leaned into the corkscrew as he twisted it into the cork. She watched the muscles cording in his forearm, his square hands so capable in everything he did.

"I like art."

Cagey, as always.

"Not so big on furniture collecting, though, huh?" she added with a smile.

"No, my ex-wife was the one who liked furniture." He gave her a wry look. "You do want wine, don't you?"

"Sure." She was pretty sure she shouldn't, but after the shock she'd just received, she could use some calming spirits. And she didn't want to be rude. He was, after all, cooking her dinner.

He pulled a glass from a rack by the wall and filled the generous bulb of it with white wine. She smelled it—crisp and oaky—then sipped. Excellent. So the guy had a successful business, a great house, incredible taste, and knew how to cook. This was getting ridiculous. He could win awards for Most Eligible Bachelor. If she didn't know better, she'd think someone was playing a joke on her.

After a second, she excused herself, went back down the hall to retrieve her tote bag and purse, and returned to the kitchen. No sense wasting time enjoying herself. She had a job to do.

"So, you were going to tell me your philosophy of dating," she said, uncapping her pen.

He was deveining shrimp at the sink. "You want me to do that while gutting fish?"

She laughed. "Those are crustaceans, not fish."

"You're right. Much more appropriate. But I'm sorry to say I don't have a philosophy. I just believe you have to go on attraction, at least at first."

"Okay, so, attraction. Then what? What are you looking for, once you realize it takes twelve coats of paint for the woman of your dreams to look so attractive?"

Joe laughed. "Attraction isn't just about looks, you know."

"*I* know. But what do you think it's about?"

"It's about . . . chemistry. Charisma. Personality. That click you feel when you get along with someone." He gave her a look that for some reason had her heart tripping.

"And what makes you think chemistry will work after all this time of it *not* working?"

He took a long, slow breath. "I wouldn't say it hasn't ever worked. I think it's worked several times."

"But not forever. Isn't forever the goal?"

"Maybe. But maybe not." He rinsed the

shrimp, then brought a cutting board over to the island where she was sitting. He flashed her a grin, then turned, opened the refrigerator and bent down to grab something off a lower shelf.

Laurel's mouth went dry. *Nice ass*, she almost said out loud. She could say that, couldn't she? Just as an impartial observer? She was, after all, writing about him as a single man. She should be able to look at him as a single man, and appreciate his . . . uh . . . single-man assets.

He turned back around with several cloves of garlic in his hand and splayed them onto the cutting board. Then he took the flat of a broad knife and began pressing on them, crackling their papery skin.

"Maybe forever is an ideal goal," he continued as Laurel gulped her wine, "but having some long-term mini-goals isn't so bad, is it? I mean, relationships are valuable, even the ones that don't last."

Laurel watched as his lithe fingers—the same lithe fingers she'd watched countless times at the coffee cart—stripped the little cloves bare.

She swallowed. "That's true. So maybe, after your divorce, you're just looking to date for a while? Not really interested in another long-term thing yet?"

He moved several of the cloves in a line and chopped them, evenly and rapidly, with the skill of a seasoned chef. Laurel couldn't help it, she found it incredibly attractive.

She raised her eyes to his face. He was watching the knife as he worked, his eyes downcast, his face serious. It was a sobriety she hadn't seen very often in him, quite different from his usual knowing smirk or challenging grin.

"No," he said, then shook his head. "No. I want forever."

He stopped chopping and his eyes met hers. She held her breath.

"Don't *you*?" he asked.

His tone was soft and Laurel's bones felt like they were melting.

"Yeah," she said. She broke their gaze and shifted on the stool, writing *forever* on the pad in front of her. "Sure I do. That's the point. I'm just going about it in a different way. I'm going about it in a way I think is more likely to get it."

Joe picked up his wineglass and took a sip, eyeing her for a moment. Then he turned, unwrapped a stick of butter and threw it in a sauté pan that had been sitting on the stove. Going back to the refrigerator, he removed a pot and set it on another burner.

"Hope you don't mind leftover rice." He adjusted the gas flame under the pot.

Dinner, Laurel concluded an hour later, after sopping up the last vestige of buttery sauce with the Tuscan bread Joe had provided, was the most amazing thing she had ever eaten. They were halfway through their second bottle of wine— her notes were forgotten on the kitchen island— and she had consumed more at one sitting than she had in a month.

"That," she said, sitting back at the kitchen table and popping the last piece of bread into her mouth, "was incredible."

She leaned forward again to pick up her inexplicably full-again wineglass and smiled at Joe.

He smiled back.

"You know, you are quite a catch, Joe Squires," she said, magnanimously admitting what she'd been thinking all evening. "You cook, you've got a great house, you're smart, you're good-looking."

His smile broadened. In the candlelight, his eyes glinted. "And you, Laurel Kane, are a little bit drunk, I think."

She must be, she thought, because his saying so didn't bother her. "I don't think that matters. Empirically, you are what can only be considered an eligible bachelor. You've got it all."

"I don't know about that." He folded up his napkin and tossed it casually on his empty plate.

She held her wineglass up in a salute. "Another plus."

He laughed and reached for her plate, stacking it on top of his. "What about you, Laurel? Don't you think you're a catch?"

"Hah!" She sipped her wine. "I'm a dime a dozen. Thirty-something women looking to get married are a dime a dozen. You heard it here first."

Joe stopped. "I don't think I could find a dozen women like you if my life depended on it."

His look was so sincere, Laurel blushed. She

waved a hand. "Oh, well, you know. I mean, generally."

He shook his head. "I've never met even *one* woman like you. Ever. Which is why I don't understand this arranged marriage thing at all."

Laurel swirled the wine around in her glass. He was being too nice to her, she thought. Like he felt bad for her. But the last thing she wanted was for him to feel sorry for her.

She stood up and moved in the direction of the living room. She didn't want to think about her arranged-marriage plan just at the moment. She was comfortable, enjoying herself, and liked the feeling of being in his house.

She got to the living room and felt along the inside wall for a light switch, but there was none. So she continued into the room anyway, afraid to feel around too much for fear of knocking some expensive piece of art over. Joe was right, she was definitely a little bit drunk.

Keeping the lights out didn't prove too brilliant either, however, because five steps into the room she tripped over an ottoman. She thought she was headed for the floor when strong arms caught her from behind.

She let out an involuntary *whoops!* as he caught her around the waist, and clutched his arm. Wine sloshed over one of her hands, but she held onto the glass.

She hadn't even heard him follow her into the room.

"Maybe a little light would help," he said, his

voice low and close to her ear. He plucked the glass from her hand and set it deftly on a table next to the chair to which the previously unseen ottoman belonged.

She turned slowly toward him, her hand still holding his arm. She wasn't sure if it was that that kept his arm around her or his own desire to keep it there, but when she faced him, he brought his other arm around her too. Their legs touched.

The feeling was hot and strange and dizzying. She wanted to lean into him, feel the length of her body against his, but she couldn't do that. That would be wrong. In fact just standing like this was wrong. It would ruin everything.

But she didn't move. Instead she looked up into his face, her hands still on his arms.

"Well, well," he said softly.

Her heart thundered in her chest. Coffee-guy Joe had his arms around her! The man who had garnered nine women's phone numbers in one evening was holding her—looking at her— touching her in a way that was definitely not journalistic.

He smelled clean and male, and he felt invitingly warm. She curled her fingers around his biceps, pulling herself just a little closer to him. Their hips met, then their torsos. His arms around her waist felt solid and sure. One of his hands rose to her face and his fingers touched her cheek.

She couldn't stop looking into his eyes, those

pale, long-lashed eyes, glimmering only slightly from the dim light down the hall. Part of her couldn't get over how weird it was to be standing like this with Joe, but that only made the circumstance more electrifying.

At this moment, more than anything, she wanted for him to kiss her. Then she thought, what the hell. A woman who's arranging her own marriage can kiss whomever she wants.

So she did.

She raised herself up on her toes and touched her lips to his.

It was a lot like the kiss at Clyde's. Tender, soft, lingering. But then his tongue touched her top lip and she thought her knees would buckle. She raised her arms up and around his neck, pressing her body into his as her lips parted. His tongue found hers, and every thought was wiped from Laurel's mind.

Joe's arms rose behind her back and he cupped the back of her head, her hair bunched softly in his hands. She could feel the urgency in his kiss, and met it with her own. Her body was on fire, as out of control as if she'd put a jet engine in her car and floored it. She wanted his hands everywhere, wanted to feel his body on hers, wanted to be enveloped by his heat, and to inhale every last breath of sweet shimmering desire from his skin.

Her hands found his face and held it for her kisses. She stood on tiptoe to get her arms more completely around his neck and he dipped his knees to help her. Then he dipped them some more and swept her up into his arms.

"Want to see the upstairs?" She saw his familiar grin in the faint light.

Part of her was jolted back to reality. *This was Regular Joe.*

A bigger part of her told the other to shut up.

"More than you can imagine," she said, surprising even herself with the sultry certainty in her voice.

He turned on no lights and the hallway went by in a blur as she buried her face in the side of his neck. The bedroom was similarly dark and she didn't even realize they were there until Joe tossed her onto the downy softness of a huge, masculine four-poster bed.

It was like something out of *Dangerous Liaisons*, and the thought made her giggle.

"What's so funny, Miss Kane?" he asked, positioning himself over her and applying those dastardly fingers to the buttons of her shirt.

"This bed. It's like you're making up for the rest of the house being empty with this one piece of furniture." She extended her arms over her head, feeling the airy cushion of the comforter beneath her. "I feel decadent just being in it."

"Exactly the point."

Her shirt was undone and his hand covered her breast, his thumb teasing lightly over the nipple. She sucked in a breath.

This was crazy. The man was too skilled, too—

She gasped as his head bent to her breast and

his tongue found her nipple. His other hand snaked behind her back and unhooked her bra before she realized he was even near the clasp.

Then he was coaxing her shirt down her arms, along with her bra straps.

Some part of her brain struggled to come to life. This was all happening too fast. "Joe, I . . ."

He slowed, but didn't stop. He pulled the shirt off and ran his hands from her shoulders to her waist and back.

"Laurel," he said softly. "How do you feel?"

"I . . ." What did he mean? Her mind scrambled for logic but was awash in confusion. Did he mean did she want to stop? *Did* she?

His hands on her bare skin undid her. She closed her eyes and felt like lava, sinking into the bed in delicious and complete relaxation.

His touch stopped and she opened her eyes to see him whip off his own shirt. Beneath it was a lean, muscled chest and she reached out a hand to it. One finger traced the line of hair from his navel to the button of his jeans.

She hesitated. Then, like plunging into a pool, she undid the button. Like the difference between being wet and dry, the action was irrevocable and they both knew it. They shed the rest of their clothing and righted themselves on the bed, meeting in the middle on their knees, skin to skin.

Joe's hands cupped her face while hers traveled up his ribcage.

"This is what it should feel like, Laurel," he said softly, as if there were others sleeping in the same room. "This," he said between light kisses, "all the time."

His words flashed along her nerves, thrilling her while raising a dozen questions she couldn't ask. For her? for him? Was it some sort of existentialist comment?

But he kissed her again and the questions flew out the window. His hand found her breast again and began stimulating the nipple. Laurel sighed as desire washed over her.

Would it really be so bad if they slept together, just this once? How much would it really ruin? This way she'd know just exactly what she was missing . . . or rather, just exactly what he was offering, to the world, the dating world. To other women.

She opened her eyes, saw his face silhouetted in the dark by the shaded windows behind him. Dim light from the streetlamps made the room nearly twilit.

"Joe . . ."

He raised a hand and smoothed her hair back with it. The touch was gentle and intimate.

"Laurel," he said.

She couldn't reply. She couldn't stop this now. Couldn't. Or wouldn't.

He lay her gently back on the bed. She melted once again into the downy covers. One of his hands touched her thigh and traced a lazy line all the way up to her hip, where he laid his palm against her belly.

His hand was as hot and dry and as strong as

if it contained some sort of healing force. The nervous fluttering in her stomach abated and the objections lodged in her throat died there.

His palm rubbed a warm circle on her abdomen, then moved downward, until his fingers could probe her, urge her legs to part.

He kissed her then, urgently, his fingers deep within her. Those quick, clever fingers she had watched so many days at the coffee cart, now doing incredible, spectacular things to her insides, making her gasp and squirm and rise up into his hand to urge him on.

She tore her lips from his and arched her back, just as a towering wave of sensation broke over her, causing her to cry out with release.

A second later she was aware of a tearing sound, and she opened her eyes to see him donning a condom. Then he was above her. She grabbed his hips as he came toward her and pulled him inside. Slick and swift, with one thrust he was deep, and she moaned with the satisfaction of it. Her body pulsed around him and he responded by plunging himself into her depths again and again.

She opened herself completely to him and he took her, took all of her, driving them both until she felt another burst of pleasure and he let loose a hard exhalation, then thrust one final time.

Nine

No. No no no no no, she thought as she tiptoed down the stairs.

Mistake, she thought. *Stupid, stupid mistake.*

A mistake that had felt pretty damn good, of course, but that didn't excuse anything. She'd made that kind of mistake before. Handsome guy, charming, appealing in some momentarily irresistible manner, but wrong for her in every way that mattered.

She didn't have time for this sort of mistake anymore.

She got to the bottom of the stairs and sat on the last step to put on her stockings and shoes. Somehow being in work clothes made the whole scene worse, so obviously *un*–thought out. So definitely the wrong choice.

She was tired of making bad relationship choices.

She stood up and looked at her watch. Five thirty A.M. How had she stayed so long? How had she slept? She was *never* able to sleep away from home. It just figured that the one time she should have been restless, she wasn't.

She cast around for her purse. The kitchen, she thought, remembering that she'd dragged it and her tote bag from the hall when she'd begun taking notes. There it was, on the counter by the wall.

She grabbed it and her bag, looked around the room to be sure she hadn't left anything else, and turned back to the hall.

In the kitchen doorway stood Joe. He looked large in the threshold, despite wearing only a pair of boxer shorts and rubbing a hand through his rumpled hair. She felt like he'd caught her with her hand in the cookie jar. Blocking the doorway, his chest didn't look naked so much as imposing and wall-like.

The effect was diminished, however, when he rubbed one eye with his hand and she could see elements of a much younger Joe.

"You're getting an early start." His voice was low and ironic, a tone that was almost comforting in its familiarity. Strangely, she didn't feel the awkwardness she was afraid of as she'd crept away from the bedroom to make her hasty exit.

"Joe," she said, taking a breath. "I was trying not to wake you. I have to go."

He looked at her dispassionately for a long moment, not moving from the doorway. "You're thinking this was a mistake." His voice was flat.

"Aren't you?" She set her purse on the counter and crossed her arms. "Come on, Joe, we both know last night was an impulse. We're not right for each other."

"We're not," he repeated.

Clarifying what she'd said, or agreeing? She couldn't tell. And she couldn't ask, because she wasn't sure she wanted to hear the answer. She blushed, thinking perhaps she'd overestimated last night's implications by assuming he might see it as anything *other* than an impulse.

His eyes were on her purse, where she'd laid it on the counter.

"Well, no," she said. If she wasn't careful, this guy would screw up her plan for a safe, dispassionate marriage of convenience. And she was *not* up for another hormonal roller-coaster ride ending in disaster. She just wasn't. "I mean, we believe in different things, clearly. This was just . . . it was just an aberration. We had one simultaneously weak moment. I'm just acknowledging that, that's all."

He chuckled softly and brought his gaze back to her.

"You know this isn't right," she pressed, feeling some urgency. "You know that, right?"

She held her breath for his answer.

Or maybe she should have just asked what he thought.

He took his time. "I have trouble," he said slowly, "with the idea of 'right' and 'wrong' in this context."

She sighed heavily. That figured.

"Look, Joe. I don't know what you think happened last night. But if you're thinking it could lead to any kind of relationship, I have to point out the obvious."

He leaned against the door jamb. "And what's obvious, Laurel?"

She flung a hand out. "That you're looking for love and magic and romance and all that stuff I don't even believe in anymore. Besides, you and I both know the only magic that went on here last night was of the physical variety. The kind of magic any unknown quantity holds. And we both know that satisfying curiosity about the unknown is a short-lived gratification at best. And—"

"Jesus, Laurel," he burst out, his expression suddenly, to her eyes, angry. "How can you be this analytical first thing in the morning? Have you really figured all this out in the few short hours since you were butter in my arms?"

"Butter?! Oh *please*." Her face flushed hot. "I'm not just figuring this out now, Joe. I've known it all along. Way before last night's error in judgment. And if you were honest with yourself you'd know you have too."

"So now I'm not being honest with myself."

"No!"

"So now you not only know what I know and

what I'm thinking, you know that I'm not being honest with myself?"

"Okay, it *seems* like you're not being honest with yourself."

He moved a couple of steps into the room, towering over her with his anger and his broad, naked shoulders. "Listen to yourself, Laurel. Is there ever a moment in your life when you can admit you *don't* know what the hell you and everyone else around you is thinking? Do you ever allow yourself even a *second* to consider that maybe you've got something wrong? That you can't just size up a situation according to your own narrow parameters?"

She took a short, sharp breath. "Fine. *Fine.* I won't tell you what you're thinking. I won't even tell you I know what you're thinking. But I'll tell you this, I know what *I'm* thinking."

They stood in silence a second before he spread his arms wide and said, "Which is . . . ?"

"That this was a mistake!" She glared at him, then decided that further discussion would be fruitless. "I have to go." She grabbed her purse and started past him.

"Who's the love-'em-and-leave-'em type now?" he said in a low voice when she passed by him.

She stopped and looked up. He gave her an ironic tilt of his brow.

A sickening thought occurred to her. "So help me, Joe, if you did this to make some sort of point—"

"And what if I did?" he returned vehemently.

She gasped.

"You wouldn't see that point if I had it pasted on my forehead. And I'm sure as hell not going to explain it to you, because it's obvious to me now that you will never understand it."

"What you mean is . . ." She stepped toward him, one finger out as if to poke him in the chest. "That I'll never *agree* with it. Understanding you is not my problem, Joe, it's seeing things your way. And that drives you crazy. You just can't stand the fact that you can't sweet-talk me into believing that you're right."

He laughed once. "And when did I ever sweet-talk you?"

Her mind fled to last night, to just a few hours ago, when he'd held her so tenderly and touched her with all the passion anyone could desire.

But he hadn't said a thing. No sweet nothings, no false declarations of emotions he wasn't feeling, no slick avowals of love.

And it pissed her off that she couldn't accuse him of playing that kind of game with her. That was where her anger came from. He wasn't acting the way she'd expected. He hadn't tried to convince her he felt anything for her at all. And she'd leaped into bed with him anyway.

It was just sex to him. And she was another Carla.

She felt sick to her stomach. She took a deep

quivering breath and looked out the window. At the base of the horizon was a fringe of light. Dawn.

"Never," she said. "You never tried to sweet-talk me. Which is fine with me. I wouldn't have believed it anyway."

She walked past him down the hall toward the front door, blindly digging into her purse for her keys with one hand. She reached for the doorknob with her other, and, fingers holding only her keys, her purse dropped to the ground. The contents spilled onto the hardwood floor. Coins rolled, pens clattered, papers fluttered, and Laurel closed her eyes and cursed.

She knelt, scooping up stuff and shoving it into the bag. From the corner of her eye she saw Joe move toward her and she held up a hand, skewering him with a look.

"Don't help. I can do it."

He stopped, his face angry again, and leaned against the banister, his arms crossed over his chest.

She got the last of her things back into the purse and rose.

"I'm sorry," she said in a hard voice, unsure what she meant. "Goodbye."

She turned the knob and went out the door. It wasn't until she'd reached the Metro and had begun wondering if she was being unreasonable that she remembered: Joe had a date that night.

* * *

Joe, rooted to the spot, watched the door close behind her. His eyes trailed down the door to the floor where her things had dropped.

Damn her, he thought. But he didn't mean precisely that. Damn her obstinance, he revised. Damn her determination to ignore what was right in front of her face.

And what is it that's right in front of her face? he asked himself.

Joe ran his hands through his hair, holding his head. Nothing. Nothing, he told himself. She was right. Last night had been a mistake. The last thing he wanted or needed was a woman who was incapable of love. Or rather, a woman determined *not* to love. So even if a shadow of emotion crossed her mind, she would fight it.

But then there was the woman he had slept with last night. Every touch, every kiss, every inch of her body had said things to him she would never say out loud.

She was passionate. Even uninhibitedly passionate. How could someone be like that and truly not be susceptible to falling in love?

They couldn't, he told himself. *She* couldn't.

His eye caught on something against the baseboard. He took a step forward for a closer look, then bent down and picked it up.

It was a small piece of metal, about the size of a dime, in the shape of a four-leaf clover. A charm. A lucky charm. It had to have come from her purse.

He started to laugh.

She wasn't so tough. And she wasn't so practical. And she wasn't, he was convinced, as immune to him as she'd like to think.

He palmed the lucky piece. Something in Laurel Kane believed in magic.

Laurel spent the weekend alternately writing the column and agonizing about what Joe was doing and/or thinking. Friday night had been pure torture. Knowing Joe was out with someone, somewhere, doing God knew what, was almost more than she could bear. Was it possible he would sleep with whomever his date was too? Two women on two consecutive nights?

It was too awful to contemplate, to consider herself just another notch on his bedpost, and yet contemplate it she did. Every time her mind wandered she found it had wandered over to Joe and whatever it was he was doing or had done Friday night.

One thing was certain, however, she wasn't going to ask him. She was not going to humiliate herself by showing any interest at all in what he'd done after sleeping with her. What she was going to do was stick to her guns that the night had meant nothing and that whatever happened it could not be repeated.

They had a professional relationship. That was all.

Monday afternoon Laurel sat at her desk with her head in her hands, exhausted from the weekend's work and mental aerobics. She'd gotten the column done and turned it in that morning, somehow, despite the turmoil in her mind. God knew how or what she'd written, but she had. Thankfully, she'd had most of it finished before the night with Joe.

A short knock sounded at the door. Laurel raised her head and was about to call "Enter" when it opened and Rulinda swept in on her cloud of Chanel No. 5.

"I read your column," she said without preamble, the British accent disturbingly absent.

Laurel braced herself. Had it been awful? Nonsensical? Full of mistakes? Ridiculous assertions?

She hadn't said anything to make it sound like Plain Jane and Regular Joe had engaged in unbridled, rapturous sex with each other, had she?

Rulinda sat herself in the chair across from Laurel and leaned forward as if about to impart something extremely complex and important.

Laurel leaned forward too. It would be just her luck to have sex with the wrong guy and lose her job all in the same weekend.

"It's fabulous," Rulinda said, in such an unusually intent voice that for a moment Laurel thought she hadn't heard correctly.

Rulinda leaned back in the chair. "I want it to be a series, open-ended. I want to put Regular Joe and Plain Jane on everyone's lips. America's answer to Bridget Jones. The column, not the book."

"I think America has answered that, actually,"

Laurel said, thinking it would be a typical *DC Scene* move to hop on that long-gone bandwagon.

Rulinda ignored her. "We'll follow these two through thick and thin. Regular Joe and Plain Jane as Everyman and Everywoman. I'm thinking this is what *DC Scene* goes big-time with. It's exactly the kind of thing that can put a niche paper on the map. Radio and print ads, buses, newsstands, kiosks. I can see it now, posters with the two of you leaning back to back."

Laurel's heart thundered in her chest as dread tightened her stomach. "That would ruin him as an *anonymous* source," she interjected, the first objection she could think of.

But Rulinda wasn't listening. "Point, counterpoint!" she crowed. "It'll be like that Spencer Tracy and Audrey Hepburn movie—"

"Katharine Hepburn."

"Where he's a sportswriter and she's—some kind of—what was she?"

"A political columnist."

"Anyway, Plain Jane and Regular Joe will be what DC's talking about. The whole column will be an antidote to DC's obsession with political society. This can be big, Laurel. Really big." She paused. "What? What are you saying?"

Rulinda's eyes were suddenly focused on her and Laurel stared back a moment before realizing she'd been shaking her head no.

"Noth—I mean, I . . . I'm just not sure Regular Joe will go for that. Like I said, right now he's anonymous."

And very likely to want to stay that way, she thought, considering his growing profile in business. Not to mention that he probably never wanted to see her again.

"Why?" Rulinda's expression showed how completely she didn't understand wanting to be anonymous. "He's good-looking, right? Or would we have to put a bag over his head?"

Laurel forced a laugh and before thinking said, "No, he's good-looking. *Really* good-looking." Way too good-looking to be the counterpoint to herself, she could add. She should have gotten someone closer to average.

"*Really?*" Rulinda shot forward in her chair, a salacious smile on her face. "Maybe I should meet this guy. We could take him places."

Laurel looked at her in horror. *Rulinda* could take him places, was what she meant, Laurel thought, picturing Rulinda on Joe's arm as they showed up at some trendy Georgetown party. She could see the Post Personalities section mentioning how the infamous Rulinda Mason was seen with the handsome owner of Hot & Sweet, J. P. Squires. She could envision the photo shot so clearly she had to close her eyes against it.

"He—he might be wanted for something," Laurel blurted desperately, then actually kicked herself under the desk as she uncrossed her legs to stand up.

"*What?*" Rulinda's eyes grew wide.

"I don't mean legally." She waved a hand and fiddled with the cord for her blinds. What on earth *did* she mean? "I mean . . . by his own company. I think they have some kind of clause, or something, you know. He couldn't advertise for another business without getting in trouble with them."

"What sort of business is he in?" Rulinda's eyes were piercing. If there was one thing Rulinda hated, it was not getting what she wanted.

Think, Laurel told herself, opening the blinds so quickly that Rulinda squinted and held one hand up to block the glare. "For God's sake, Laurel."

She closed the blinds completely. Both of them blinked in post-glare blindness.

"Well?" Rulinda demanded. "His business?"

"Uh, uh"—Laurel's mind spun—"underwear."

Rulinda's eyes lit up again. "That could be perf—"

"That is, undergarments for men. Body shapers. Like, male girdles and stuff. He's got a little paunch himself." She wrinkled her nose as if trying to put it nicely, but she couldn't help picturing Joe's rock-hard torso as she said the words.

Rulinda let out a small *wuff* and sat back in the chair. "Never mind, then. We don't have to say who he is. Forget the posters. The series'll be great."

Laurel sat back at the desk and exhaled. "Still, I'm not sure he wants to be part of something that big. I think he was just in it for the, uh, the one shot."

Or the one shot at her. Didn't he say he'd slept with her to prove a point?

"Nonsense." Rulinda dismissed the notion with an impatient look and a be-ringed hand. "From what I just read of him, I'm sure he'll go for it. *DC Scene* will pay for his dates, we'll arrange for him to meet people, we'll foot the bill for any sort of makeover or alterations he wants to make in order to meet women. Hell, we could send him to Weight Watchers if he wanted. He'll be thrilled to be part of that, if for no other reason than to have someone else funding his romantic excursions. Trust me."

As if Joe needed a makeover. If Rulinda ever laid eyes on him that would be it, there'd be posters of him plastered from here to the Capitol advertising the column.

"What about Plain Jane? Doesn't she have a choice?" Laurel asked.

"Well of course. We'll do the same for you too, hon." On Rulinda's lips the endearment came out as something less than dear. "We'll fix you up, get you some new clothes, makeup, whatever. You want to get a decent hairstyle, jazz up your wardrobe a little, *DC Scene*'ll do it for you. From now on, we're taking your dating life seriously."

Laurel's hand rose to her hair. Her hair was *fine*. So were her clothes. She looked down at her black skirt then back up at Rulinda. "I don't have a dating life. I'm—"

"Not now you don't, but you will. We're going to juice up your quest for a husband, give it some legs. We'll show the world just what Dr. Nadalov's theories can do. Did I not *tell* you that book was fabulous? Did I not *tell* you you'd want to live by it?"

Laurel remembered the conversation despondently. "Yes. Yes, you did."

She just thought she could live by it by herself. Well, aside from that initial column, the one she'd thought would be a one-time thing.

God, how was she going to go back to Joe and ask him to participate in another column? Or another ten columns? She couldn't. She just couldn't. She'd been having enough trouble figuring out how she was going to buy coffee from him again. Asking him to help her career would be like begging him for mercy, admitting wrong, crawling to him for sympathy. She couldn't do it. Could she?

"I just don't know if Regular Joe will go for it," she said again, at a loss for how else to get out of this.

Could she just never ask him and tell Rulinda he'd refused? Rulinda didn't know who he was. She'd never find out the truth.

But it was not Laurel's policy to avoid the truth. She'd always believed that if a situation required a lie, you were standing on the wrong side of the issue.

Was she standing on the wrong side of this issue?

"Laurel," Rulinda said, leaning forward again. "Do you have any idea what this could do for your career? Your name on everyone's lips. Your column the buzz of DC. Your next words the ones that everyone's hanging on. I don't need to tell you that when that happens, a columnist becomes extremely valuable to a publication. And promotions come with value, Laurel. *Raises* come with value."

Laurel put her head in her hands, feeling as if her brain might explode. Would she be selling her soul for a promotion and a raise if she went back to Joe and asked him to help? Or would refusing just be furthering the self-indulgent mistake of sleeping with Joe?

"I'll talk to Regular Joe," she said finally.

"Do it." Rulinda sat back. "Make him see the benefit of participating."

Laurel exhaled slowly, knowing he would see right through any spin she might put on this to make it look good for *him*. "I'll let you know as soon as I have an answer."

"Get me a yes by tomorrow." Rulinda stood up and headed for the door, where she turned. "I want this column to run weekly. I'm going to talk to marketing right now and have them work up some promotional ideas for it immediately."

The moment Rulinda was gone, Laurel's entire body drooped. She was going to have to see Joe again, and not just at the coffee cart. She was going to have to actually *work* with him again.

And that would be dangerous. The guy was trouble. It was almost as if he was sent to test her resolve. To give her an opportunity to show she wasn't going to fall for the illusion of love with a handsome, charismatic, unreliable kind of guy.

She needed to stick to her plan.

She drummed her fingers on the desk and looked at the papers scattered across the top.

Pages of notes from her interviews with Joe. Another pile of notes on the guys she'd met at Short Stops. Her glance fell on a note in quotes. "It's not as bad out here as it seems." Stan had said that, thinking she was perhaps freshly back in the dating game and finding it intimidating. On the contrary, she thought, she'd been in the game way too long. That's why Short Stops had seemed so promising—an opportunity to interview men and let them know right off the bat her philosophy and why it would work.

Maybe she'd just been there on a bad night. Maybe that particular batch of guys had been unusually romantic. But really, how romantic could someone be if they were hoping to meet their one true love in an eight-minute date? They had to be practical, at least some of them.

She pushed some papers aside. Her fingers found the stick-on nametag—LAUREL, she'd written in decisive black capitals—and unearthed the coupon for the next Short Stops, Inc., event.

She picked up the phone and dialed.

"Short Stops, Inc. Cindy speaking!"

Ten

"Hey Angela?" Laurel called as Angela passed her office door later that day.

Angela peered around the doorframe.

"Would you get me another latte?" She picked her purse up off the floor by her feet and rummaged around for her wallet.

She could do without seeing Joe, without struggling to see if he looked at her differently or if he treated her the same way he always had—she wasn't sure which would be worse—but she couldn't do without her lattes.

"Sure." Angela came into the office, a slight smirk on her pixie face. "But you know, the last time I ordered an extra latte he looked at me really funny."

Laurel handed her a five. "What do you mean,

he looked at you funny? Does he have some kind of limit now on the number of coffees a customer can buy?"

"No, silly." Angela rolled her eyes. "Like he knew it was for you. He even asked about you this morning, if you were sick or something."

Laurel stopped. So he'd expected to see her. Or rather, did not expect her to avoid him. That was good, wasn't it? He wasn't angry with her.

But then . . . did he expect her to think last Thursday was nothing? Because she hadn't meant to say she thought it was *nothing*. Just not a prelude to a romantic relationship. But did *he* think last Thursday was nothing? Sure, they'd argued, but the more she thought about it, the more it seemed to her she'd misunderstood what he was angry about.

"What did you tell him?"

Angela shrugged. "That you were really busy."

Laurel exhaled, her tensed muscles relaxed slightly. "Good. It's true."

She folded the Short Stops coupon and put it in her wallet. On it she'd written the time and place of the next event. Cindy had been thrilled she was trying it again.

Zero response quotient be damned, Laurel thought. She'd show them her way could work. She had to.

"Anything you want me to tell him this time?" Angela asked, folding the five forward and back.

Laurel looked at her. "Yes. Tell him I want a latte."

"I mean besides that."

Laurel smiled. "Angela, I know what you're thinking, but there's no drama going on here. I'm just busy. I had to finish the column Friday, along with my editing, and now Rulinda's given me another assignment. In fact, a weekly assignment." She paused. "Come to think of it tell Joe I do need to talk to him." She paused again. "In fact, never mind. I'll go down in a little bit and get my own latte."

Angela's brows rose. "All right."

Laurel sighed. "It's really no big deal."

"Okay." Angela's voice was sing-songy as she deposited the five on the desk in front of Laurel. "Whatever you say."

She left with a devilish smile. Laurel picked up *Love Is Not the Answer* and leafed through it. Nadalov had several workbook-style exercises for people to try and she looked for one she could propose to Joe for the next column. Preferably one where she wouldn't have to watch him capture the hearts of ten women in one evening.

Or hear about some date he'd arranged on his own . . .

If, that is, he agreed to work with her again.

She couldn't think of one reason why he would.

She settled on "Interviewing a Successful Couple." She would interview a couple who had had an arranged marriage, and Joe would interview a love match. Each would accompany the other on interviews, and then they would share their observations, preferably all in one evening so she didn't have to see him more than once.

She didn't actually know any people who had married by arrangement, but she remembered a colleague who wrote a piece a few years ago on Americanized young people from India still opting for arranged marriage. He could probably provide her with someone to interview.

She put down Nadalov's book and sighed, looking at her watch. It was four thirty. She ought to go down now and talk to Joe. That way she could tell Rulinda today that there was no way in hell he wanted to participate in another dating scenario of any sort with her.

She could still follow the book, however, and write about it. It wouldn't be quite the unique column Rulinda was hoping for but hey, if Laurel was clever enough she might still see her face on the side of a bus. In an ad, that is. Not plastered there by some timing error in crossing the street.

The coffee cart stood empty. No customers, which didn't surprise her at this hour, but no Joe either. Surely he didn't just leave the thing sitting there unattended. But, she supposed, if he wanted to do something unavoidable, like go to the bathroom, he couldn't exactly put everything away.

Great, she thought. She'd finally gotten her nerve up to talk to him—and *not* ask him about his date—and he wasn't even here.

She decided to wait for his return and looked around for something to sit on. There were no benches or planters or windowsills, just a lamppost suitable only for leaning against.

She rounded the cart to see if Joe had a camp stool or chair. He didn't. When she turned toward the side of the cart, she caught sight of him in a doorway down the sidewalk, holding a camera to his eye.

He looked like a photojournalist in his jeans and faded sweater, as if he were holed up in the doorway of a bombed-out building in war-torn Bosnia. His short blond hair and hard-cut features, the way he propped one arm against the entryway and focused the telephoto lens with a broad, long-fingered hand, all contributed to his look of rugged capability. For a moment she recalled those fingers touching her with thrilling skill and surprising gentleness.

Then she noticed what he was taking pictures of. Across the street, three women were emerging from the doorway of an unoccupied building.

Laurel stared from him to the women, then beyond them to the building. It was a run-down storefront, with a blackened plate glass window, that had long been rumored to house a "massage parlor," the kind specializing in massages of the disreputable sort.

Certainly the three voluptuous women sauntering down the sidewalk did nothing to dissuade her from believing the rumor.

And there was Joe, taking pictures of them. He

even appeared to be taking pictures of the upstairs windows, as if the telephoto lens could penetrate the glass of the upper floors.

She crossed her arms over her chest and leaned back against the lamppost. Shallow, superficial jerk, she thought. She should put this in the column. Looking for true love indeed.

Once the women were gone, and Joe had given up taking shots of the upstairs windows, he headed back to the cart. Halfway there, he spotted her and grinned.

Typical, she thought. He was not even ashamed of himself.

"She returns!" he said when he got close. "I thought you were gone forever, but for the tell-tale sign of latte orders coming from the *DC Scene* office."

"Wishful thinking, no doubt. I was busy."

"So I heard." He was looking at her intently, she thought. Or had he always looked at her that way? She couldn't remember, and not remembering made her flustered.

"You're looking pretty busy yourself." She looked pointedly at the camera.

He held it up. "Yeah. Just taking some shots of that building. Maybe tomorrow I can get a look inside and see what kind of work it needs."

"The *building*?" she repeated.

He looked confused. "Yeah. For the new shop." He glanced over his shoulder at it again and another woman exited. He chuckled, turning a knowing look on her. "Oh, I get it. You thought I was taking pictures of the girls." He laughed again, taking the lens cap off. "You don't have to be jealous, Laurel. Here, let me get a shot of you."

"Jealous!" Laurel held up a hand but it was too late, Joe had just clicked the shutter.

"Hey, can I get just a regular cup a coffee here?"

They both turned to see a short square man with a buzz cut standing in front of the cart.

"Sure." Joe stowed the camera in a metal cabinet at the bottom of the cart and plucked an insulated cup from the stack. "Want cream and sugar, or just black?"

"Black."

Joe served the man while Laurel told herself again that she was *not* going to say anything about their last parting, *nor* was she going to ask about his date. Instead she pondered how best to word her request for his participation in the column. Though she was reluctant to have to see him, she knew that it was only with the two of them that the column would be most successful.

Unless . . . a thought dawned on her. Regular Joe didn't have to be *this* Joe. In fact, she could find someone a lot more *regular* than this Joe, who, it turned out, was wildly successful in addition to being good-looking, charming and her worst nightmare.

So she'd just ask him, flat out, if he wanted to participate and when he said no, it'd be no big deal. She could tell Rulinda—without having to lie—that he wouldn't do it, but that she could find someone else to take his place. Easily.

Then she wouldn't have to hear about his dates—or gag herself to keep from asking about them.

The stocky man left and Joe put his money in the money box.

"So, latte? Or is there some other reason for your visit today?"

"Let me get this straight," she said, her arms automatically crossing over her chest—he followed suit, no doubt to mock her. "You slept with me just to make a point, a point which I could argue with at length, and now you want to treat me as if nothing happened?"

That was not at all what she'd planned to say.

"Hey, *you're* the one who said it was a mistake. So how do you want me to treat you?"

She put her hands on her hips and, since she was on a roll, said the first thing that came to her mind. "Apologetically, for a start."

He smiled over his crossed arms. "All right, I'm sorry if you thought I slept with you to prove a point. That was really just a side benefit. But—"

"Oh I hate that kind of apology." She held a hand up.

"What kind?"

"That I'm-sorry-you-feel-that-way-but-I'm-in-no-way-responsible kind. But you know what? It doesn't matter. That's not what I came down here to talk to you about. And anyway, sleep-

ing with you does *not* prove that I am susceptible to romance. It only means I am susceptible
to basic human hungers, just like everyone
else."

"Uh-huh." One raised eyebrow.

"Are you trying to say you think I have some
hidden feelings for you? That romance won out
and *that's* why I slept with you?"

Joe smiled serenely. "I don't think I ever actually *said* I'd slept with you to prove a point."

"Maybe not, but you said it was a 'side benefit.'"

"Did I?"

"Oh, for God's sake, never mind. I came
down here to talk to you about something else,
anyway."

He tilted his head inquiringly.

She clenched her teeth. The faster he said no,
the better. "Rulinda loved the column and she
wants to make it a series. She wants you to continue to participate and me to continue writing
about us doing things like the speed dating. We
won't pay you, we never pay sources, but we will
foot the bill for the dates and events we use in the
column. This could go on indefinitely. What do
you say?"

She'd delivered the information in a tone she
thought made none of it sound interesting.

Which was why she was surprised when he
said, "Great. I'll do it."

She eyed him warily. "You understand you
won't be paid."

"Yes."

"And you'll have to get together with me on a somewhat regular basis."

A smile tugged at his lips. "Yes."

"And when you get together with me you'll have to keep your hands to yourself and forget all about what happened the other night."

He laughed, the deep dimples and creases by his eyes making his whole face participate. "Maybe you didn't notice, but *I* haven't brought that night up once."

"Not yet," she said darkly.

"Nor have I brought up the fact that *you* were the one who started it. You kissed me first."

"What?" The memory came back to her as if at his bidding. Her decision to kiss him, to see what she was missing . . . "*You* kissed *me* at Clyde's," she shot back. "That was first."

"Touché." He laughed.

She exhaled slowly. This was getting them nowhere.

"Do you mind if I ask why you don't mind doing this?" she asked. "Participating in the column?"

He lifted one shoulder and let it drop, cocking his head, the remnants of mirth clear in his face. "I think it's fun."

"Fun."

"That's right."

She thought for a moment. "Rulinda said she might even want to do some advertising with the two of us."

He paused. "What kind of advertising?"

"She was talking posters. The two of us, back to back, that kind of thing."

"Photographs."

"Right."

Would he turn her down now? Had she pushed him to the limit? Part of her wished she hadn't brought up the advertising, which Rulinda had dropped anyway. No doubt the part that remembered their night together with erotic fondness.

But her brain was glad. Her brain hoped he'd balk and she could then find someone more suitable. Or rather, more manageable. Thank God her brain was in charge.

"Seems a lot to ask of an unpaid 'source,' " he said. "Wouldn't I be more of a partner or co-author or something at that point?"

"When you start writing, I'll fight for your right to be paid. Until then, we're not the *National Enquirer*. We can't afford to pay for stories. And believe me, finding someone else willing to do this for free would be a piece of cake."

He chuckled. "Relax, I don't care about being paid. I just don't want to be photographed. Deal?"

She exhaled with something like relief, though she was not about to analyze it. "Okay, deal. Do you want to know what I have in mind for our next column? It'll take some preparation."

He held out his hands. "Fire away."

"We'll each pick a couple . . ." She told him the gist of her idea.

"And we go to these interviews together, right?" he asked.

"Right."

"Not just you to mine," he clarified, "but I get to go to yours too, right?"

"Right. Why?"

"Just," he shrugged, "because I want to make sure what you write in the column is accurate."

She chuckled. "You'll probably think it's not no matter what I write, but hey, tough luck. It's my column."

"Don't I get a rebuttal?"

She laughed. "I don't think so."

"I think I should get a rebuttal," he insisted. "Think about it, it'll just add to the point-counterpoint flavor of the thing."

"Oh God." It was just what Rulinda had said. She'd even used that phrase, 'point, counter-point.' Thank God he was an anonymous source and Rulinda couldn't get to him on her own.

"What?" Joe was watching her face.

"Nothing. Just—I'll think about it." He was probably right, some kind of rebuttal from him would make it more interesting. "Here's what I'm thinking the format will be. I'll write the column from my point of view, then I'll take some direct quotes from you about your views and let you edit those to be sure they're accurate. How's that? *And* I'll make it clear to readers that the bulk of the column is my point of view. Does that sound fair?"

"Fair enough," he said. "So when do we do the interview thing?"

"This week. Rulinda wants the column to be weekly now, so we'll have to be quicker than we were with the speed dating. I'm thinking we arrange it for Thursday night, both interviews and our comments. I'll write it over the weekend."

"Works for me."

She nodded and glanced at the cart. "And I do want a latte."

He laughed, and she couldn't help smiling with him. Maybe they could forget about the other night and go back to being just friends. They *had* been friends, in a way, hadn't they? Before they'd accidentally slept together?

She reached for her purse to pull out the five she'd given to Angela earlier, but Joe shook his head, his eyes on the steaming milk.

"It's on the house today," he said.

She started to protest but gave up before the words reached her lips. She knew enough about him to know that a) he'd expect her to object, and b) he could be stubborn when he wanted to be and would refuse her money until she relented.

Instead she just said, "Thank you."

His look of delighted surprise made her smile as their eyes met.

She could only hold his gaze for a moment, though, and dropped her eyes to his hands again.

Her skin tingled as she remembered their intimate exploration of her body. What they'd done to her, those hands. How confident they'd been.

Laurel turned her head away, forcing her gaze down Connecticut Avenue. Despite the cold winter day, she felt inexplicably hot.

The Patels—a young Indian couple Laurel's journalist friend had interviewed four years before—lived off of Massachusetts Avenue near the DC border with Maryland. Joe met Laurel at her office and since Laurel had taken the Metro to work, they decided to go in his car.

They pulled into the Patels' driveway and Joe got out of the SUV, coming around to open her door despite the fact that she'd gotten out on her own.

"So, you'll interview these people and I'll interview my friends?" he asked as they crossed the driveway to the front walk.

"I don't think it needs to be that structured. If you want to ask a question, go right ahead. No doubt you'll think of an angle I've missed."

Joe shot her a grin. "No doubt."

They reached the door and Laurel rang the bell.

A small, beautiful Indian woman with lustrous black hair in a long braid answered the door in a flowing sari. Her smile was sincere as she beckoned them inside.

Surya and Hakim Patel had set up in their living room with trays of hors d'oeuvres and a large pot of tea.

Laurel introduced herself and then Joe. She spoke a little about what they were doing, then pulled out her pad. She was surprised when Joe took a small pad out of his back pocket too. As she watched him flip some pages over the spiral binding, his eyes slid slyly to her and a smile teased his lips.

She suppressed a smile of her own.

After a few minutes of pleasantries on both sides, Laurel got down to business.

"So your marriage was arranged by your parents, is that right?" Laurel asked.

"Yes, yes, that's right," Surya said.

From their earlier phone conversation, Laurel knew she spoke a very Americanized English. There was only the slightest trace of an Indian accent, which in Laurel's opinion just made her sound more cultured.

"My parents are still in India," Surya continued, "and they found Hakim's family. We were both here in DC, so in some ways it seemed fated!"

Hakim nodded at them with a pleasant smile.

Laurel looked down at her notes.

Joe said, "How long have you been married?"

Surya put her hand on Hakim's where it lay on his knee and said, "Four years."

"Any kids?"

"Oh yes. Two. Four months and eighteen months. They're sleeping now."

"And the two of you didn't meet until the wedding, is that right?" Laurel asked.

"Oh no, we met before the wedding." Surya patted Hakim's knee. "We had, I think, three dates, but I didn't let him kiss me. Not even on the cheek, good night. Just three dates to see if we could, you know, carry on a conversation." She laughed brightly. "Mostly it was me, carrying on. Hakim's very quiet." She smiled over at him.

Hakim laughed self-consciously. "I thought she was very beautiful. Very beautiful."

His accent was stronger. He looked at his wife through deep brown eyes that seemed to glow at the sight of her.

"So you had to make sure you had common interests and goals. That's what you talked about?" Laurel asked.

"Oh yes, at great length," Surya said. "I asked him about his opinions on everything. From cooking to politics. We agreed on almost everything. So much that I started to wonder whether he was telling the truth!"

"What convinced you that he was?" Joe asked.

Surya looked at the ceiling, thinking, then looked at her husband. "I don't know. I think . . . I think I just believed him. My brain was telling me to question it, to be suspicious. But there was just something really . . . really trustworthy about him. A feeling I got."

"Hmm," Joe said, casting a glance at Laurel, then writing something down on his little pad. "A feeling."

"I know it sounds silly." Surya laughed, a musical sound, and patted Hakim's knee again. "But that feeling was the most important thing to me. My instincts had to be satisfied."

"Doesn't sound silly at all." Joe leaned back smugly.

Laurel nodded, keeping a smile in place. "But, in arranging this union, you had to get both of your families to approve, right? That was very important too?"

"Oh yes," Surya said. "They came over here before we even met, to make sure that we suited. They had to investigate our backgrounds, you know, make sure everything we said about ourselves and our families was true."

"And if they didn't approve, you wouldn't have gone through with it?" Laurel asked.

Surya frowned. "It would have been very difficult to go through with it."

"Do you consider yourselves happy?" Joe asked. "You think the right decision was made for you?"

"*We* made the decision," Surya corrected, with a gentle smile at Joe. "We could have said no, if one of us had not liked the other. Or we could have said yes, even if our parents disapproved, though their disapproval was unlikely in this case."

"So you essentially arranged your own marriage. The two of you," Laurel said.

"With our parents' help." Surya nodded.

"And it works without romance," Laurel added, shooting a quick gloat at Joe.

"Oh *no*." Surya shook her head.

Laurel's eyes snapped back to her.

"Hakim is very romantic. He..." She grinned over at her husband. "Shall I tell them? He writes me poetry," she said without waiting for an answer. "Incredible poems, with such depth and love."

"We are very much in love," Hakim said, in his deliberate way, as if searching for the right English words. "I could tell, when we met, that I would fall in love with her."

Laurel's hand gripped her pen. "But you weren't in love, when you met. Even when you married. You didn't wait to fall in love before making the decision to marry."

"No," Surya said thoughtfully. "But it was my greatest hope, to fall in love with my husband. And it has come true." She smiled at Hakim. "Love came true."

"This is the quick-date woman?" Bennett Bridges asked Joe out of the side of his mouth as Laurel entered the house.

"Speed dating. Yeah." Joe made sure Laurel was out of earshot, watching her as she greeted Bennett's wife, Sandra, with a warm smile. "She's working through some book on how you don't need love to find a husband."

"Really?" Bennett said. "What do you need, a lasso and a branding iron?"

Joe chuckled, shaking his head. "According to this book, it's the right résumé, or maybe a herd of goats."

Bennett's brows rose and they both chuckled as they followed Laurel and Sandra into the living room.

Laurel had been suspiciously quiet as she scribbled rapidly on her pad from the Patels' house to the Bridges'. Thoughts were flying, Joe could tell, on ways to spin the fact that Surya and Hakim Patel were in love and had hoped for love, even while arranging their own marriage. They had also relied somewhat on attraction and instinct in deciding on the union.

He'd made a point of not commenting on how completely they disputed Laurel's main contention —that Love Is Not the Answer—knowing she would just dig in her heels. With his good friends Bennett and Sandra as the second interview, he was sure she'd have no choice but to concede that love *is* in fact an answer, and the best one at that.

"This is a wonderful house." Laurel's eyes took in the high ceilings, the turn-of-the-century door moldings and the elaborately carved mantelpiece.

"Thanks," Sandra said in her soft cool voice. "But it's been a bear to remodel. That molding isn't made anymore. We've had to special-order it so His Highness can tell his buddies it's all original." She rolled her eyes toward Bennett.

"It *is* all original," he objected, "except for a couple places upstairs. One bedroom door and the bathroom. Part of the den."

"Which he tells everyone anyway so you

wouldn't think we'd *need* to special-order everything to match perfectly."

"Just get the coffee, woman," Bennett said and Sandra laughed.

"That's his fallback argument," she said. "Pretty sophisticated, isn't it? So what can I get you? Coffee, tea, beer, wine?"

"Coffee for me," Laurel said.

"I'll take a beer," Joe said.

"Me too." Bennett waved toward a couple of armchairs to one side of the fireplace. "Have a seat, you two."

"So how do you and Joe know each other?" Laurel asked, smiling at Bennett.

"We work together. I'm his accountant."

Laurel laughed. "The stories you could tell, eh?"

"You bet. I've known this guy for almost twenty-five years."

"But he would never tell," Joe said with a significant look at his friend. "Since I have just as many stories about him."

"Empty threats, my friend." Bennett laughed. "Sandra knows all my stories."

"And a few more Joe doesn't know yet," Sandra said, reentering with a tray bearing all of their drinks.

"Yet?" Bennett repeated.

They all laughed.

Sandra had a glass of white wine, making Laurel the only one with coffee. A testament to her uptight nature, Joe thought, sending her a grin and raising his beer to her in a toast.

She gave him a dark look, which pleased him. She always seemed to know what he meant.

"So," she said, turning a much more pleasant expression to Sandra. "Thank you both so much for meeting with us tonight. I don't know if Joe explained to you the scope of our project?"

"He said you were writing a paper or something," Bennett said. "About how you don't need love to find a husband?"

"No, I said she was writing *for* a paper. About how you don't need love to find a husband. Accountants," Joe shook his head, chuckling, "they never get words right."

"It's not accountants," Sandra said. "It's just Bennett."

Laurel smiled, looking from Sandra to Bennett as the two of them put up their dukes in mock fighting position. Joe could tell she was enjoying them, which boded well for him driving his point home.

"It's a column for *DC Scene*," she said. "And it's more of a dating theme. Joe and I are comparing dating for love and dating for practical purposes."

"Dating as a prelude for marriage," Joe said.

"That's right. But actually having to get married seemed a bit much for the sake of a column," Laurel said with a laugh.

Joe sat forward on the couch and pulled his notepad from his back pocket. "That's why we're interviewing you guys. You're my example of a successful love match."

"Oh honey." Sandra laughed, that great full-throated laugh she had, and leaned toward Laurel. "You have to take the position that you don't need love to find a husband? How did you get stuck with *that* job?"

Laurel's cheeks turned pink and she picked up her spoon and lifted the lid on the sugar bowl. "Actually, I think it's true. I think, what with the state of marriage in today's society, maybe marriage can, or should, be built on something other than love. Maybe it would last longer."

"But if you don't love a man, what on earth do you need him around for?" Sandra's question was facetious, but her eyes appeared genuinely questioning as she looked at Laurel.

"For support, partnership. Children." Laurel spooned sugar into her cup with the words and stirred.

"Sure, okay." Sandra's tone was clearly doubtful. "Maybe you can find someone who gives you that. But if you want to keep him, you got to have love."

Holding her cup carefully, Laurel turned toward Sandra. "So you think men need to be loved in order to want to stay in a marriage?" The hand not holding her coffee snaked into her purse, no doubt searching for her pad and pen.

"No, I think women need to love 'em to keep from killing 'em ten times a day." Sandra's smile was wide and candid, her expression toward Laurel a tiny bit pitying.

"Yeah, and *we* need it to keep from wanting to be dead," Bennett added with a so-there nod at Sandra.

Joe, Sandra and Bennett laughed, but Laurel's face was concerned. "That sounds as if you've dealt with your share of adversity."

"Hasn't everyone?" Sandra asked. "Marriage is a difficult business sometimes."

Laurel nodded. "And when did your marriage become difficult?"

"*Become* difficult?" Sandra looked up at Bennett, her brow furrowed with the question. "I wouldn't say it's a constant state."

"Just a temporary condition," Bennett said. "Every once in a while."

"But you just said you wanted to kill him ten times a day, Sandra." Laurel looked down at her notes.

Joe watched her, wondering if she was being deliberately obtuse or if she really believed that's what Sandra had just said.

"Sure, but that's not the marriage. That's him." Sandra elbowed Bennett playfully in the side.

"Yeah, I can be difficult. I hear that all the time." Bennett laughed. "It's my cross to bear."

"*Your* cross!" Sandra shook her head. "No, what I meant was more that marriage is an *effort* . . ."

"Yeah, frequently an effort," Bennett concurred.

"But worth it. Worth it every single day, even when it's a big pain in the ass." Sandra laughed.

"I once heard it said about marriage," Bennett said, "that when you're happy, you're twice as happy. And when you're sad you're only half as sad. That about sums it up for me."

Sandra sent Bennett an intimate smile that had Joe glancing at Laurel to be sure she'd seen it. There was something about these two, Joe had always thought, that advertised the best things about marriage. It was love, he thought now. True, enduring love.

But Laurel wasn't looking at them. She was gazing at her pad thoughtfully.

"Can you think of some things that, generally speaking, each of you does that love helps you tolerate?" she asked.

Bennett and Sandra looked at each other consideringly.

"Everything," Sandra said, at the same time Bennett said, "Pretty much everything."

They laughed, Sandra laying her hand on his leg as Bennett's arm came around her along the back of the couch. She leaned into him.

"So you don't think you're naturally compatible?" Laurel asked, scribbling on her pad.

Joe ran a hand through his hair. This was ridiculous. She was working hard to slant whatever they said to suit her own point. "Hey, this is supposed to be *my* interview. I get to ask the questions here, don't I?"

"Sure." Laurel finished her written thought

and looked up at him, her eyes simultaneously troubled and challenging. "I just wanted to get a couple in because I know you're not going to ask them anything hard."

"Why should I? I'm not here to figure out who leaves the top off the toothpaste and who doesn't hang up their clothes. I'm here to show you, and your readers of course, a good example of successfully marrying for love."

"Yes, but you've got a bad habit of looking on the sunny side of things and then pretending there's nothing else to look at."

"Yeah, bad habit." Joe laughed incredulously. "Much better to go through life looking for the dark side."

"As a journalist, I have to look at both sides. Otherwise whatever I write won't be balanced. If you want the whole picture you have to look at everything."

"So when things are bad, you go looking for the bright side?"

"Of course."

Joe shook his head. He'd never met anybody who knew herself less than Laurel did. "I didn't see much evidence of that Thursday night. Or rather, Friday morning."

Laurel went scarlet and glanced from Joe to Bennett and Sandra. Bennett and Sandra looked with interest at Joe, their expressions identically amused.

"So," Joe said, turning to them, "I really have

only one question for you guys. How did you two meet?"

Bennett raised a brow at Joe and chuckled, but let the moment pass.

Sandra leaned back against her husband and nudged his arm. "You tell it, honey."

"Uh-uh. If I start to tell it you'll just interrupt me and change everything." Bennett squeezed her shoulder with one of his big hands. "You tell it, and I'll interrupt."

This was exactly why Joe had picked them. The story was great—or maybe it was just the way they told it. In any case, Joe had heard it dozens of times, and always thought it illustrated perfectly how misperceptions, expectations and a rigid view of life could screw up your chances of seeing what was standing right in front of you.

Sandra had hated Bennett when she'd first met him. Bennett had found her irresistible, but hadn't wanted to get involved with, let alone married to, anyone until he'd finished his MBA. Sandra had wanted to marry someone artistic, and Bennett had thought she was enrolled in the business college, like *he* was. In reality she'd been commissioned to do the mural in the foyer of the building. To this day there is a briefcase-bearing black man with bird-droppings on his shoulder in the background of the business-hall mural, an illustration of Sandra's initial feelings for the man who was eventually to become her husband.

Long story short: When they'd both set aside their own ideas about who they should end up with, they'd fallen head over heels in love with each other. That had been nearly twenty years ago.

Joe watched as Laurel got caught up in the story, smiling and laughing in all the right places, then sighing—he could swear in satisfaction—at the conclusion.

Joe looked at his watch. "We should go. Got to go fight the dark side of life now, make sure it doesn't take over the story," he explained to Bennett and Sandra.

"Very funny," Laurel said, then turned to his friends with a sincere smile. "Thank you so much for this evening. It really was a pleasure to meet you both."

They'd said their goodbyes and were standing at the door when Bennett said, "Good luck to you guys. Something tells me you're both going to learn more about yourselves together than you would alone. That's how it was with Sandra and me."

Laurel looked alarmed. Joe started to say something, when Sandra slapped Bennett in the gut.

"*They're* not a couple, you fool," she said.

"I didn't say they *were*." Bennett placed a hand on his stomach as if injured, his other arm still around her shoulders. "I just said—"

"We all heard what you said. Just you shut up now." Sandra turned a beaming smile on Laurel. "Good night, Laurel. Hope to see you again sometime."

"Me too," Laurel said, with a self-conscious glance at Joe.

"What did you tell them about us?" she asked quietly as he opened the car door for her.

His gaze slid toward her. "I told them that you are a pain in the ass but that I like you anyway."

"You *like* me?" she repeated. Something about the phrase brought back seventh grade and she wondered if he *liked* her, liked her, or just liked her.

"Yeah, is that okay?" He stepped back, holding his hands up as if being robbed. "I mean, if I don't touch you or anything."

She gave him a smirky smile. "You can like a woman without touching her?"

He pointed a finger at her as he headed around the hood of the SUV to the driver's side. "Get in the car, smart aleck."

She settled into the passenger seat and watched him fold himself behind the wheel.

"That's not too close, is it?" He looked, mock-worried, at the space between the two bucket seats.

"Very funny."

He put the key in the ignition and the engine rumbled to life.

"I never said you couldn't *touch* me, Joe," she said after a minute.

His eyes shot to her. "Yes, you did."

"I meant I didn't want you to get any ideas about repeating the other night, not that you have to treat me like I've got the plague."

"You don't want me getting ideas," he repeated.

"You know, I just don't think it would be smart. Because we believe different things, about relationships."

"You mean because I believe in love and you don't."

"Exactly." She hoped she didn't sound egotistical. Like she thought he was dying to repeat the other night. God knew Joe Squires could have other options if he so desired. Probably any other option he wanted.

She felt his eyes on the side of her face and turned to look at him.

He was grinning. "Does that mean I can touch you if I promise not to fall in love with you?"

Eleven

For some reason, that was not what Laurel wanted to hear, even though she herself could have guaranteed any number of men in her past that she would not fall in love with them. That was always the problem. She couldn't sustain it.

Hearing it from Joe, however, didn't make her feel any better about their situation. She supposed it was always hard to be told that someone could promise not to fall in love with you.

Laurel leaned back on the Explorer's seat, and tried to concentrate on Sandra and Bennett. How close they seemed, even though they'd been together so long.

"So how long have Sandra and Bennett been together?" she asked.

"Almost twenty years. Pretty good argument for love, don't you think?" Joe asked with a grin.

"I liked them," she admitted. "But you have to admit that some of their answers showed a certain laying aside of that love in order to make the marriage work."

"What?" He looked at her, scandalized. "What are you talking about? Everything they said reflected that love was the point."

"Not when they said it was an effort."

He glanced from the road to her and back. "Is that what you thought that meant? Is that what you think love means? 'Never having to say you're sorry'?"

She laughed. "Now you're quoting *Love Story*?"

"Yes, because it's bullshit. Love means having to say you're sorry all the damn time, even when you don't mean it. *Especially* when you don't mean it."

She looked at him with interest. "Is that what you really think?"

"I don't think it, I *know* it. I've *done* it. It *is* work, it *is* difficult, but it's impossible without someone you love. That's my point. You love someone, you put up with their idiosyncrasies."

"I don't think that's true. Or, rather, that *might* be true, but love is also fraught with a whole lot of expectations—like expecting the other person to put up with idiosyncrasies that maybe they'll get tired of. Then what do you think? That they don't love you. And maybe they don't. But if you're not dealing with that love factor, if you've got a deal, a mutually satisfying deal, then each person holds to their end of the bargain so that the other holds to theirs."

"Jesus, Laurel, that's the way you want to live? In a permanent Mexican standoff? You do this for me and I'll do that for you. Stop doing this and I stop doing that. That's more like a nuclear non-proliferation treaty than a marriage."

She sighed. "You're deliberately misunderstanding me. Obviously I meant that you do it for mutual gain, not to avoid mutual destruction."

"No you didn't. You meant don't shoot me and I won't shoot you."

"More like you wash my back and I'll wash yours."

"Great. A Mafia marriage."

She laughed. He was so indignant. It was kind of cute. A big strong guy like Joe outraged about a situation in which nobody was whispering sweet nothings to anybody else.

"How did you get to be such a romantic, Joe?"

"I think it's a natural state. From what I've seen, you have to really work at it to be any other way."

"No, I mean it." She canted sideways on the seat to face him. "From all I've heard, even the most amicable divorces are tough. How is it that your faith in love survived a broken marriage?"

He thought a long moment, long enough for her to wonder if maybe she shouldn't have asked, then he exhaled heavily. "I guess because I see the mistakes I made, why it went wrong."

Laurel sat quietly, dying to ask what the mistakes were but certain that it was way too personal a question.

But after a minute, Joe continued. "I took it for granted. I thought we were married so it was forever, but I didn't *feed* it, you know?" He looked over at her.

She nodded. "I think so."

"And Renee, well, she wasn't great at telling me when there was a problem. Maybe it was the Southern thing . . . she was from Georgia. Always polite and smiling and sweet. She wouldn't argue or yell. There'd just be a mood, like when I got home. But then I was able to tell myself that it was probably because of something else, like she'd had a bad day or was frustrated at work. But I didn't explore it. I never asked." He laughed once, cynically. "I probably didn't want to know."

"Communication is up to both people," she said lamely, feeling that without any marriage experience herself, anything she said would be invalid.

"That's true," he said and nodded. "That's true."

They were both quiet for a minute before he added, "I guess I feel like I'd know how to do it right this time. I'd know how not to blow it. And I'd know how to pick the right person."

She looked at him for a long moment, then sighed softly. "It must be nice, knowing that."

In the dashboard light, his face was set. They drove in silence for many minutes, the only noticeable sounds being the tires on the road and the occasional thumping of the struts as they encountered the newest cold-induced potholes.

"Do I get to read the whole column when it's done, or just my quotes?" Joe was weaving through traffic on Massachusetts Avenue faster than Laurel would have liked.

"You can read the whole thing," she said, gripping the armrest on the door. "Buy a paper."

"I mean *before* it runs. I have the feeling you're going to slant this unreasonably toward your own ends."

Laurel pressed an imaginary brake with her foot as Joe narrowly skirted a car, stopped to make a left turn, then breezed through the intersection at the Naval Observatory.

"I'm going to write what I saw, Joe. It may be slightly slanted but you'll get your say, just like we talked about."

He cocked an eyebrow at her. "Slightly slanted? I could tell the conclusions you were drawing, Laurel, and I think they were more than *slightly* slanted."

Laurel took a deep breath and looked out the side window. Better to watch the scenery whipping by than to take a year off her life trying to control a car with only her nerves.

"Do you even want to know what I saw, Joe, or do you just want to disagree with whatever I say?"

She glanced at him.

"Okay, tell me. Tell me how you're going to twist Bennett and Sandra's story to show that they're incompatible."

Laurel crossed her arms over her chest. "I'm not going to twist their story."

"But you're going to portray the Patels as the very picture of marital bliss and Bennett and Sandra as, what, struggling?"

"What makes you say that?"

He slid his eyes her way with a knowing expression. "You seemed to get caught on that 'marriage is an effort' point."

He seemed upset, and she thought again that she shouldn't have brought up his divorce. Still, she didn't need to take it personally. If he were just another reporter on the same beat, she wouldn't give a damn what he thought.

"You didn't think the Patels seemed happy?" She folded her hands in her lap.

"That's beside the point. The point is—"

"You think I'm biased."

He shot her a hard smile. "Yeah. I think you're biased. Just a little."

She straightened in her seat. "Well, guess what, Joe, I'm supposed to be. That's what columnists do, we write our opinions, our biases, and let people agree or disagree. You, my idealistic friend, are free to disagree."

"Which I will. I'm sure."

In her lap, she kneaded her fingers. She was not going to be pushed around by a man who thought he knew exactly how the universe should be ordered, not just for himself but for everyone else too. If she could just get out of this damn car, she would remember that she didn't have to worry about what he thought. That he was just a tool, a foil, a warning.

She turned to him. "Are you angry at me, Joe?"

"No, I'm not angry," he said angrily. "I'm just . . . I just . . . I don't agree."

"With what? What is it you disagree with, exactly?"

"I disagree with you portraying the Bridges as anything but a successful marriage. A successful marriage based on good old-fashioned falling in *love.*"

Laurel let the statement hang in the air a moment. Let him think she was plotting her argument, she thought, as they rounded another left-turning car and she gripped the armrest again. Let him believe all the negative things about her he wanted.

She began, "First of all, I don't intend to sugarcoat anything—"

"I *knew* it!" He banged the heel of his hand on the steering wheel, then braked, hard, to stop for a red light.

She let out a slow breath. "I also have no intention of portraying them as unhappy. Or unsuccessful."

He slid her a suspicious look.

"I think they're a great example of what a good marriage can be. Maybe the best example we could have found."

He continued to look at her from the corner of his eye. "But . . . ?"

She inclined her head. "But I don't think they're necessarily representative. And I think the Patels were a good example as well. Honestly, I thought both couples seemed equally successful."

"And both couples were in love with each other."

"Yes. So?"

He turned to her fully. "So, going by this experiment, love *is* the answer, to negate Mr. Nadalov."

She let herself smile, glad that his anger seemed to be diminishing. "No, love is the *result*. Dr. Nadalov says that love is just the psychological outcome of sexual intercourse."

A bark of laughter shot from Joe. Someone behind them honked their horn. He looked at the green light and floored the accelerator.

"So why aren't you and I in love after last Thursday night?" His challenging grin was back. "I mean, if any sex is powerful enough to result in love, I'd say last Thursday was right up there."

Joe rounded Sheridan Circle barely touching the brakes. At her silence, he glanced over and added, with an endearing touch of uncertainty, "Right?"

Laurel clutched the edge of her seat, leaned into the door and couldn't help laughing. Maybe it was the combination of adrenaline and relief that he was no longer being so combative. But the flash of insecurity in his question made her heart quicken with empathy. He wasn't so different from her, perhaps just more extroverted. He hid the holes in his confidence with laughter, and she hid hers with . . . with what? Anger? The thought made her ashamed of herself.

"If that was what Dr. Nadalov meant, then yes. I'm sure we'd be heading for the altar right now." She smiled in the dark. "But I think Dr. Nadalov's point was about *regular* sexual intercourse. Obviously you don't fall in love with everyone you sleep with."

"But if you sleep with them enough, you do?" He slowed the car and stopped at the light at Florida Avenue.

They were mere blocks from his house, and Laurel's mind couldn't help picturing Joe's darkened living room, where she'd tripped and he'd taken her into his arms. How delicious it had felt. How gratifying and exciting and—and *wrong* it had felt. But it was the very wrongness of the moment that had increased the excitement.

"Within a properly arranged marriage," she said, taking the opportunity of the red light to breathe easily, "where both families approve and the social foundation is sound, where the two parties treat each other with respect, then yes, regular sexual intercourse within the marriage context usually results in love."

"So you're saying that if you and I went back to my place . . ." The light turned green, he crossed Florida Avenue and headed for Dupont Circle, bypassing the route to his house without a glance. "And we repeated—"

She felt her body go hot. "No I don't mean that. You and I are not in a sanctioned arranged marriage. Love doesn't just grow out of sex alone."

He held out a hand, palm up. "But Dr. Nadalov—"

"What he's referring to is the commitment. And for all your talk of love, Joe, I don't see you making any commitments."

"To you?" His brows rose and he looked at her as they exited Dupont Circle.

"No, not to me, to anyone. How was your date last Friday, by the way?" Laurel scrunched her eyes together and turned her head toward the window. Dammit. She hadn't meant to ask that. And except for the occasional pang, she'd even stopped thinking about it. Why had she brought it up now?

He paused for a long moment, but she wouldn't turn her head from the window.

"Are you going to include this in the column?" he asked.

Laurel's palms began to sweat. "If you don't want me to, I won't. I just thought it might be an interesting aside, you know, how your pursuit of love is going outside the context of Dr. Nadalov's exercises."

"Uh-huh." His pace slower now, he turned right to follow Massachusetts Avenue as it jogged to avoid New York Avenue.

He looked over at her for such a long moment she was tempted to grab the wheel, though he was driving perfectly straight and not in danger of hitting anything.

"What?" She turned her head to look at him. "Does that mysterious look mean, 'No, Laurel, I'd rather not talk about it'?"

He turned back to the road. "No, I'll talk about it. Whatever you want to know. Just, no particulars about the girl. She hasn't signed up for the life-as-an-open-book treatment like I have. And you have."

Protecting her, she thought, her breathing growing uncomfortably shallow. He was protecting whoever the woman was who'd come after her last weekend. The *real* date. The woman he'd actually asked out, maybe dressed up for, maybe been excited to see.

Not the woman he'd slept with on the spur of the moment to make a point.

She hated the spurt of humiliation that shot through her. This was exactly the kind of thing she didn't need.

"Speaking of which," he added, "is the fact that Regular Joe and Plain Jane slept together going to show up in the column anywhere?"

"Absolutely not!"

He laughed. "Why not? I think it's relevant. Besides, people will probably be wondering."

Laurel's mouth dropped open and she gaped at him. "People won't be wondering that. Why would people be wondering that?"

"Because people always wonder that when a man and a woman spend time together. I'd think they'd particularly wonder about it in this context."

"So you want me to tell the world that we slept together? What are you, some kind of exhibitionist?"

"Now Laurel. You know the whole world doesn't read *DC Scene*. Besides, nobody knows who Regular Joe is."

"But they know, or probably suspect, who Plain Jane is. And I'm not about to start serving up sexual experiments for the entertainment of my readers. That's nothing but porn."

"Sexual experiments? I was a sexual experiment?" One hand spread out on his chest and his expression feigned shock. Or maybe it was real, it was hard to tell.

"That's right, bucko." *That is right*, she told herself. Let him see how that felt. Honesty was a tough policy.

His eyes darted toward her and his hand dropped back to the wheel. "Seriously?"

"Sure. I was A Point and you were An Experiment. No big deal."

The Capitol rose up before them, lit up like a postcard against an inky dark sky.

Joe was silent. She stole a glance at him but could tell nothing from his profile. Had her assertion stung? Had she gone too far? Could she possibly have hurt his feelings?

He hadn't been an experiment, she knew. She'd just caved in to an overwhelming sense of attraction to him. But she couldn't tell him that, even though it seemed fairly obvious. If she did, he'd just take the ball and run with it, no doubt making another of his infamous "points" and making her feel bad in the process.

"You said Fourth Street?" he asked after a minute. She directed him around the Capitol to the street of half-renovated, half-dilapidated row houses where she lived.

"It's that one." She pointed to the one under which her apartment crouched. The street was what could be called "transitional," which was the only thing that made it affordable.

He peered through the side windows at the row houses on either side, then pulled into an open spot half a block down. He turned off the engine and the lights, then turned to face her, one wrist draped over the steering wheel.

He could have double-parked while she got out, she thought. Did he expect to come in? Instead of being hurt by what she'd said, had he thought it meant she might be amenable to another experiment?

Was she?

No, of course not. She mentally shook herself. Of course he'd parked, because he knew they had to share their views on the evening so she could write the column with his opinion included. She had planned from the beginning to offer coffee for that very purpose.

But now that they'd agreed last Thursday's transgression had been, well, off-the-charts-fabulous sex, could he be thinking they might repeat it?

Or was it just her thinking that?

Laurel looked at her watch. Ten thirty.

"Well . . ." she said, hating her own indecision. This was business. She knew what she had to do, she had to get all the information she needed for the column and then write the damn thing. She turned to him decisively. "Do you have time to come in for a minute?"

One side of his mouth kicked up. "Into your apartment?"

"For coffee." She picked her purse and briefcase up from the floor by her feet. "And conversation. I want to get this all over with in one night so I can write the column tomorrow."

She opened the SUV door. The overhead light cast an uncomfortable glow that made her squint as she looked over at him.

He squinted back at her, his mouth quirked with amusement. "I don't know. I'm pretty sick of coffee."

She laughed. "Water then. Or soda. Orange juice. I might even have some wine. I'm sure I can come up with something other than coffee."

He didn't move and she started to feel as if she were out of line to be asking him.

"Hey, you're the one who wanted your opinion in this thing." She stepped out of the car and looked back at him nonchalantly. "Either come in and tell me what it is or let me write the column without it. Up to you." She slammed the door and headed down the sidewalk toward her apartment.

A second later she heard his door slam, then the chirp of the remote setting the locks. She smiled to herself, pulled her keys out of her purse and turned down the steps to her apartment.

As she put the key in the deadbolt she felt him come up behind her. Her mind strayed to the memory of his arms catching her from behind. She could almost feel the solidity of his chest against her back, his arms as they encircled her, his eyes laughing as she turned and he looked down at her. *Well, well . . .*

She pushed open the door and stepped into the dark living room/dining room of her apartment. Dead ahead was the kitchen, and behind that the bedroom, shotgun style. She flipped the overhead light and the room brightened, but the smell of mildew assaulted her as it always did after a day away from it.

"Sorry about the mildew." She crossed the room to turn on another light and deposited her purse on the table by the kitchen. She turned back, taking off her coat.

He shrugged. "Basement apartments. What are you gonna do?"

"Trust me, there's nothing you can do. I've tried everything. You can just hang your coat on one of the hooks by the door. I'll be right back."

She slipped past the kitchen into the bathroom, where she'd suddenly remembered leaving stockings hanging on the shower rod. The last thing she'd need would be for him to use the restroom and see her intimate apparel strewn about.

While in the bathroom, she checked her face in the mirror. Her makeup, as usual by the end of the day, appeared to be gone. Her cheeks were pale and her hair was flat. Yet another reason to be glad she wasn't interested in dating Joe. She didn't have to worry about things like how her makeup looked, or what she was wearing, or whether he was paying enough attention to her or if he was looking at her the right way.

In an arranged marriage those things didn't matter. In an arranged marriage being clean was enough. As well as being honest and loyal and trustworthy and all that.

Still, she didn't need to look like a corpse.

She yanked open the door to the medicine cabinet and reached for her blush. But the thought of reappearing with fresh makeup, and more important, his *noticing* the fresh makeup, had her putting back the blush and ruthlessly pinching her cheeks. Which was stupid, because she really did not care what he thought about her. That was the whole point.

She ran a brush through her hair—anyone would do that—and pulled open the door. Joe was standing in the darkened kitchen, directly across from the bathroom, with the refrigerator door open.

"Mind if I drink one of these seltzer waters?" he asked, peering into the light. The contrast of shadow and light conspired to make him look as if he'd been artfully lit for a photograph, to capture the clearness of his eyes and fine bone structure of his face.

She stood in the kitchen doorway. "Help yourself. Do you want a glass?"

He straightened, popping the top on the can of seltzer. "No thanks. Can I get you one?" He held the can out for her.

"No, nothing for me."

She moved back into the living room, away from him, away from the nearby bedroom door, and sat on the couch. Pulling her tote bag toward her, she angled herself so that she leaned against one arm and could brace her pad and pen against her knees, which would be between her and Joe. Uninviting, unassuming, impersonal.

He came out of the kitchen, looking like a movie idol who'd stepped off the screen and into these familiar surroundings. He held the can of seltzer water in one hand as his gaze swept the room, lingering on the few prints she had hanging on the wall—nothing so original and artistic as his—touching the books in her bookcases, grazing the dozen vanilla candles she had on a set of nesting tables, finally lighting on the framed photographs set up along the top of a barrister's cabinet.

He picked up the one of her and Ethan, shiny and red-eyed in the poorly exposed shot, but it was a picture she'd liked because they both looked so happy. It was one of the rare times they'd laughed really hard over the same thing—in this case Sue's drunken manipulations of the camera—and she'd kept the photo out because it made her feel good to remember that they had, occasionally, connected like that.

"Is this . . . uh . . . ?" He was obviously striving to remember the name. "Tiny Tears?"

She couldn't stop a small laugh. "It's Ethan, yes."

He nodded. "You look happy. Both of you."

She sighed. "I know. That's why I put it out. We didn't look that way very often."

"No?" He looked up at her, his eyes curious.

She shook her head. "In fact, he not only didn't ask for a copy of that picture, he didn't even notice I'd framed it and put it out." She shook her head again and laughed dryly. "You know, they can cry when you dump them, but when they spend the whole relationship not seeing you, not even *trying* to be interested in who you are, it's hard to feel too bad about it."

She waited for a cynical comment from him but he made none. She worried that she might have hit a nerve. After what he'd told her about his marriage she wondered if he'd done the same thing to Renee. His expression remained thoughtful, however, as he turned and put the picture back in its place.

After a minute he said, "For someone who doesn't believe in romance, you sure have a lot of candles." He picked up a six-inch pillar from the collection on the nesting tables.

She blushed. "They're for the mildew. The smell. Those're vanilla scented."

He chuckled. "Ah. That explains all the little bowls of leaves."

"Potpourri."

"Right." He was quiet again.

She wondered what he was thinking, looking at her personal things. Just last week they'd been so intimate and now here they were striving hard to keep an *impersonal* air. At least he seemed to be. Ordinarily he would have said a lot more about Ethan, she was sure. Did he feel as out of step as she did?

What *was* he thinking?

"So how was the date?" she asked, breaking the silence he hadn't seemed to mind as he looked at the books on her shelf.

He turned back to her, amused.

"You said I could ask." She made her voice light.

"It was fine."

"Fine, ooh. High praise." She slipped her shoes off, pulled her feet in toward her and wrapped her arms—pen, pad and all—around her knees. "Doesn't exactly sound like true love."

He looked down at the floor, crow's feet crinkling and his mouth barely smiling. "No. Probably not." He shrugged, looked back up, his gaze candid. But he didn't elaborate.

"Where did you meet her?" She let go of her knees, propped the pad on them and scribbled a blue circle on one corner of the paper.

"At a party. Couple weeks ago. She invited me to a concert at the Birchmere. I'd actually forgotten about it until she called the day before."

Laurel felt something inside her break loose, some tension she'd been carrying for days. He'd had the date *weeks* before he'd slept with her. *And* he hadn't even asked for the date. *The woman had asked him*. She felt tremendously better.

"So, what . . . wasn't she *attractive* enough?"

Joe slowly rounded the coffee table. "Depends on how you define attractive."

"I don't know, Joe, it's your philosophy. Attraction, you know. So, what are you, a leg man?"

He smiled slowly. "I like yours."

Laurel looked at her pad and ran her hand through her hair, messing up what she'd just brushed. "You know what I mean. Generally."

"Attraction is a multifaceted, multiphased thing." He sat down on the couch next to her and crossed one ankle over his knee. He laid an arm along the back of the sofa, lounging comfortably, his hand dangling near where her knees leaned against the back cushions. "And since you claim to have used the method and had it fail, I don't think I need to explain it further."

He tilted his head, pinning her with a contemplative gaze. "But we haven't defined what it is *you're* looking for," he continued. "We've spent a lot of time talking about what you *don't* want. What is it you *do* want, Laurel?"

Laurel scrunched a little farther back into the arm of the couch and looked down at her pad. "You want me to give you a list?"

"I'm sure you've got one. If you're not looking at a man to see if you're attracted to him, what are you looking for?"

"That's easy." She raised her chin and looked at him. "I'm looking for someone stable, intelligent, gainfully employed, loyal. You know, the kind of man who can make a commitment and stick with it."

He tapped two fingers on the back of the couch as he studied her. "And what about you, Laurel? Can you make a commitment and stick to it?"

The question, as expected as it should have been, caught her off guard.

"I—I don't know." She blurted out the words before she could qualify them.

Hadn't that been the problem in the past? Hadn't it always been *she* who'd fallen out of love? Or never been in love in the first place?

"I think I could make a commitment to be loyal," she said, adopting a confident tone, "to adhere to the contract. That's different from making a commitment to love. Which frankly I think is impossible."

Her eyes dropped, she gazed at his thigh, which just happened to be in her line of sight. The faded denim lay flat over the curved, hard muscle of his leg. She knew those legs were hard because she'd run her fingers over them just last week, as they'd flexed and moved over her with such power and precision.

She lifted her gaze to his. "You can't make a commitment to a feeling, because you can't stop feelings from changing. You can't help not feeling love anymore."

The look in his eyes grew from challenging to sober. Then—and she might have imagined this—he looked sad. His hand slid from the back of the couch to her knee. Despite herself, she liked the warmth of it.

"You haven't been hurt by love," he said softly, as if figuring something out for himself. "You've been hurt by yourself, haven't you?"

Her breathing became shallow. Because, she told herself, she couldn't decide whether to ask him to move his hand or not. In any case, she couldn't take her eyes from his. "I'm not sure what you mean."

His hand moved down her leg, his palm against her calf. Not suggestively, just . . . calming. Reassuring. "It's not men. It's not relationships. It's not even dating. It's *you*. You don't trust yourself."

Her heart pounded as if she were on the verge

of confessing a crime. As if some huge truth were about to come out and change her life forever. "Does it matter? Whether love didn't last for someone else or for me, does it matter? Love didn't last. Love *doesn't* last."

They sat looking at each other for a long moment, Joe's hand warm and sure on her leg. Laurel felt as if she couldn't catch her breath. As if she were running a marathon and couldn't stop.

Meanwhile Joe looked at her with such compassion she thought she might cry. Maybe this was why Catholics said confession was good for the soul. Telling all, confessing all, really showing yourself to even one other person made all the demons seem less real.

Or maybe it was *more* real. So real they could be slain.

"I need to go into a situation that I know I can control," she said in a voice that rang with certainty. "Because if I can control it I can keep my promises. I can make sure that the circumstances leading me to make that decision stay the same, because they're circumstances I choose."

"So it's all about control." Joe's eyes were so intent she couldn't tear hers away.

Joe sat forward and the hand holding her calf pulled her leg down, so it lay flat against the sofa behind him.

"Yes." Laurel nodded, her heart fluttering like a sail in an unsteady wind. "You can't keep promises if you're out of control."

"So being out of control is bad." His hand

took her other leg and straightened it as well. Slowly, deliberately. He moved to the edge of the couch, facing her as if she were an invalid and he the doctor.

"Y—yes." Her brows furrowed as he shifted closer to her, their hips next to each other.

"And were you in control last Thursday?" His hand rose to her cheek, moving a lock of hair behind one ear.

"*No.*" She raised her hand to clasp his wrist, but she didn't fling his hand away as she'd planned. She just held onto his wrist. "That's why it was a mistake. That's why it was—"

Her next words were swallowed by his lips coming down on hers.

She caught her breath.

His tongue plunged into her mouth and the savageness of the kiss gave her no choice but to respond. Not that her body would have given her another choice.

Her heart accelerated and a ferocious desire swept over her.

Her mouth opened under his and her grip on his wrist grew tight. Her neck tensed against the onslaught, pressing back into him, while his other arm took her by the waist and pulled her close.

Her back arched. Her chest pressed into his. The heat from his body enveloped her.

Her right arm reached around his neck, her hand gripping his shoulder, releasing the tension in her back and neck. She dropped her head back and gasped.

His lips found her throat. Chills of pleasure swept up her spine as his tongue traced a line from just below her ear to her collarbone. His arm behind her back had her arching into him. His hand, hers still on his wrist, slid to her breast, then to the buttons of her shirt.

She felt his fingers on the flesh just above her bra, then they pulled her shirt away and he kissed her, sucking softly at the tender skin of her breast.

A wave of pleasure washed downward within her and she recognized the moment when physical hunger overruled any composure her brain might have had to offer.

She ran her fingers through his hair, impossibly soft, and held his head to her breast as she reveled in the current of desire that possessed her. Her limbs felt molten, her nerves alive.

She didn't need love for this, she told herself. She didn't need anything but passion, this moment, this temporary feeling, to augment her saner life, the one she'd get back to tomorrow.

Her hands moved to his shirt, pulling at the sides so it came untucked from his pants. His head rose and his eyes dove straight into hers as her hands found the skin of his back.

"Where's the bedroom?" His voice was low and sent a hot wave of carnal pleasure through her.

"Behind the kitchen." Her whisper was incongruous in the living-room light, but she didn't care. She did not want to stop this feeling. She refused to consider this a mistake. Not again. She'd been honest with him. She could have what she wanted.

Joe stood up, his hair ruffled and his shirt untucked, and Laurel thought she'd never seen anything so sexy.

He pulled her to her feet so roughly she rammed into his chest, her hands on his pectorals. She looked up at him, her lips parted, and wasn't sure she cared if they made it to the bedroom. Her hands found the bottom of his shirt and rose to feel the skin of his back again, hard, muscled, long and hot.

His hands held her shoulders and he bent to kiss her again, plundering her mouth as he moved her backward.

Just as she was melting into him again, he grabbed her shoulders and pushed her so that he could look into her face. His cheeks were flushed, his eyes gleaming, and his mouth was quirked in a small but devilish smile.

"Behind the kitchen." He turned her by the shoulders and marched her down the narrow hall between the kitchen and bath.

The bedroom door was closed, but before she could open it he reached around her, his lips finding that spot below her ear again, and pushed the door open.

The room was dimly lit from the hallway light, the air cooler than the living room, as they took two steps into it and fell onto the bed. Joe pushed the door closed with his foot and it slammed, throwing the room back into darkness.

Emboldened by the dark, Laurel clutched at Joe's shirt, pulling it up, then over his head as he rose up. She flung it behind her as he worked on the buttons of her blouse, the cool air inching down her torso as the fabric fell away.

Smoothly, he reached behind her back and with a silent snap of his fingers her bra loosened. She raised her arms as he pulled both blouse and bra away, then lowered his head to her breasts, taking one nipple in his mouth and one in his fingers.

Laurel sucked in a breath, her hands diving through his hair, her back arching up toward him, her hips pressing into his.

She could feel his hardness through his jeans. Her hands moved to his back pockets, slid inside and felt the hard flexing rounds of his buttocks.

His lips moved to her arched neck and after both of their hips pressed forward simultaneously he raised his head and groaned. "Ah God, you feel incredible."

She smiled. His words made her feel heady, powerful, like someone she'd never been before.

Her hands fled to his button fly and his to her skirt zipper. As quickly as they could they shed what was left of their clothing. Joe leaned over, grabbed a condom from the wallet in his jeans and donned it quickly.

He ran his hands down her rib cage, then

pulled her back up so her head was on the pillows and her body under his. He knelt above her, hands running from her collarbone to hipbone and back up. The touch was electrifying, the feeling one of reverence, appreciation, admiration. She'd never felt so beautiful.

His hands descended to her thighs, then he moved over her. One fist depressed the mattress by her head, his arm coiled and muscular, supporting his weight. Her eyes looked up into his as his hand urged her legs to part.

Want spiraled up her back, lodged in the back of her throat, as his fingers found the hot, fluid spot within her and slid over it, then back, over it, then back. She gasped. He slid his fingers again, torturing her with deliberation, a touch—a pause—then another. She threw her head back, gulping air as his weight shifted and she felt the head of his penis touch the spot just next to his fingers.

"Laurel," he said low. "Tell me . . ."

Her eyes snapped to his. Her breathing was fast and uncertain.

It was dark but she could feel his eyes upon her.

"Are you in control now?" His fingers slid over her again and she jerked, sucking in air. The sensation was incredible, mind-jumbling, torturous.

"Are you?" he insisted.

The fingers slid again, and she swallowed, wanting to be taken wherever he wanted to take her, not caring where, just wanting to go, do, feel, *now*.

She shook her head, raising her hips to his hand, feeling his penis slide inward just a little, then back out of her reach. "No."

He teased her a moment more.

"Do you want to be?" His voice was warm in the dark room. Soft, slow, convincing.

She *didn't* want to be. She wanted to be taken, hard and sure and fast, by this man who seemed to know exactly what would drive her insanely, deliciously mad.

"*No.*" The word sighed from her.

He hesitated just a second, passing his fingers over her once and again. Then he plunged into her.

She moaned with pleasure, grasping his back.

He thrust forward and she responded. He thrust again, and again, and they built a rhythm that escalated—faster, harder, deeper—taking them both into a world of clinging limbs and sweat-slick bodies joining, melding, forging a oneness that gathered them in its grasp and did not let them go.

Until finally, Laurel's body shuddered and stars broke behind her eyes, cascading across her skin, flying out with her breath.

Joe thrust hard, three times, two times, once, until he let out a final guttural cry of release, and lowered himself, still quaking and pulsing within her, to her side.

Twelve

Laurel stretched languorously in bed and tried to remember what it was she'd been dreaming about. Flying, she thought, because she was in a happy, centered state of mind, a state she didn't often wake up in.

The covers were warm and the bed cozy, and when she turned to her left side she faced the broad smooth back of Joe Squires.

She jerked back, her mind instantly alert.

Oh yeah. She'd done it again.

She rolled the thought around in her head to see what objections it might hit, and found she didn't feel nearly as strongly as she had last week that the night was a mistake.

In fact, she couldn't bring herself to think of it as a mistake at all.

Her stomach fluttered as she remembered the things he'd done to her, the way he'd touched her, the feeling of physical harmony they'd had together. She felt as if she'd suddenly become an Olympic gymnast, her body capable of things she'd never dreamed possible.

And that was way better than any mere dream of being able to fly.

No, this time sleeping with Joe was not a mistake, because she'd gone into it thinking it would just be sex. Knowing it would just be *fantastic* sex, and being totally okay with that. What's more, she'd been honest with Joe about it.

No, there was nothing to feel bad about here.

And there was a helluva lot to feel good about. Namely, that she'd never felt as physically fulfilled and awakened in her life. The guy knew her body better than she did. And was happy to share.

She lay on her side, looking at the ridge of his spine between the muscled planes of his back. She loved the way his shoulder lay like a round-topped mountain over those planes, the way his rib cage tapered to a slim waist beneath the covers. His skin was golden, honeyed, slightly tanned. She wondered if there'd be a bathing-suit line at his waist, but she didn't want to move the covers to see. She reached out a hand to touch his skin but hesitated before making contact.

Spontaneous, heat-seeking sex at the end of a night was one thing. But waking up cozy and touching each other in the morning light was another completely.

She tucked her hand back under the covers and frowned at his back. His rib cage rose and fell lightly as his lungs filled and emptied of air. Her eyes trailed up his backbone to his neck, to the line where his hair was neatly trimmed. There was something so boyish about that spot that she had the strange sensation that her heart was crawling into her throat. She wished she could lay her lips against it without waking him.

Instead, she turned over and slipped out the other side of the bed. The air was chilly as she tiptoed toward the bathroom, but before closing the bedroom door behind her she glanced back at Joe's sleeping face.

And paused.

God, he was beautiful. His hair was perfectly tousled. His face softened with sleep just enough to show that the fine bone structure was not just a product of expression. He was sculpted like a piece of art.

She closed the door and stepped into the bathroom. Flipping on the light over the mirror, she glanced at the clock—6:04—then at her own rumpled face and sighed. No artwork here. She grabbed her robe off the back of the door, donned it, and scrubbed what was left of yesterday's makeup off with a washcloth. Running a brush through her hair, she opened the bathroom door, tossed the brush into the basket on the back of the toilet, and went to make coffee in the kitchen.

* * *

Joe rolled over in bed, stretched an arm overhead and sighed. He felt as if someone had stolen all his bones.

Opening his eyes, he took in the room that was Laurel's most private domain. The first thing he noticed was the absence of clutter. The closet doors were closed, and he supposed they could contain a mountain of unwashed clothes, but he doubted it.

The second thing he noticed were the candles. Half a dozen of them alone on a shelf near the bed.

Across the room, two sets of bookshelves lined one wall, crammed with books. Hardback, paperback, big, small, some stacked flat on top of the rows, others piled on the top of the unit. There had to be hundreds of them.

A high window, with an ant's-eye view of the back terrace had a ledge filled with little flowering plants that appeared to be thriving. In fact, from where he lay, there didn't appear to be one dead leaf among them. He wondered if she talked to them. For all her practicality, anyone who carried a lucky shamrock charm could easily be the type to talk to plants.

All in all, the room was neat as a pin. White standard-issue rental walls held a few framed art posters—Georgia O'Keeffe, Van Gogh, a local artist he was familiar with named Frederick McDuff—and what looked to be an original etching in a bentwood frame.

He rolled onto his side and saw a stack of books on the bedside table. The top one, of course, was *Love Is Not the Answer*. Beneath that was a biography of a wronged woman caught up in a political scandal, and beneath that a novel called *Spare Me Lies* by a woman he'd never heard of. He didn't have to think hard to guess what that was about.

His eyes trailed to the clock.

6:27.

He sat bolt upright in bed. It was Friday, dammit. For a moment there he'd convinced himself it was the weekend.

He threw the covers aside and pulled open the door. The aroma of fresh coffee—French Roast, he could tell by the smell—greeted him like a rebuke.

Laurel sat at the table in a green flannel robe, reading the paper. A narrow V of creamy skin—that he happened to know was as soft as chamois—showed between the lapels. She wore reading glasses, he noted with brief surprise.

"Hi." He gave her an involuntary, probably blinding smile. Something about her nearly always brought one out of him.

She started, looked up, blushed, and offered a self-conscious smile in return. "Hi."

Her eyes moved from his face, down his torso, then flew back up to his face, her blush deepening. That's when he remembered he was naked.

He nearly laughed. Uninhibited as a showgirl last night, she was nothing but prim behind her glasses this morning. It made him regret even more the fact that he was almost an hour late getting started.

"Mind if I hop in the shower?" He gestured toward the door to his left.

"Please." She nodded vigorously. "Go right ahead. Towels are in the closet."

He gave her another smile and ducked into the bathroom.

It smelled of vanilla, just like the other rooms, and he quickly found the ubiquitous grouping of candles on the ledge of the frosted window.

He turned on the faucets and, as he waited for the hot water to flow, he examined the array of shampoos. There had to be six or seven different kinds, including conditioners. He opened one and sniffed, wondering which scent he'd recognize, but one glance at the clock on the wall told him there would never be time to sample them all.

He was in and out of the shower in minutes. No time to head home and change, he just had to grab the cart and go. Those early risers were the most inflexible about getting their first cup of coffee on time. If he wasn't dependable, they'd go somewhere else and never come back.

He dressed quickly and walked into the dining room. She'd laid out an extra plate and mug, he noted, and there were bagels in the middle of the table.

"This scene's almost too cozy to leave," he said, pulling on his sweater as he crossed the room toward her.

She looked around as if noticing it for the first time. "It's nothing special. I just—"

"Yeah, yeah, I know. You're not doing anything for me you don't normally do." Before she could protest, he leaned down and planted a kiss solidly on her lips.

She looked startled.

"I'm sorry to do this but I've got to run." He pulled his watch out of his pocket and strapped it to his wrist.

"That's okay." She looked as if she meant it.

"No, it's not." He picked up a bagel and took a bite as he headed for the door. "I'll call you later."

"You don't have to!" she said, turning on the seat.

Her face was intent—determined to set him straight—but he just grinned and stepped out the door. "I know."

He'd call her, she thought. What did that mean?

Well, of course, she knew what it meant. And at first it had made her feel all warm and fuzzy inside—exactly the way she shouldn't feel about him. Or anyone.

She was two hours into the workday and hadn't gotten a thing accomplished. All she'd done was worry about Joe.

She was a disaster in relationships. An unqualified disaster. And in this case she wasn't even sure what kind of relationship she was in. It certainly wasn't romantic. Were they friends? Were they sex buddies?

She had no idea. All she knew was that when it came to men, she was a failure.

"Hey!" Angela grinned at her from the door, but the moment Laurel looked up she sobered. "What's wrong with you?"

Laurel shook her head. "Nothing. Just under the gun here."

"Oh." Angela strolled into her office. "I wanted to tell you, I was at Car Pool last night and saw Ethan Connelly."

That got her attention. "Ethan was at Car Pool? He always said he hated places like that."

Angela made a face. "Yeah, it is kind of a meat market, but maybe his date wanted to go there." She sat down across from Laurel.

Laurel leaned back in her chair. "He had a date?"

Angela laughed. "Yeah, can you believe it? And she looked like she was about nineteen!"

Laurel's surprise turned to shock. Ethan had always expressed contempt for men who dated much younger women.

Angela's expression became concerned. "Should I not have told you? I thought it would make you feel better. You know, less guilty about breaking up with him."

Laurel shook her head. "No, no, it's good that you told me. I'm just . . . surprised, I guess."

But why? Why should anything Ethan did

bother her? It wasn't his fault the relationship ended, it was hers. She hadn't fallen in love. So he was free to contradict himself, even if that meant going to pick-up joints with teenage girls.

She thought about all the other times she hadn't fallen in love. All the relationships of varying lengths that had eventually become unsatisfactory. Each time the feeling she'd started out with had disappeared, almost as quickly as it had arrived. Swift infatuation fading to nothing, the way smoke disperses in the air.

It's not men. It's not relationships. It's not even dating. It's you. You don't trust yourself.

Joe's words haunted her. He'd been right. Exactly, dead-on right. When he'd said it she'd felt like she was running from a freight train. Well, the train had caught her now, and she finally realized what her fears were all about. And why she should never stray from her plan to arrange a marriage.

She was incapable of falling in love.

"Jesus," she breathed, absorbing the realization.

"Laurel, what's wrong?" Angela leaned forward. "Should I get you some water?"

"I'm fine." She waved a hand distractedly.

Something Dr. Nadalov said echoed faintly in her mind and she shuffled around her desk for the book.

"Do you need something?" Angela asked anxiously.

"Listen to this. Hang on." Laurel found the

book and flipped it open, pushing through the pages. "Here it is. 'In the same way some people are deficient in seratonin, creating depression, others are operating with less dopamine, resulting in an inability to achieve the sensation known as falling in love.'"

She slapped the book shut and looked at Angela. "You *see*? That's my problem. I'm *incapable* of love. That's why I broke up with Ethan—why I've broken up with everyone—because I wasn't in love and I thought I should be. But that was before I realized I couldn't be!"

"Laurel, everybody can fall in love. I think you're taking this way too seriously."

She shook her head. "No. I'm not. It's just all finally making sense. My whole life is finally making sense."

Only why did she now feel just the opposite? With Joe . . . as if she might fall in love and she shouldn't?

She leaned back, answering her own question. "Because I can't. I know that I can't fall in love, so I shouldn't even entertain the thought that I can. It'll fade like all my infatuations and people will only get hurt . . ."

But who? Joe? Joe wasn't in love with her.

"Laurel," Angela said, looking at her with all the certainty a twenty-something could possess, which was quite a lot. "*Everyone* can fall in love. Maybe you just haven't yet. Although . . ."

Laurel looked at her. "'Although'?" If Angela had any wisdom on the subject, she was more than willing to hear it. If there was one thing she needed right now, it was wisdom.

Angela shrugged with a coy smile. "I think you have."

"You think I have what?"

"I think you have fallen in love. You just don't know it yet."

Laurel laughed, sadly. "I'm in love and I don't know it? That doesn't make sense. Love is a state of mind—you can't be in it if you don't know it. It's a mutually exclusive proposition."

Angela shook her head. "No it isn't."

Nobody was ever as sure of anything as a young woman on the subject of love. Laurel almost felt sorry for her.

"So who am I in love *with*?" As soon as she asked the question, she wished she hadn't.

Angela beamed. "With Joe! And what's more, I think he's in love with you."

Laurel blushed and turned swiftly back to the computer. "Don't be ridiculous. Joe's not in love with me, and believe me, I am *not* in love with him."

Angela stood up. "I wouldn't be too sure," she sang.

Laurel fixed her with a steady eye. "Angela, if you convey any of this little theory to him, I will personally string you up and beat you to death."

"I don't need to convey it to him. He already knows it, I'm sure. What's more, I think it's good for you. *He's* good for you. He's just what you need."

"Angela—"

"I'm going! I'm going!" She giggled and danced out of the room. "But I'm right!"

Laurel refocused her eyes on her computer screen. Falling in love with Joe was *not* what she needed. She needed to finish this damn column, *that's* what she needed.

Then she needed to get home and change for her Short Stops encounter.

She took a deep breath and thought about the evening ahead. She was excited about this event. She'd perfected her spiel, even practiced her delivery, and she was confident she'd be able to chalk up at least a couple of dates this time. Dates she could then share with Joe, so he didn't think he was the only one participating in the actual "going out" part of this experiment.

And so he knew she wasn't sitting around thinking she was in love with him, or wondering when he was going to call. For the thousandth time, she rued the fact that he'd had to run so fast this morning. She'd had her nonchalance all in order, ready to use on him and show him that their second night of sex—*fabulous* sex—meant nothing more to her than the first.

But then he'd bolted, saying he'd call, and she was left feeling like a cliché. A woman he had to run from with a placating promise to call.

Laurel finished the column, laid it on Rulinda's desk and rushed home to change. With Sue on the phone, she plotted her evening's ensemble.

"Just because you're espousing a nontraditional mating dance doesn't mean you shouldn't strive to look traditionally, well, *hot*," Sue said. "Knock these guys off their feet, if that's what they want. Then tell 'em what they have to do to win you."

"Win me," Laurel scoffed.

"Honey, don't sell yourself short."

"All right. Here's what I've got. I've got my short gray skirt."

She held it up in front of her as she looked in the mirror. It was short enough to show off her legs—something, she had to admit, she might not have done without Joe's compliment of the night before.

"And a black sweater, black hose, and my new black ankle boots. How does that sound?"

"It *sounds* good, but have you got it on? How does it look? And try not to think about the fact that it's you you're looking at."

"Hang on." Laurel took a minute to strip off her work clothes and don the outfit, then looked at herself. Or rather, her body. If she blocked out her head in the mirror she could almost evaluate herself as another person. "It looks . . . uh . . . well, it looks okay. Pretty good."

"Good for you!" She could hear the laughter in Sue's voice.

She bit the inside of her lip, letting her hand drop from where it had blocked the view of her head. "There's a lot of leg showing, though. Am I too old for that, do you think?"

"Too old? Since when is having great legs a matter of age? Look at Tina Turner."

"Regular Joe said I had nice legs." She turned sideways, checked out the width of her thighs. Was that a run? She leaned in, no. Just lint.

"You do. You've got great legs. But what's this Regular Joe character doing checking out your legs? And when are you going to send me the first column?"

"I'll put it in the mail tomorrow. That's when it hits the newsstands. And Joe is way too complicated to tell you about now."

"Hmm, too complicated. Sounds intriguing. Where did you say you found him again?"

"He runs the coffee cart out in front of my building."

"Ah. Another overachiever." Sue snickered. She'd just been complaining about her brother's perpetual unemployment.

"Oh, he's an achiever, all right. But I'll have to tell you about that later, too." Laurel glanced at the clock on her bedside table. "It's getting late and you know how I like to arrive early."

"I've known and loved Miss Early Bird for years. Even if I've never understood her." Sue laughed. "All right, sweetie, have a good time. And let me know how it goes, okay?"

"All the gory details. I'll call you tomorrow."

Laurel was just picking up her purse to leave when there was a knock at the door.

Joe, she thought, and tried to feel exasperated. Instead she thought, *Good*. She could tell him what she was doing, show him she wasn't waiting around for him to call. Plus maybe he'd say something complimentary about her outfit that would send her off to this thing with some confidence.

Not that he would think trying it again was a good idea. He hadn't liked Short Stops the first time, either for her or himself.

But it wasn't Joe. It was—to her true exasperation and dismay—her mother.

Not that she didn't love her mother. She did. It was just, she was kind of overbearing. And impossible to get rid of. And she would never understand Short Stops, Laurel's plan to arrange her own marriage, or, more immediately, her 'hot' outfit.

"Mom, hi. You're back in town!" Laurel, who had thrown the door wide in anticipation of Joe, now brought it back to her side as if addressing a pizza delivery person.

"Laurel!" Her mother's eyes dove from Laurel's curled and brushed hair, down her clingy sweater to the short skirt, black hose and ankle boots. "I hope I haven't caught you in the middle of anything. Were you changing clothes?"

Laurel could practically see her mother restraining herself from making a prostitute comment.

"Actually I was just going out." Laurel flipped the switch for the outside light and a yellow glow bathed her mother in the well of the stairs. "I wish I'd known you were coming. How was the trip?"

Her mother stood stiffly at the threshold, clutching her elegantly sized Coach purse, her gray-white perfectly-coifed hair bright above her black cashmere overcoat.

"Oh it was fine. Better before your father lost at golf to Gerald Morganfeld, but you know me, I don't want to complain."

"Yes, I know you," Laurel murmured.

Her mother seemed to be trying to peer around Laurel into the apartment, as if Laurel might be hiding someone there. "I just stopped by because I'm meeting Evelyn and Regina for dinner at Racine's and I was hoping you could join us. It's very last minute, I know. But Regina got some good news this morning."

"Oh?" Laurel groped behind her for her coat on the rack. "What news is that?"

"Her daughter got *engaged* last night. To that dentist she met at the Wellness benefit last year."

At the pointed look on her mother's face, Laurel was tempted to say, "Well, your daughter got laid last night."

But even that, at this stage in Laurel's spinsterhood, could have her mother checking out reception halls and canvassing caterers.

"That's great, Mom, but I've got a date."

"Really?" Her mother's face was all astonishment.

Laurel frowned. "Well, more of an encounter, really."

Her mother glanced around behind her, disapproval quickly replacing delight. "He's an encounter if he doesn't pick you up, is that it? Or . . ." She made a quarter turn and looked up the stairs toward the sound of footsteps coming up the sidewalk. "Is this him?"

Her face was back to delight and Laurel's stomach fluttered. She stepped forward on the threshold and glanced up the steps.

Joe was just passing under the nearest streetlamp as he approached the basement stairs.

She had to admit, he looked great. He trotted down the steps with the grace of an athlete and gave them both a smile. He was wearing khaki pants and a leather jacket and looked like something out of a Ralph Lauren ad—an association that would not be lost on her mother.

"Hi, sorry, am I interrupting something?" He looked politely from Laurel to her mother.

"Two things, actually." Laurel folded her coat over her arm and stepped out the door. She closed it resolutely behind her. "Mom, this is Joe Squires. Joe, this is my mother, Lillian Kane. I'm actually on my way out."

"Nice to meet you, Mrs. Kane." Joe took Lillian's hand and smiled easily into her keen eyes.

"Joe Squires. Why does that name sound so familiar?" Laurel's mother said, apparently covering for her—as if Laurel should feel bad for not having mentioned Joe to her before. Her mother was very big on rules and etiquette and the inflexibility of social convention.

"Joe's not my date, Mom. He's just a friend." Laurel shrugged into her coat and shuffled as far forward as she could politely in the narrow stairwell, but neither Joe nor her mother took the hint.

"My father has been a businessman in Washington for years," Joe said, still holding her hand and looking at Lillian warmly. "Joseph P. Squires, Senior. His name used to pop up in the paper every now and then."

"Oh? And what sort of business is he in?" her mother sniffed.

Joe's demeanor, if anything, became more relaxed in the face of her mother's snootiness. "He's retired now, but he was a restaurateur. He owned the Eden on Connecticut Avenue and Fiddler's Green on Wisconsin."

"The Eden!" Lillian gasped. "Why, for years that was my husband's favorite restaurant."

"Your father owned the Eden?" Laurel repeated, stunned.

It had been one of the premier restaurants in Washington up until about ten years ago, when it closed in a hail of media sadness and fond farewells. It had been a meet-and-greet for senators, congressmen, even presidents.

"And Fiddler's Green? I went there for my senior prom," Laurel added, remembering how impressed, and embarrassed, she'd been that her date had spent that much money on a dinner she'd been too nervous to eat.

Joe's eyes lit with interest. "Did you, now? I might have waited on your table."

No, she'd have remembered a great-looking waiter.

"I can't believe I didn't know that about you." Laurel's brain spun, trying to remember what she knew about the Squires family.

"How long have you two known each other?" Laurel's mother was beaming at the two of them.

"Feels like a lifetime." Joe gave Laurel a brazen wink.

Laurel turned to her mother. "About a month and a half. But I can't stand here and chat about it now, I've got to go." She looked at her watch. She was verging on being late.

"Oh come now. Surely it's something you can postpone," her mother said indulgently. "Why don't you and, and . . . and Joe, was it? Why don't the two of you come to dinner with me? We're eating at Racine's," she said to Joe. "It's not the Eden, but it's quite good. Do you know it?"

"Yes. In fact I think the chef there, Claude-Henri," Joe said with perfect pronunciation, "is one of the best French chefs in the city right now. His *pâté de campagne* is incredible."

Lillian gasped again. "I have that every time!"

Laurel nearly rolled her eyes. Another conquest for Joe, she thought, mentally pronouncing his name with a flawless French accent of her own.

"Can we continue this another time?" Laurel said, one hand on her mother's arm. "I really do have to go."

Joe turned toward the steps and offered his arm to Lillian. "Oh!" Laurel's mother laughed like a young girl.

Laurel plodded up the steps behind them.

"So where are you off to, then?" her mother asked as they stood in the circle of the street-lamp. "What's so important that you can't have dinner with us?"

Laurel glanced guiltily at Joe, who raised his eyebrows in polite, if exaggerated, inquiry. A smile played at his lips.

"I told you, I've got a date." Her eyes flicked over to Joe. His expression didn't change. He wasn't even embarrassed to have stopped by the house of a woman on her way out for another date.

"I thought you said it was an *encounter*," her mother said.

Joe's eyes widened with comprehension.

Laurel sighed. "I'll tell you both about it an-other time. Good night, Mother. Joe, I'll talk to you next week." She turned and started down the sidewalk toward her car.

"Well, there's no need to be rude about it," her mother said. "Perhaps *you'd* like to join us for dinner, Joe?"

Laurel stopped dead in her tracks and turned. Surely he wouldn't say yes. Surely he had some-thing better to do with his time than go to dinner with her mother.

"Well, thank you, Mrs. Kane, but I can't to-night. Got a date of my own."

"A date?" Laurel repeated.

"An 'encounter'?" Joe's voice rang with amusement.

"Fine." Laurel turned again and kept moving.

"Hi! Welcome to Short Stops!"

Cindy was still perky, so Laurel guessed she wasn't too late. And since she'd done this before, she didn't have to make Cindy go through the setup and rules and warnings, etc. She just took her seat, filled out her nametag and slapped it on her chest. Taking her pad of paper from her purse, she smiled as the men took seats across from the women.

"Hi, my name is Laurel," she said to the tall slim man who sat down across from her. She held out her hand and he took it in a firm, warm grip.

He was probably about her age but looked older, with thinning hair and a somber demeanor. His eyes, a light, faded hazel, were intelligent and kind, she thought, and his handshake had felt almost comforting.

"I'm Robert," he said. His voice was low and resonant. She could picture him in a church pulpit, reassuring the congregation of God's love. She would believe him, she decided.

"Nice to meet you. You've got wonderful eyes," she said, leaning forward with a smile. *Knocking their socks off, Sue*, she thought.

"Why, thank you." He inclined his head modestly. "I'm the one who should be complimenting you."

"Oh no." She laughed and waved a hand. "Eight minutes is not enough time for flattery. Let me tell you a little about myself and what I'm looking for and then you can tell me some of your thoughts."

"An excellent idea." He smiled, and her mental critic did a double take. The smile didn't suit him. It seemed . . . thin. Incongruous.

She gave him her speech, honed to a trim three minutes but adorned with smiles and warmth and a touch of humor. Sue had advised her, excellently, not to come across as a hard-ass looking for someone to join up or get out. She could in fact seduce someone into seeing things her way, Sue said.

Laurel finished up and smiled at Robert. His expression had not changed. He still looked kind and intelligent and older than his years, but though she'd stopped he was continuing to nod understandingly. As if she were still talking.

"So . . . ," she concluded, "why don't you tell me what your goals are, Robert?"

He took a deep breath and stopped nodding. "Well, I suppose I could admire what you're doing," he said slowly, in a tone so modulated she at first didn't realize the words were vaguely insulting. "But frankly, in my business I have it brought home to me every day how important it is to, how shall I say, live life to the fullest. Seize the day, as it were." He nodded again. Slowly. Deliberately. With all the vivacity of a man afraid to seize the next word without reconsidering it several times first. "Experience shouldn't be dodged, but faced. Feelings should not be controlled, but celebrated."

He sounded like a series of motivational posters. *Hang in there, baby.*

"Well, Robert, I—"

"In my business," he continued, running her over in that same modulated voice, "I don't meet many people who are, how shall I say, receptive to dating. So it's difficult for me to find eligible women, in the workplace. That's where most people meet potential mates, you know, in the workplace. But in my business, it's not, that is to say, it's not . . . exactly . . . feasible."

Laurel mentally crossed Robert off her list. "What *is* your business?"

He smiled the thin smile again. "I'm a mortician."

Cindy's whistle blew and Laurel jumped.

"Well, uh, Robert. It was nice to meet you." She held out her hand again, glad she didn't have to come up with a rejoinder for his last statement.

"Nice to meet you too, Laurel. And thank you again for the compliment. About my eyes." He took her hand and smiled, then placed his other hand on top of their two. "You know, you have nice cool hands."

Thirteen

"Um, I'm sorry, Miss Kane." The young girl's voice on the phone was nervous. "But you had what we call a, um, a zero response quotient?"

Cindy had answered the phone at Short Stops, but had put this young girl on when Laurel had said why she was calling.

Now she knew why.

"Oh come on." Laurel didn't believe it. There was no way this could happen twice. Especially not when she had gone out of her way to seem, well, normal. Even attractive, to the best of her ability.

This time it *had* to be an error.

"Um, what that means," the girl was continuing, "is that none of the—"

"I know what it means," Laurel said, with an involuntary edge.

"You do?" Wonder colored her voice.

Before the girl could humiliate her further, Laurel said, "But I think there must be some mistake. I made a good connection with at least two of the men there. Roger and Steve? Could you just double check?"

"Um. Do you want me to, like, look at their files?"

"That would be great."

"Okay . . . I think . . . I think I could do that. Make sure we wrote everything down right on your sheet."

Laurel sighed. Steven had even flirted with her. They'd talked about going to the National Cathedral, where there was an ongoing series of lectures he was enjoying, then laughed about the idea of getting married there on the first date. She had to be on *his* list, at least.

Besides, it would be too unbelievable if the same thing happened twice.

"I'd appreciate that," Laurel said.

"Um, okay, sure. Do you want to hold?"

Angela appeared in the door to her office.

Laurel waved her in. "Would you mind calling me back with that information?"

"Um, okay, sure."

They confirmed the number and Laurel hung up. Angela sat in the chair across from her desk.

"What's up?" Laurel asked.

"Good news." Angela beamed. "We've already gotten twenty-seven e-mail responses to the column. And Mitchell said three advertisers have called about buying space in the next issue if your column's going to be doing a followup."

Laurel felt some of the heaviness from her Short Stops conversation lift at the news. She may not be able to get a date, but dammit, she could write.

"That's incredible. Did Mitchell tell them it's an open-ended series?"

"Sure did. Rulinda's thrilled," Angela reported. She crossed her legs and one shoe slipped off her heel. She let it dangle from her big toe. "She said to tell you if she hadn't had to meet Senator Ladbroke for lunch she'd have been in here giving you a big sloppy kiss."

Laurel laughed. "Thank God for small favors, huh?"

"I'll say. I once saw her give a big sloppy kiss to Lloyd after one of his restaurant reviews generated a lot of controversy." Angela made a face. "He didn't seem to like it at all."

"Speaking of which, anybody like the book review?" Laurel asked.

Angela shrugged. "Nobody said anything about it specifically, but Rulinda wants me to call around later in the week to some bookstores to see if *Love Is Not the Answer* sales have spiked at all. I bet they will."

Laurel smiled. "Thanks, Angela."

She flipped her shoe back up onto her foot and put her feet back on the floor. "No, I mean it. I didn't think much of the book. You know, what you read to me. I still don't think much of what it says, but your column was terrific."

Laurel was touched. To her surprise, Angela's opinion meant a lot to her. And here she'd thought she didn't care what anyone but Rulinda thought. Rulinda, who was in charge of raises and promotions.

"Who were the advertisers who called, do you know?"

"Actually, this'll make you laugh. One of them was Short Stops, Inc."

As if on cue, Laurel's phone rang.

Angela stood up. "I'll let you go."

Laurel waved and picked up the phone. "Laurel Kane."

"Um, is this Laurel Kane?"

"Damn, Squires, she made you sound pretty good," Bennett said, sitting across from Joe in Joe's office. *DC Scene* was unfolded in his lap, his legs on Joe's desk.

"You think?" Joe leaned back in his chair, his legs on the desk too. He gazed out the window.

Bennett read, " 'With his mega-watt smile, *GQ* style, and Bow-Flex body, it wasn't surprising that Regular Joe turned the heads of all the women in the room.' That sounds pretty good to me."

Joe nodded idly, thinking he not only hadn't turned the head of *every* woman in that room, he hadn't turned the head of the most important one.

" 'Though Regular Joe is drop-dead gorgeous,' " Bennett continued, " 'I suggest the lopsided outcome was the result of another principle of attraction. Confirming years of my own empirical data, the women at the Short Stops encounter seemed to fall prey to the age-old problem of wanting the one who didn't want them. Regular Joe said he was not using this tool deliberately, though he certainly could have, but it was clear to anyone watching him that, though charming, he was aloof—a near-lethal aphrodisiac to too many of us.' "

"If only we'd known *that* in high school." Joe forced a laugh.

Bennett read on silently, then started chuckling. " 'Regular Joe claims he simply did not find any of the women attractive, and in fact found the whole encounter to be distasteful.' "

"That part's true enough. What I don't understand," Joe said, turning to his friend, "is how she can go on and on about how great the system was for her, despite what she and anybody reading that column is going to consider a failure. Nobody—not one of those guys—wanted her phone number. Does that make any sense to you?"

Bennett shrugged and folded the paper. "I think it was pretty obvious she failed because she was trying something different. Scaring men off with the idea of marriage before even getting one date."

"So why would she try it again?" Joe couldn't

get the thought out of his mind. Since he'd stopped by last Friday and her mother had let slip that she was going to another *encounter*, he'd been obsessing about it, which was unusual for him. "Why would she set herself up for more rejection like that? Why would she go back with the same spiel to try it all over again?"

"Because," Bennett said, "if she'd been playing the game like everyone else, she'd have gotten responses. I mean, the girl's hot. Maybe she went back with a different spiel. One more like yours."

Joe's feet dropped to the ground. "You think that's what she did? You think she went back to play the thing out for regular dates?"

"Hell, I don't know. But that's what I'd do."

"Shit." Joe stood up, then, without an actual destination in mind, turned to the window. It made sense. After all, why would she bang her head against the same wall twice? It made much more sense to go, act like everyone else, get a few dates and *then* drop the bomb on them.

"What? What's wrong with that?" Bennett asked. "So she's changing her tack. So what?"

Joe stared out the window. But suppose she went back for regular dates? Suppose she'd dropped the spiel altogether? Then it was just *him* she was resisting, just *him* she didn't want. Her going out on a date meant this wasn't an ideological rejection he was receiving from her, it was the real thing. And he knew from experience there was no combating that.

"If she did that then she's not playing by the rules," Joe said. "She's abandóning her own plan, her own philosophy."

"Uh-huh." Bennett's voice was skeptical. "So you're bothered because she's cheating on her own philosophy."

"Yeah." Joe turned around to face Bennett. "She's made a big deal out of this arranged-marriage thing. You should hear her go on about how love relationships don't work and how you should squelch every natural desire or feeling of attraction you have. If she's going out on regular dates then she's a hypocrite."

Bennett tented his fingers together and looked at Joe over them. "Maybe she's just doing the arranged-marriage thing for the column. You ever think of that?"

"Oh no." Joe shook his head, running a hand through his hair. "She's doing it for real. She's resisting every normal, healthy desire she's got because of this . . . this"—he searched for an appropriate adjective, but none even came close to describing what he thought of her plan—"this idea."

"Really?" Bennett's voice was suddenly very interested.

Joe looked over to see him smiling.

"And you know this because . . . ?"

"Because I talk to her. A lot. Because she tells me that attraction doesn't mean anything to her." *That I don't mean anything to her.*

What the hell was he sticking around for? The

woman was hell-bent on being with anybody but him, and he just kept coming back for more.

Oh sure, he knew he could get her into bed. He knew that sex was something they were perfectly compatible for. But if he tried for anything else, anything more, he knew she'd throw up a roadblock faster than he could say Nadalov.

What was wrong with him? What was it about him that he couldn't let her go? The girl was nuts, obviously.

I suggest the lopsided outcome was the result of another principle of attraction.

Joe sat down hard in his chair.

She'd pegged it. In the column. He had fallen prey to the age-old problem of wanting the one who didn't want him.

So it was true. She'd been rejected again. One evening, ten men, ten rejections. A perfect record.

The phone rang. Laurel looked at it malevolently. She had the brief ugly fantasy it would be Short Stops calling back to say that not only didn't anyone in her group want her phone number, but they'd interviewed all the men who'd ever come to a Short Stops encounter and none of *them* wanted her phone number either.

She let the phone ring until just before it would roll back to the receptionist, then picked up.

"Laurel Kane," she said in a busy, hassled voice, though she'd just been sitting at her desk, staring at last Friday on her desk-blotter calendar, the day of her failure, but also the day Joe'd said he had a date.

In between dwelling on her second spectacular failure, she'd been remembering how he'd looked like a Ralph Lauren ad that night. And wondering how he justified to himself stopping by her apartment—she, whom he'd made mad passionate love to the night before—on his way to taking out another woman.

Not that she expected him not to date—but really, weren't there some rules, even in a purely sexual relationship?

"Laurel, hello. It's Surya Patel."

Laurel would have known who it was from the first two words, so rich and musical was Surya's voice.

"Hi, how are you?" She made a supreme effort to change her own hard tone, thought briefly about how rich and musical she might sound if she had arranged her own happy marriage.

"I'm well. Thank you."

"Good." Laurel skimmed reasons why Surya might be calling—to reneg on their participation in the column, to ask to read the column before it came out, to change things they'd said, to add some information, or to try to glean what Laurel had thought of her and Hakim.

"I hope I'm not imposing," Surya said. "But I've been thinking about our meeting."

She wanted to change what she'd said, Laurel thought. Maybe she wasn't so happy after all?

Laurel didn't know how she'd feel about that, then decided that she'd lost any shred of decency she'd ever had to think she might be glad.

"And I wanted to tell you," Surya continued, "that Hakim has a friend, at his work, a man named Peter?"

She paused, so Laurel said, "Oh?"

"Yes, his name is Peter Lowery. And Hakim was telling him about the article you're writing, and how you came to interview us."

Laurel wondered how on earth so much information had come out of Hakim, the quietest man on the planet.

"Peter has been thinking for some time about marrying in the same way that Hakim and I did. But he is not Indian, you see, so he does not know how to go about it."

"Oh, I see." Laurel's mind clicked into information mode. "Tell him about Dr. Nadalov's book *Love Is Not the Answer*. It's excellent. I can give you the ISBN number if he'd like to order it."

She pushed some papers around on her desk, searching for the book she knew was buried there somewhere.

Surya laughed. Laurel remembered her broad, easy smile, the lovely way her subtle lipstick had complimented her smooth dusky skin.

"Actually, I told him about *you*." Surya laughed again. "And he would very much like to meet you. I thought, perhaps, Hakim and I could help the two of you with this, since neither one of you has family who are educated about the process."

Something in Laurel's stomach flipped like a fish suddenly finding itself out of water.

Surya was offering to help find her a husband. Surya, who *knew* about arranged marriages, who *knew* how to find an appropriate mate, who had actually *done* it. Surya could make it all happen for her.

She, Laurel Kane, could be making plans to get married in *three dates*.

Laurel felt sick.

"He is a very nice man," Surya continued. "I have known him several years. Hakim has known him longer than that. And he is doing well at his job; he has an excellent future. He has a lovely home in Bethesda. And he is very close to his mother, who lives in Maryland as well. He also is a writer, of technical journals, but still a writer, like you."

Laurel swallowed over the queasy ripple in her esophagus. "Well, that's . . . uh, that sounds . . ."

Amazing. Terrifying. Surreal.

An awkward silence stretched long as Laurel's mind went and stayed blank.

"But perhaps I have misunderstood," Surya said, filling the void apologetically. "Perhaps you were just writing about this and not really planning to do it. I will understand of course, if you don't want to."

"No, no." Laurel laid her forehead in her palm. She *wanted* to do this. This was a golden opportunity. "You just took me by surprise, that's all. I'm sorry if I seemed . . . seemed . . . well, anyway, I would love to meet, uh, I'm sorry, what was his name?"

Surya laughed again. "Peter Lowery. He is a most wonderful person. We know a great deal about his background and have even met his family."

"Wow. Well, great. Uh, I guess you don't know much about me, though, do you?" Laurel laughed nervously. She felt as if suddenly things were moving too fast. If Surya and Hakim decided after three dates to marry, she'd be a third of the way there—closer than she'd ever been— simply by agreeing to *meet* this guy.

"I could ask you a few questions now, if that is all right?" She paused momentarily. "Or we can talk after you have met Peter. For this first meeting the background work is not so important. Mostly you just want to see if you like each other. You can tell a lot from the first meeting."

"Yes, yes, I'm sure you can." She thought about the first time she'd met Joe. What could she tell about him?

She remembered the ear-flapped hat. The way she'd noticed his hands, which she still noticed regularly, and the crow's feet at his eyes. Which made her think of him smiling, of those eyes crinkling as he grinned at her, which he'd done that first day, in fact. As he'd needled her.

He was, she told herself for the hundredth time, a classic example of attraction leading her astray.

"Well, this sounds perfect," she said decisively. "I definitely want to meet Peter, and please thank Hakim for thinking of me."

She and Surya agreed that Surya would give Peter her phone number and they would arrange their own first date. Then, if they appealed to one another, Surya and Hakim would step in to help with the ensuing tasks. Laurel tried to imagine what those 'ensuing tasks' might be. Investigations? Interrogations? Wedding plans? What came next in a situation like this?

When she hung up the phone, Laurel took several deep breaths to calm the fish still flopping in her stomach. It was just a date, she told herself. She could change her mind at any time. Just because she was exploring this arranged-marriage thing didn't mean she had to settle for someone she wasn't sure of. She didn't have to do anything she didn't want. Surya and Hakim had said that about themselves. She wouldn't be untrue to her goals if she didn't like this guy.

She put her hands together and rubbed their slick surfaces over each other. This was ridiculous. She was actually afraid to meet the man.

The phone rang and she nearly leaped out of her chair.

"Laurel Kane."

She heard a clearing throat, realized she'd answered before the first ring had stopped, thereby catching whoever it was off guard.

"Hi, Laurel. This is Peter Lowery, Hakim Patel's friend? Surya said—"

"Oh yes, Peter, hi." She hadn't meant to interrupt him but she was on adrenaline overdrive.

She glanced at her watch. Had it even been three minutes since she'd hung up with Surya?

"Hi," Peter said again. "As you know, Surya gave me your number—"

"Just moments ago," she said, laughing nervously. Again, she hadn't meant to interrupt him. She felt like a ninny.

He cleared his throat again. "Yes, well, I like to, uh, strike while the iron is hot, I guess you could say."

"Well, why not," she said, thinking a 'what the hell' attitude was just what this situation needed.

"So . . . uh . . ." He gave an uncomfortable little laugh that Laurel recognized. She'd used it several times in her conversation with Surya.

She took a deep breath and leaned back in her chair. "I know. It's weird, isn't it?"

Relief shined in his ensuing laugh. "It is." They were both silent a moment, then he added, "But I think that's okay."

"Yeah," she said thoughtfully. "It is. It is okay."

Laurel woke up the next morning feeling good. Smug, even. *She* had a date this Friday. She did. Not Joe. Well, okay, maybe Joe did too, but *she had a date*, with a man who was not going to reject her because of her "unorthodox" idea.

She smiled to herself as she got dressed. She smiled to herself as she ate her breakfast. And she smiled to herself as she boarded the Metro and thought about the coffee she was going to order, and the smooth way she was going to drop into the conversation that *she had a date on Friday*.

Peter Lowery had a nice phone voice, she'd absorbed well after the fact. After she'd realized what she'd set in motion.

He'd had a nice phone voice and a nice low laugh. She'd also liked what he'd said about the weirdness being okay. It was okay. It was good, even. It meant they were both taking this seriously, and that's exactly what she wanted.

It was a cold February morning, so she'd had to bundle up. She'd refused to wear a hat, however, because she was having a good hair day and didn't want to flatten it right off the bat. Later, at the end of the day, it wouldn't matter.

As she did most mornings, she ran into Angela on the train.

"You're looking spiffy this morning," Angela said, looking closely at her face.

Laurel glanced down at her wool winter coat, the same one she wore every morning. "How can you tell?"

"You're wearing makeup."

"I always wear makeup."

Angela looked surprised. "Really?"

They shuddered as they rode the escalator up out of the Metro. A cold breeze was whipping people's hats off and playing havoc with the trash in the gutters.

"Oooh, I *hate* winter," Angela said, chin slumped into her coat like a turtle. "Philip says the only way we can appreciate spring is to hate winter, but that doesn't explain the Californians."

Laurel glanced at her. "What?"

"You know, it's always kind of springlike out there, and they seem to love it."

"That's because they all grew up in places like New York and Chicago."

Laurel spotted Joe as they turned down the sidewalk leading to their building. He was wearing the ear-flapped hat, and she had to smile.

She was heading for the cart when Angela said, "See you up there," and veered off into their building.

"Don't you want a coffee?" she called back, stopping.

"It's too cold!" Angela gripped her shoulders with her hands and backed into the revolving door. Things must be getting serious with Philip if she didn't want to flirt with Joe.

"I'll get you one," Laurel called.

Angela beamed. "Thanks!"

There was a line, as usual in the mornings, and Laurel got in it. She slapped her shoulders a little as Angela had and rued her hatlessness when the breeze kicked up and chilled her to the bone. She tried to push her hair behind her ears with one gloved hand, but the wind just whipped it away again.

Her toes were getting numb and she'd had coffee at home. Why was she putting herself through this?

Because, she told herself honestly, *you want to tell Joe about your date.*

She wished she'd gone on up to her office, because wanting to show off this modicum of success was petty. But she'd been in line for five minutes now, and she couldn't just leave. He'd already seen her.

She made it to the front and Joe's hands, busy as always, wiped down the cart as he said, "Latte?"

His manner was brusque, she thought. "Yes. And a cappuccino for Angela."

"Comin' right up." He set to work immediately, concentrating on his job and barely looking at her.

She tapped her foot, shoved her hands in her pockets and tried to remember if there was something she'd done that might have made him mad.

"So," she said brightly, "how was your date last Friday?"

His glance flicked up to her face. "I didn't have a date."

"What?" Surprise made her forget the cold and her foot stopped tapping.

After all the things she'd thought about his stopping by on his way to a date . . . well, she should have known. He might not be her type, but he wasn't a skunk. Then comprehension dawned.

"Well, I guess I can't blame you," she said. "I'd have said the same thing to avoid dinner with someone's mother I didn't even know."

He started steaming the milk, assessing her with his gaze as the machine made a chorus of hissing, screeching sounds. "That wasn't why I lied."

Wind blew hair in her face again and she wiped it away with one hand, her eyes on him. "It wasn't?"

"How was your *encounter*?" A shadow of his normal grin flickered across his face, but he watched intently as he poured the coffee into the steamed milk, making the little leaf pattern he always made in the foam when the cup was full.

Discombobulated, she answered truthfully, "Exactly the same as the last one."

His eyes shot up to hers, their expression openly surprised. "Really?"

She started to laugh as he handed her the latte and began making the cappuccino. "Only better, really. Last time I was rejected by a bunch of normal guys. This time . . ." She glanced at the man in line behind her. "Well, remind me to tell you about the mortician sometime."

Joe's smile widened. "So, you gave them your usual spiel?"

"I wouldn't call it *usual*, I've only done this twice."

"I mean, you told them about arranging your own marriage and all. You did that again? Same thing?"

She eyed him. "Yes. Pretty much. Though I did try to dress up a little more this time. And I tried not to come across as too . . ."

"Militant?" he supplied.

She laughed. "Exactly."

He was quiet a moment, then looked at her with a kind expression in his eyes. "I'm sorry, Laurel. I don't know what's wrong with those guys."

She wasn't sure what to say in response. His kindness almost made her feel worse about it.

"I don't understand why they can't see beyond the words to the hot chick saying them," he added with a cocky smile.

She laughed, relieved. She hated it when he felt sorry for her.

"Are you going to write about it?" he asked.

She shrugged, hunching into her coat and turning her back to the wind as it kicked up again. "Probably. I'll mention it."

"Be sure to mention that you did look like a hot chick that night."

"Thanks." She blushed at the compliment. Why was he suddenly being so nice to her? It made it so much harder to gloat about her date.

He handed her the cappuccino and she decided she could wait to tell him about Peter Lowery. She handed him a ten but he waved it off.

"Cold-weather discount," he said.

"Joe, no. Let me pay."

"*I'll* take it," the guy behind her in line said.

Joe pointed a finger at him. "That's double for you, Ken."

The guy laughed.

"Well, thank you." Laurel inclined her head.

"Hey, what's on call for this week's column?" he asked as she started to step away.

She swallowed. She'd been thinking she'd write about his date last Friday as opposed to hers, this Friday. But since he hadn't actually had one last week, she wasn't sure what to do.

"I'll talk to you about it later," she said, backing toward her office. "I've got a few details to iron out." She turned away.

"Laurel?" he called after her.

She turned back.

"You forgot your sugars." He met her halfway back to the cart and pushed two bags of raw sugar into her pocket since her hands were full.

She started back to her office, then turned again. "Oh, what about Angela? What does she take in her cappuccino?"

He looked at her, shaking his head, a funny kind of half-smile on his face. "I have no idea."

Fourteen

Friday evening Laurel had every candle in the living room lit, the roast in the oven smelled delicious, and once she put the rolls in, the smell of wet cement ought to have been pretty thoroughly eradicated. It had rained earlier in the day, so the distinctive basement fragrance had reared its ugly head again, much to her dismay.

She'd dressed nicely. Not the short-skirt-and-ankle-boots kind of nicely, as she'd worn to try to impress the men at Short Stops; more the meeting-the-in-laws kind of nicely. She wanted to look respectable, stable, competent, to meet this potentially arranged mate.

The phone rang. She looked at the Caller ID. Sue.

"Marriage Mart," she answered the phone.

Sue started laughing. "Is he there yet?"

"No. He's not due for another twenty minutes."

"Good. I wanted to tell you one other thing."

They'd spoken earlier in the day. Sue had given her a detailed list of questions she should ask Peter, as well as a list of things to look for, like how old were his shoes, did he have clean fingernails, and, if he had to, could he drag her from a burning building.

"If you're only going to get three dates with this guy," Sue said, "maybe you should sleep with him tonight."

"Sue!" Laurel said on a burst of laughter. "I thought you old married people were supposed to be conservative and advise caution."

"I am! I'm advising you to be careful you don't marry someone lousy in bed."

Laurel sat down on the couch and tried to look at the room through a stranger's eyes. A stranger looking for a mate. "I assume you're not saying that because Kevin's lousy in bed," she said wryly.

Sue giggled and Laurel heard her passing the comment along to Kevin in the background.

"He said almost exactly the same thing," she came back on. "Or rather, he said he wanted me to tell you that's *not* what I meant. Anyway, I just wanted to give you my permission to check out this guy's . . . uh . . . prowess." She laughed again.

Laurel closed her eyes, tried to picture herself in bed with the man she'd constructed from Peter

Lowery's phone voice. Tall, thin, intellectual-looking, kind of nerdy. The more she thought about it, the more she realized he looked like Ralph Nader.

She opened her eyes, sputtering a laugh. Thank goodness people almost never looked the way you pictured them from the phone.

"Well thank you, Sue, but there's no way I'm sleeping with this guy tonight."

She couldn't even imagine it. Aside from not being able to imagine sleeping with Ralph Nader, she couldn't imagine sleeping with anyone who was not Joe.

Not because she felt any loyalty to him. No no no, she was sure he was out having a *grand* time with *his* date tonight. No doubt he'd sleep with whoever-she-was too. No chance *he'd* end up married to someone bad in bed.

Laurel paused over the thought, felt angry with herself for having it, then forced her thoughts back to Peter Lowery.

No, the reason she could only imagine sleeping with Joe was because she'd slept with him so recently. And she'd never slept with two men in one month in her life. Heck, she'd never slept with two men in six months.

"Hey, one other thing, what's Regular Joe doing while you're meeting Mr. Right?"

"He's going out with someone his friend Bennett fixed him up with."

Laurel recalled her conversation with Joe earlier in the week. She'd told him on Wednesday

that they each needed to ask a friend to fix them
up with someone the friend deemed appropriate.
This was another of Dr. Nadalov's exercises—
one she'd initially thought to pass over but that
now fortuitously seemed perfect.

Then, Thursday, she'd told him about Surya's
fix-up.

He hadn't said much about it after asking the
guy's name and what he did. Then he looked at her
kind of oddly and said, "Friday? That's Valentine's
Day, you know. I would think you'd be home
burning paper hearts in protest or something."

She'd laughed sarcastically and they'd agreed
to meet on Sunday to compare notes.

The doorbell rang and Laurel shot to her feet.

"Oh my God, that's him."

"Oh my God," Sue echoed. "Call me tonight,
I don't care how late it is—"

"Okay," Laurel said, but could hear Kevin in
the background.

"No wait, Kevin's got to get up early. So call
me tomorrow, *first thing*, and tell me how it
went."

"Okay. I gotta go." She looked in panic at the
door, wishing she could ask Sue how she looked.
Like a Stepford wife, she could hear Sue saying.

"Promise?" Sue demanded, half-laughing but,
Laurel knew, dead serious.

"Promise!" she laughed and hung up the phone.

She caught her reflection in the glass of a
framed poster and ran her hands lightly over her
hair, smoothing it. Then, noticing her palms

were damp, ran them down the sides of her meet-
the-in-laws skirt and walked to the door. Not for
the first time, she wished she had a peephole.

Taking a deep breath, she opened the door.

A short man with elfin features wearing a
puffy down parka—the old Michelin-man
style—stood in the stairwell. He held a bouquet
of roses that might have dwarfed him had it not
been for the wild wealth of curly brown hair that
encircled his head like a halo.

He smiled nervously. "Laurel?"

She smiled back, her eyes jumping from the
enormous bouquet of flowers to the enormous
bouquet of hair. "Peter?"

"I guess I've got the right house."

"Please, come in." Uncertain what to say
next—every thought having been blown from
her head by the flower/hair combination—she
shivered dramatically. "Brr, it's gotten cold out."

She stepped back from the door, glad for the
cold because it kept her from actually breaking
into a panicked sweat at the sight of him.

She didn't know what she was expecting, but
it wasn't this man. Not that there was a thing
wrong with him. The hair, sure, but she'd
schooled herself not to be put off by appearance.
The problem was that he was *real*. He was no
longer a theory, an idea, a voice on the phone.

And he was really here, to talk about really arranging a real marriage.

"I brought these for you," he said.

She considered joking that she'd thought they

were part of the outfit, but that seemed a little too close to the truth, and she didn't want to offend him.

"Thank you. But you didn't need to do that." She took the roses from him, their syrupy scent enveloping her. "My goodness, they smell heavenly."

My goodness? Heavenly? She had morphed into June Cleaver.

"Let me just put them in some water." She started toward the kitchen, then stopped and turned around. "I'm sorry, I should have taken your coat."

And thrown it out. Did they still make coats like that, or was it really left over from the seventies? But she was being petty. Appearance—*attraction*—meant nothing. She was clear on that, if nothing else.

"No problem." He shook his head with a nervous smile.

"If you don't mind," she continued, "you can just hang it up on the rack by the door."

She made it to the kitchen and looked around, wondering what in the world she could put this many flowers in. She inhaled the sweet scent again and thought *That should make short work of the mildew.*

She took slow deep breaths as she opened her bottom cabinets to look for a bucket.

Peter seemed like a perfectly nice guy. He was just . . . surprising. But he certainly wasn't ugly, by any means. Just . . . different from the picture she'd conjured from his voice.

"Can I help?" His voice sounded from the kitchen doorway, and for a fleeting second she expected to see the man she'd pictured after their phone conversation. Ralph Nader, in her kitchen. She nearly chuckled.

She straightened and cast the real him a smile. "I'm just looking for something big enough to hold these gorgeous flowers."

He was wearing a black cotton tee-shirt that was very tight. It wasn't tucked in, but adhered to a bony build that was slender but for a small mound of softness around his belly and hipbones —what she used to call 'love handles' but wouldn't utter tonight for all the money in the world. The tee-shirt lay flat over the top of his jeans to about mid-hip. The jeans were dark blue, of the kind that appeared to be denim-colored rather than actual denim. The yellow stitching on them stood out like the centerline on a two-lane highway.

"How about a bucket?" he suggested.

"That's just what I was looking for."

"I'm sorry they're so big," he said sheepishly.

"Don't be silly. They're lovely," Mrs. Cleaver replied.

"I actually wanted to buy you a small bouquet of lilies, but since it's Valentine's Day, they were out of everything but those." He nodded toward the roses, which leaned like an exasperated film star over the sink faucet. "Apparently someone hadn't picked them up."

"Lilies? I love lilies," Laurel said, trying to look at him in a new light. "They're my favorites."

He smiled. He had dimples and high round cheeks. "Mine too."

They stood there a moment, and for no reason at all Laurel thought of her bathroom trash can. It was a dark blue cylinder shape that would be big enough to hold the bouquet.

"Hang on just a second. I've got an idea." She moved past him to the bathroom, took out the fresh plastic bag she'd put in the can earlier, and brought it back to the kitchen. "I hope you're not offended, but I think a trash can is the only thing I have big enough to hold such generosity."

"Oh hey, no problem," he said again, blushing.

She rinsed the bin inside and out—wondering if she'd just committed a Freudian slip by saying she could only hold someone's generosity in a trash can—filled it halfway with water and began to unwrap the bouquet.

"Can I get you a glass of wine?" she asked, wrestling with the plastic around the roses. The flowers shook their heads dramatically, one of them flinging itself off the counter in despair as she finally found the tape holding the plastic together.

"Sure, great," he said.

She started to reach for the bottle, but another of the roses threatened to follow the first, and Peter took hold of the wine.

"I'll do it. I seem to have incapacitated you for doing anything else. I'm sorry."

She laughed. "Please don't apologize. They're wonderful. The corkscrew's in that drawer there."

They finally got the flowers straightened away and the wine opened and they moved back out into the living room.

"It smells great in here, by the way." Peter took a sip of wine.

"Oh good," she said, relieved. How could he have known it was the best thing he could say? She set the flower-laden trash can on the end of the dining-room table. "Like roses?"

"Actually I meant the food."

"Oh, thank you."

They sat on the couch, one on either end, and Laurel couldn't help remembering how close Joe had sat last week. How his hand had felt on her leg. How he had looked in all his gorgeous glory as he'd said *You don't trust yourself.*

Her heart fluttered and it wasn't with the memory of Joe's looks, or his hands, or the devastating way he'd touched her. It was with the memory of how completely he'd seemed to understand her.

She swallowed more wine and looked at Peter, whose beady brown gaze was circling the room.

"So, Peter, where do you live?"

"In Bethesda—"

"That's right." She nearly smacked her forehead. "Surya told me that."

She glanced down at his hands, pale white and doughy with a bloody hangnail on one thumb, and tried to imagine them touching her, or even just taking her hand.

She swallowed more wine. She had to stop thinking like this. Of course she couldn't imagine being touched by the man, she'd only just met him.

But she felt repulsed. *Isn't that a little extreme?* a voice in her head asked.

And if you can't stand the thought of him touching you on the first date, the voice continued, *what makes you think that in two more you're going to want to marry the man?*

They finished the first bottle of wine well before dinner was served. The brie and crackers she'd set out on the coffee table also went quickly. It seemed they were of like minds when it came to nervous behavior. Both gulping wine and loading crackers, if only to give the other person the obligation to speak.

They agreed on virtually everything, it seemed, to the point where she started to wonder if he was pandering to her.

Then it occurred to her that he could think she was pandering to him. But looking at his guileless face, his high round cheeks when he smiled, his thin arms as he reached for a cracker, she knew he would never think that.

He was too agreeable, too malleable. He had, she thought, too little backbone.

They talked politics and had the same views.

They had similar upbringings—suburbs, one sibling. Had nearly identical views on the number of children to have—two, max. Both knew what order they'd like to have them—girl first, then boy, with the understanding that they of course couldn't actually control this. They even knew the type of education they wanted for them—private schools, preferably same sex, at least for a while.

Peter said he was truly impressed by her work, by her talent and ambition, and said he would never dream of telling his wife whether or not to work.

Laurel, for her own part, was impressed with Peter's responsiveness. He was quick witted, understanding, and was extremely knowledgeable about integrated circuit boards, whatever those were.

The guy really had no obvious flaw, except for the small one of not being attractive to her. Otherwise, he seemed perfect.

Finally, after consuming the appetizers like a pair of wild dogs, Laurel served dinner. She opened a fresh bottle of wine and sat down across from him, ignoring the unlit candles on the table and leaving the lights high.

The roses, in their blue plastic trash-can vase, sat on one end of the coffee table, where she'd moved them before she set dinner out. Their scent lingered in the air.

"So what has led you to making the arranged-marriage decision?" Laurel asked. She scooped up some mashed potatoes and put them neatly into her mouth as he prepared to answer.

He took a deep breath, seemed about to speak, then sighed. "I've never had great luck with relationships. I mean, I always found people to love, but they never seemed to love me back. At least not for long."

He cut a piece of meat and pushed it around in the juices on his plate. "Except for this one woman. We had a four-year relationship that ended two years ago. I'm afraid I . . . well, I didn't handle the breakup all that well. I was very upset, and couldn't seem to stop calling her, thinking if I could just talk to her, find the right words, she'd remember what was best about us, why we should stay together."

He put the piece of meat in his mouth and chewed vigorously, looking at his plate.

"Hmm." Laurel frowned.

She'd been on the receiving end of just that sort of phone call before and always wondered how someone thought they could *talk* you back into loving them.

"Then I realized," he continued, pausing to take a bite of a liberally buttered roll, "that I wasn't doing anything but driving her farther away. That's when I gave up."

"You mean . . . on relationships?" From the intent way he was chewing and not looking at her, she feared he might mean he'd "given up" in the much broader sense.

He shrugged, ate another piece of meat.

"Yeah. I thought I'd just live a celibate life. Get a cat. Be one of those weird sexless people who lives for their work."

The mention of sex—even within the term "sexless"—had her looking at his lips and trying to imagine kissing him. A bread crumb near the corner of his mouth disturbed her too much to get very far.

"What changed your mind?" she asked.

He took another bite of his roll and thought for a second. "I haven't, I guess. I mean, I gave up on that kind of relationship. You know, the passionate kind."

She tried to picture Peter *passionate*, could envision his cheeks flushed and glistening lightly, his small brown eyes bright, his smile eager, his hopefulness pushy. Like an irritating little dog you felt bad for shoving away.

She shook the idea from her head. Just because she wasn't attracted to him didn't mean she had to mentally turn him into a freak.

"Then I met Hakim," he continued, looking at her now. "And I saw him go through the process of finding Surya, meeting her, then marrying her, all with the understanding that they were making a marriage and they were committed to making it last. No fireworks, no emotional water-testing."

She nodded, looking into his eyes and seeing the earnestness there. "No mistaking infatuation for love, or uncertainty for excitement."

He looked at her, impressed, she could sense,

that she knew exactly what he meant. "That's right. Just a commitment."

"And they're happy now," Laurel said, hands splayed.

"They certainly are." He nodded.

She nodded with him. They were on the exact same page. What she saw in Hakim and Surya, he saw too; and they both wanted the same thing. He was a nice man, she told herself, looking into his intelligent face. A truly nice man.

"And they're very much in love," he added, with a quick crooked smile. "So I thought, I could do that. I'm forty-five years old. I could make that promise and keep it. And I could probably fall in love with the woman who would make that promise to me. I really think I could."

He looked at her over the rim of his wineglass, and Laurel noticed for the first time how red his eyes had become. Had hers? Was he drunk? Was she?

In that instant, she started to feel vaguely uncomfortable. It sounded to her like Peter was still looking for love, whether it was in the guise of an arranged marriage or not. And it was love that Laurel was incapable of.

The other thing that disturbed her was how much Peter sounded like he was running away from something. From past failures, or future ones. From the risk of heartbreak. Or the possibility of rejection. As if, once he got a woman to marry him, he could be free to love her, perhaps too much, and it wouldn't matter.

Was she doing the same thing? Did she want to get a man to marry her so that she could *not* love him and it wouldn't matter? Was it possible she was doing this because, as Joe had put it, she was afraid of *herself*?

"Well," Laurel said briskly, standing with her plate in hand, "let me clear a few dishes here."

She marched into the kitchen, aware that her knees were not terrifically steady, and set her plate by the sink. Then she rested her hands on the counter and dropped her head.

I could probably fall in love with the woman who would make that promise to me. I really think I could.

Had Peter Lowery just told her, three hours into meeting her, that he could love her?

He was also looking at her in a way that, if pressed, she could describe as moony. Could it be that he was interested in this arrangement because it was fast? Speed marriage instead of speed dating?

She heard his chair scrape and knew he must be leaving the table, so she rinsed her plate and put it in the dishwasher. She was just straightening when he came into the kitchen.

"Let me help." He put a hand on the small of her back and, standing next to her, put his plate in the sink.

She stiffened. What if he had a best friend who at the beginning of the evening had advised him to sleep with her, if he could, to avoid the possibility of marrying someone bad in bed?

Her fears were fanned to a flame when he didn't remove his hand from the small of her back, but stepped close enough for his body to be up against hers. With the open dishwasher beside her, she was trapped.

So, the objective part of her thought, maybe he *wasn't* so malleable. If nothing else, this proved the man had some backbone. Or some audacity.

His eyes were about level with her nose, so he was not a lot shorter than she was, but he was small enough that she didn't feel physically threatened. Just awkward and extremely uncomfortable.

She thought of Surya saying that when they were dating she never let Hakim kiss her, not even good night, just as Peter moved in for the kill.

She was immobilized by her own indecision about just how open-minded she should be. So she wasn't attracted to him. She did, she thought, *like* him. He was nice, funny, interesting, for the most part. If he was someone she worked with, she'd probably enjoy going to lunch with him. Should she let him kiss her? Just to see how it was?

His lips found hers and the feeling was so strange, so soft and smooth, like kissing a girl, that she wasn't sure what to do. Her hands itched to push him away, but her mind kept telling her that they agreed on everything, right down to what to name their son, if they had one—they had both, it had turned out, always liked the name Evan.

After a second, Peter shifted position, putting

his other hand at her waist and pulling her closer. At the same time his tongue, small and pointed, shot between her lips like a mouse darting out of the shadows.

She backed up, her calves hitting the open dishwasher door and clattering the plates together. At the same time, the doorbell rang.

Laurel used the opportunity to push him back by the shoulders and turn quickly away with a strangled, "I should get that."

She wanted to go straight to the bathroom and brush her teeth. She wanted to scrub a washcloth all over her face and come out to find Ralph Nader in her kitchen, perhaps checking the energy efficiency rating on her dishwasher.

Instead, she bolted out of the kitchen, her face burning and the back of her hand pressed to lips that felt too wet and vaguely violated.

For the first time that evening Laurel realized what bothered her most about Peter Lowery. She knew, without a shadow of a doubt, that with a man like this she could run the show. That she *would* run the show, for the rest of their lives, until she hated first him, then herself.

She made a beeline for the door, stopping only once she got there to realize it was nearly eleven o'clock on a Friday night and she had no idea who this was. Damning the missing peephole again, she decided she would rather be mugged than go on kissing Peter. She opened the door.

On the doorstep, looking like every woman's wet dream, stood Joe.

Fifteen

"Hi." Joe leaned against the doorjamb and wondered if he'd gone too far. He'd debated this move, then decided, What the hell—even if it didn't work out for him, at least maybe he would help Laurel see that her plan had all the earmarks of a catastrophe.

She stood with her mouth open, so obviously stunned she was having trouble recovering.

"What on earth are you doing here?" she finally said in a half whisper. She sent a quick glance over her shoulder.

Joe followed her gaze and saw her date emerging from the kitchen. He was a small, innocuous-looking man with an amazing head of hair. His face was curiously flushed.

Laurel too, he noted, looked a little flustered,

and he wondered—in a skeptical sort of way—if he'd interrupted something.

He wouldn't be upset if he had. That was, after all, the intent.

But really, Laurel and . . . *that guy*?

"I'll tell you." Joe sauntered past her into the living room. He gave the date—Peter Lowery, she'd told him earlier in the week—a friendly nod. "I had a better idea for this month's column. Instead of us just comparing notes—you know, 'My date was fun, we went to the movies, or I . . . ' "—he glanced at the dining table—" 'I cooked dinner, my date was' "—his eyes slid over to Peter again—" 'nice.' "

He turned back to her again, his expression as friendly and open as he could make it, as if he'd just run into her at the grocery store.

"I thought instead I would come over here and interview *your* date." He gestured toward Peter. "Ask him what he thinks of *the plan*, how he thinks the evening went, what the next step is, all that. Maybe I'll even let you two try to talk me into your way of thinking."

He put his hand back in his pocket.

"So whaddya think?" He grinned at her. "Isn't that a lot more interesting than His Date, Her Date?"

Laurel, still stunned, just stared at him, speechless.

"Laurel?" Peter said uncertainly.

They both turned toward him. Joe scanned the man's body, taking in his height, his arms, his ability to take a punch. And were those vinyl jeans?

Laurel said, "I'm sorry, uh . . ." She turned back and gave Joe a puzzled, half-angry look. "This is, uh . . . um . . ."

"Peter!" the man exclaimed.

"Of course, Peter, this is Joe Squires. Joe, Peter Lowery."

Joe put on his best smile and strode over to Peter. They shook hands, Joe making sure to squeeze just a little too hard. "Nice to meet you, Peter. Say, I didn't interrupt anything, did I?"

Laurel's gaze skittered away from his. He thought she looked pale and faintly sick. It wasn't like her to be so quiet when he was doing something arrogant.

"Well, actually—" Peter began.

"You were interrupting *a date*, Joe," Laurel said, her hands moving to her hips. She was starting to recover. "But you're here now, so what is it you want?"

"Okay, good." Joe took his notepad out of his back pocket and settled himself on the couch, feet on the coffee table just to piss her off. "I'd like to ask Peter here a few questions. I've learned a lot about journalism the last couple weeks." He smiled up at her and pressed a hand to his breast pocket. "Hey, Laurel, have you got a pen?"

"Oh my God," she muttered, shaking her head. "Do you want a glass of wine too?"

She was being sarcastic, but he said, "Thanks, that'd be great."

"Laurel," Peter said again, less hesitantly than before. He took a step toward her.

Laurel had walked to the phone table at the end of the couch and picked up a pen. A good sign, Joe thought. A very good sign.

She handed it to him. "I'm sorry about this, Peter. It's just, well, it *is* my job."

Joe raised his eyebrows at her. Unusual acquiescence to the situation. Had something happened with Peter Lowery?

"Who *is* this man?" Peter asked, his little eyes glittering a tad too brightly.

Joe's muscles tensed. He didn't like how intently the guy was looking at Laurel. How nearly angry he seemed.

"He's the guy who works with me on the column. He's Regular Joe." Laurel tipped her head in his direction, crossing her arms over her chest.

"*Regular Joe?*" Peter repeated irritably, obviously confused.

"Sure, don't you read Laurel's column?" Joe scribbled an insane-looking face on his pad. "Where have you been, Pete? All of DC's talking about it."

"That might be overstating it a little." The look she shot him was full of wry humor and he made another note on his mental pad, with his mental pen, the one he always had with him.

Laurel wasn't mad at him. In fact, if he wasn't mistaken he'd say she was *glad* he'd shown up.

"So, Peter, what *do* you think of this arranged marriage thing?" Joe perched the pen on his pad like a steno-pool secretary and looked at Peter with the eagerness of a cub reporter.

"Am I going to be part of that column?" Peter asked Laurel. He did not look happy about the prospect. "Is that what this was all about?"

"As you can see, Peter, I wasn't exactly expecting *this* to happen." She looked sharply at Joe.

Joe cleared his throat. "What do your parents think of you arranging your own marriage, Pete?"

Peter ignored him again, glaring at Laurel. "You were planning to—to *use* me. Just for some stupid column?"

"Of course not," Laurel said. "Not without your permission. And I wouldn't use your name."

"Aren't you serious about all this?" Peter's voice rose an octave. He had pasty hands that he held out to his sides. They were shaking, Joe noted, in true psychopath style.

"Of course I am." Laurel's body went still, countering his rising ire with exaggerated calm.

"I *mean*," Peter said, "I thought you were serious about finding a husband. Surya did not say anything about me being some sort of . . . some sort of . . . of *experiment*."

"Hey, don't knock it till you try it," Joe volunteered from the couch.

Laurel sent him a scorching look.

"You'd do that to me?" Peter squeaked. "You'd take me on a ride, all for some two-bit column in a third-rate paper?"

Laurel flushed. "As I said, I would not have included you without your permission. And I went into this with the most serious intentions in the world."

Peter's expression went from angry to hopeful in an eerie flash. "Really?"

"I am sorry to hear you feel that way about my work, however," she added. "I was under the impression that you'd read the column. If you had, you'd know I use a lot of my personal experience in it."

Peter blushed and stammered. "Well, I—uh—Surya told me about it."

A taut silence stretched across the room.

Joe decided to break it. "Wasn't someone getting me a glass of wine?"

"Get it yourself." Laurel did not take her eyes off Peter.

"I thought we were really hitting it off." Peter held his hands out toward her in a conciliatory way. "We can talk about the column thing, if you want. I just didn't realize . . . you know . . . I didn't realize what it was all about."

"So, what *did* you all talk about?" Joe asked.

"Listen, Peter, you're a very nice man," Laurel began. "But—"

"Isn't that what you're looking for?" Peter interrupted, obviously having heard that opening before. Probably more than once. Probably more than ten times. "Isn't 'a very nice man' what every woman *claims* to be looking for? A nice man is just what you want in a husband, isn't it? I thought you were one of the smart girls, one of the ones who realized that nice guys really are the best husbands. *I* would be the *best* husband, Laurel, I would."

"I'm sure you would be." Her voice was low.

"Then you do like me?" His tone had gone oddly nasal and he clasped his hands in front of him. "Because I like you, Laurel. In fact, I could love you, Laurel. I know I could."

He looked like a weirdly insistent beggar, Joe thought as he slowly took his feet off the table and put them on the ground.

"Peter, of course I like you." She was talking to a small child now. One who maybe had a really sharp knife in his hands.

"So I can tell Surya to contact your parents? Can I tell her that everything went all right tonight?"

This was actually painful to watch, Joe thought. The man was pathetic.

"Peter, I . . ." Laurel was shaking her head, her expression soft and pitying. "I just don't think—"

"Oh, I get it." Just like that, the man's demeanor went from pleading to nasty. "You probably want somebody like *this* jerk." He flung a hand out at Joe.

Joe sat up straight and tried to look offended. "Hey."

"There's no call for that," Laurel said. "He's just a friend."

But her expression showed she was catching on. She was looking nervous, thinking maybe this guy was different than he'd let on.

Joe sat like a coiled spring on the sofa.

"Pete, sorry to interrupt again, but did you talk about past relationships, for example?" Joe interjected. "I know Laurel's got a—"

"Shut up, Joe," Laurel tossed at him.

"Listen, just ask him to leave and let's go back in the kitchen." Peter was back to pleading. "I know I can show you what a good husband I can be."

"In the kitchen?" Joe said.

"We're *not* going back in the kitchen." Laurel's voice was firm.

Joe looked at her in surprise. What was in the kitchen?

"Let me talk to Surya," Peter said again. He stepped toward Laurel. She backed up. "*Please.* Let me just get this thing started—"

Joe stood up. "What about you, Pete?"

Laurel was to his left, standing in the center of the room, her arms across her chest. Peter was to his right, moving toward her, though he stopped when Joe stood.

"Did you talk about *your* past relationships?" Something in Joe's tone seemed to catch Peter's attention. He stopped where he was and turned fierce little eyes to Joe.

"What do you mean?" His pale hands clenched into fists at his sides.

Joe looked at him a long moment, giving the guy a chance to own up or get out. "I guess what I mean is, did you mention Renata?"

Peter looked as if he'd been struck. "My old

girlfriend?" His eyes flicked nervously toward Laurel. "Sure, I mentioned her."

"Girlfriend? That's not how she saw it. You only dated a couple months," Joe continued. "That doesn't really qualify as a *relationship*, does it?"

Laurel looked slowly from Joe to Peter. "You said it was four years."

"It—it—" Peter looked desperately at Laurel, then turned to Joe. "It was more than two months!"

Joe shifted his gaze to Laurel. "Somewhere between two months and four years." He looked back at Peter. "Though the police report said two months."

Laurel's head jerked back to Joe. "What are you talking about?"

"Nothing," Peter said. "He's bluffing."

"*Bluffing*? About what?" Laurel put her focus on Peter. "What in the world does *he* have to bluff about? Do you two *know* each other?"

Peter shrugged. "I don't know. I've got to go. Laurel, if you want to call me, Surya has my number."

He moved awkwardly past her, plucked an enormous coat off the rack by the door and exited hastily.

Laurel silently watched him go. Then she strode to the door and flipped the deadbolt.

She turned to Joe. "How do you know all of this about *him*?" She gestured toward the door behind her.

Joe sighed and sat back down on the couch. He tossed the pad and pen onto the coffee table and leaned back, hands behind his head.

"Renata was a woman he apparently dated for a couple months about two years ago, and when she tried to break if off he became a little obsessed. She had to get a restraining order against him."

Laurel leaned back against the door with a thud. "*What?*"

"It's true." Joe dropped his hands to his lap. "He wasn't dangerous, just harassing."

Her face flushed pink and she pressed her palms to it. "How—what—how on earth do you know that?"

He ran a hand through his hair and laid his head on the back of the couch. "The Internet. It's amazing what you can learn about people with just the tiniest bit of information to go on. By the way, you owe me forty-nine ninety-five for the background check."

"You did a *background check* on my *date*?"

She pushed herself off the door and glared down at him on the couch.

"You're welcome," he said.

She put her hands back on her hips. "That's—that's very close to stalkerlike behavior, you know."

He raised his head. "You think so? I thought it was one friend looking after another. Besides, what's worse? My doing a background check, or the fact that you just nearly married a man whose ex-girlfriend had to file a restraining order to keep him away? I know which one I'd vote for."

"I did *not* nearly marry the man. And I want to know why you did a background check on him."

He gazed at her, from her hairbanded head to her high-buttoned blouse to her long wide skirt. "What have you got on?"

"Joe," she warned, but she looked down at her outfit.

"I mean it. You look like someone's mother."

She rolled her eyes. He thought he could see a smile pulling at the corners of her mouth.

"Where are the little black boots?" He leaned forward to look at her feet. "Hell, where are the *legs*?"

"Joe. Look at me."

He raised his gaze to hers.

"Why did you do a background check on my date?"

He leaned back. "I was bored. I was on the computer and I was looking up people I knew and I ran out of them, so I decided to look *him* up. Lo and behold, up came some reference to a Peter Lowery in the police log from some small Montgomery County paper. I just followed the lead from there."

"How did you know it was the *same* Peter Lowery?"

"I didn't." He smiled slowly. "But I do now."

Laurel looked at him a long moment, her expression exhausted and sad. Finally she sat on the armchair next to the couch.

"God, what a night." She put a palm over her eyes.

Joe stood up to leave. The last thing she needed was him sitting there, witnessing another failure. Though he could not have been more glad that the evening had failed. When she'd told him about Surya's fix-up, he'd had a flash of real fear that her arranged marriage plan might actually work.

She took her hand off her eyes and looked at him. "Are you leaving?"

Her voice was small. And she looked so discouraged he wanted to take her in his arms and comfort her.

But the time wasn't right. He could tell she was eager to have the whole night over with.

He stepped around the coffee table closest to the dining room so she wouldn't have to move her legs. On the table were the remains of a roast beef, a bowl of mashed potatoes and a bowl of peas.

"Looks like Sunday dinner, Mrs. Brady," he said, turning back to her with a smile.

She laughed despondently. "Doesn't it?" She sighed heavily and closed her eyes. "How pathetic."

"It looks good," he said softly.

She opened her eyes and smiled at him. "You're a nice guy, Joe."

"Oh no," he laughed, holding up his hands.

"Don't pin that one on me. I'm leaving, already."

She laughed. Then she stood up and reached for the huge bucket of roses on the end of the coffee table. "Take these for me, will you? Take them and throw them away. Or give them away. I don't care what you do with them, just get them out of here."

He smiled, taking the bouquet from her hands. "No problem."

Upon touching the bucket, he realized it wasn't a bucket at all and tipped his head to look under the abundant foliage.

"Is that a trash can?" He headed for the door.

"Yeah, it was the only thing I had big enough to hold them."

He chuckled as she opened the door for him. "Kind of prophetic, huh?"

She laughed, her first genuine one of the evening. "I'll say."

"I'll bring you back the can."

She shook her head. "Don't bother. I'll never look at it the same again. In fact, I'm going to get rid of everything ever associated with this night."

"That's my cue." He started for the steps.

"Hey Joe?"

He turned around, saw her framed in the doorway in her Suzie-homemaker dress and her sad face, and thought he'd never known a more beautiful woman. Why she thought she had to make herself into something other than what she was to find happiness was beyond him.

"Thanks." She nodded her head as if to say *really*.

He looked at her seriously. "Anytime, Laurel. Anytime."

Laurel woke up the next morning as tired as if she'd never gone to sleep. Indeed, she'd tossed and turned all night, dreaming first that Peter had tried to kill her, then a wild sex dream involving Joe woke her in a sweat around 4 A.M. *Murder and sex*, she thought. *My life as a made-for-TV movie.*

She turned to look at the clock. Nine-thirty. She still didn't feel like getting up. What would happen if she just lay here all day? What would happen if she didn't get up until Monday morning for work?

The phone rang. She groaned and rolled toward the bedside table.

"Hello?"

"*Well?*" It was Sue. "How *was* it?"

Laurel exhaled long. "Oh God, Sue, it was awful. Just awful."

"Oh no." She sounded genuinely disappointed.

Laurel told her the whole story, ending with Joe taking away the flowers and noting how the roses in the trash can had been a bad sign from the beginning.

"Oh honey," Sue said, but Laurel could tell she was barely restraining a laugh.

"Go ahead, get it out." Laurel laughed reluctantly herself.

"I would have said the hair was the first bad sign," Sue said, giving in to her mirth.

Laurel took the extra pillow and put it briefly over her face, halfway between laughter and utter humiliation. She lifted it to say, "There were bad signs everywhere."

"Yeah, but not until he was there and it was too late to do anything about it," Sue said.

Laurel tossed the extra pillow beside her again. "That's true. Well, not completely. Did I tell you I lost my grandmother's charm?"

"That four-leaf-clover thing?"

"The one she got from her *one true love*," Laurel confirmed. "Guess my good luck left me along with it. I'm sure if I still had it, Peter Lowery would have turned out to be the man of my dreams."

"Didn't he die in World War I?" Sue asked. "Your grandmother's love, that is?"

"Yep. And my grandmother mourned him till the day she died. She even had that charm in her shoe when she married my grandfather, whom she seemed to despise."

"Doesn't sound like a good-luck charm to me." Sue laughed. "Hey, I read the first column online, by the way. It was *fab*ulous! I mean it, truly fascinating."

"Thank you." The praise did a little to lift her spirits, but not much.

"Now, tell me again why you're not going after this Regular Joe character? You made him sound like chocolate decadence for dessert."

Laurel pushed herself up in bed, looking around at the tangled sheets and remembering her dream. Then she remembered the night Joe had stayed here and the dream had been real.

"Because," she said steadily, "that's exactly what he'd be like. Dessert. Something delicious and sinful and ultimately bad for me."

She pictured him at the door last night, holding that ridiculous bouquet. *Anytime, Laurel. Anytime.*

"He was good for you last night," Sue pointed out, echoing Laurel's very thought. "That was an incredibly considerate thing for him to do. Not to mention brave. Can you imagine barging in on a date of his?"

"Maybe I should." Laurel laughed. "Wouldn't that make a great column. Oh my God." She put a hand to her forehead and dropped her head back against the headboard.

"What?"

"I've got nothing to write about. No column. Oh my God and it's due Tuesday."

"What do you mean, you've got no column?" Sue's voice was outraged. "You're not going to write about what happened last night? My God, it's hysterical and—and horrible. It's a cautionary tale for all women."

"Particularly women stupid enough to think they can arrange their own marriage."

"Yes!" Sue exclaimed. "I mean, no!" She laughed. "Not that you're stupid, but wasn't that what this whole thing was about? To see if it worked? If it doesn't, you need to show that."

"Sue, I can't write about last night. Not without exposing Peter to all sorts of horrible press, not to mention humiliation."

"Oh come on, the guy deserves it. Besides, who would know? You wouldn't use his real name either, right?"

"Surya and Hakim would know, for one thing. But whether he deserves it or not, if I wrote it, it could be actionable."

"What do you mean?"

"Libelous." She imagined facing that angry little man in a court of law.

"Not if it's the truth!"

Laurel shook her head. She couldn't get Peter's enraged face from her mind. It had freaked her out, the way he'd gone from whining to infuriated and back again. "I can't write it. Not without turning it into fiction first. I mean, the guy was seriously creepy, Sue. The last thing I want is to piss him off even more."

Sue paused. "Hmm, yeah. I hadn't thought of that. If his ex-girlfriend needed a restraining order to break up with him, you'd probably need a bodyguard after you exposed him as a nut in the newspaper."

"She wasn't even really a girlfriend. They'd only gone out a couple months. For all I know, I *already* need a bodyguard."

Laurel thought instantly of Joe. What would she have done if he hadn't shown up last night?

What would *Peter* have done? She shuddered to think how the evening could have ended up.

"You should hire Regular Joe," Sue said, and Laurel wondered if she were possibly telegraphing her unspoken thoughts across the country.

The Call Waiting beeped and Laurel asked Sue to hang on.

"Hello?"

"I've got the answer to your problems," Joe said.

Before she could think, Laurel's heart flipped. "What do you mean?"

"What's your biggest problem this morning?" She could hear the smile in his voice.

She smiled too and settled back into her pillows, cradling the phone close. "Well, gee, Joe, after last night it's really hard to pick just one."

He laughed. She inhaled deeply, her tense muscles uncoiling.

"What are you going to write about this week?" he asked.

She closed her eyes. "Damn. Yes, I guess that is my biggest problem. Or at least my most immediate."

"I've got the solution."

Saved again, she thought.

"Well, don't keep it a secret. What is it?" She laughed.

"Nuh-uh. Not on the phone. Can you meet me tonight? Seven o'clock? Vespucci's?"

The last of her tension seemed to melt away as

she imagined sitting in the cozy atmosphere of Vespucci's with a giant glass of red wine and Joe. "Sure."

"Great. Seven o'clock. Don't be late."

"Hah! The pot calling the kettle black. I'll be there."

He laughed and hung up.

Just before hanging up, Laurel remembered Sue. She switched lines. "I'm so sorry to keep you so long. That was Regular Joe."

"Oh really?" Sue said in a knowing voice. "And what did he want, first thing in the morning?"

"To save me," Laurel said, feeling happier than she had a right to be after last night's debacle. "Again."

Sixteen

The night was cold, and a frigid wind tossed trash from the gutters across the city streets as Laurel walked up Connecticut Avenue from the Metro.

Vespucci's was crowded, with people standing just outside the door, not quite in a line but obviously waiting to get in. Laurel sighed. Valentine's weekend. Unless Joe's in with the chef was foolproof, they'd never get a table tonight. Not without first suffering severe frostbite on their extremities.

She stood out front, not looking at all the other people, just as they weren't looking at her, and paced back and forth to keep warm. She scanned the street for Joe's Explorer but didn't see it. She knew he'd be late; why had she been on time?

Because she wanted to see him, she thought. Because she was *looking forward* to seeing him. She closed her eyes against the thought, but felt contentment settle deep within her.

She couldn't arrange her own marriage. She couldn't ignore her emotions, though she had certainly tried. Maybe marrying by arrangement was right for some people, maybe for those brought up with the idea, whose culture required it. But for her, she couldn't set aside how she felt.

And how she felt was . . . well, it was . . . like nothing she'd ever felt before. She was overwhelmed, consumed, enthralled, and, strangely, comforted. All of this *by Joe*.

She hated to admit it. Hated knowing that she not only had failed in her determination to marry sensibly, but that she was doubtlessly setting herself up for some kind of heartbreak.

Because Joe didn't want to marry her. He wanted to sleep with her, sure. He wanted to tease her, argue with her, challenge her, perhaps even see what she does next. But he did not want to marry her. If he did, how could he have watched her go on all these dates? How could he have *helped*, even?

She had to admit now, at least to herself, that every time he'd been with another woman she'd felt a little crazy. She'd wondered, imagined—all right, *obsessed*—with far too much intensity about what he was doing, with whom, what the woman looked like, how he was feeling about her, where he'd found her, if she was smart, if he was giving the woman that same teasing grin he always gave her.

She'd tortured herself with these questions, only realizing now the reason why. Only realizing now that she'd wondered if the way he was treating her was as a friend, or as someone with whom he could—just maybe, possibly, if luck were on her side—fall in love.

God, she was sick. She put her face briefly in one hand.

And now, here she was, meeting him for dinner.

What was he up to? And what did he want from her, exactly? While he had been pretty open about his disbelief in her philosophy—had told her quite bluntly that he thought it would fail—the only thing he'd ever offered her himself was sex. Mind-blowing sex.

A commotion arose at the door of the restaurant —patrons leaving—so maybe the line would diminish somewhat. It occurred to her that she should go in and at least put their name on the list, when she saw that the person coming out was Joe.

He spotted her and beckoned her over. He was coatless and wearing a dark brown button-down shirt with dark dress pants. Stylish yet casual. He did it so effortlessly. *Chocolate decadence for dessert*, is right.

But what if he isn't just dessert? she asked herself, walking toward the door. What if—she indulged the thought—he wanted her too?

Giddiness butterflied in her stomach and she gave him a tremulous smile.

"Hey, hope you haven't been waiting long." He put one hand on her coat between her shoulder blades as she edged into the doorway beside him, past the other waiting patrons. "It's arctic out here."

"Not long," she said.

Just long enough to figure out that she'd been right to fear him in the beginning. He was going to be her undoing, and if he didn't laugh at her for falling for him, he would at least have to feel completely vindicated in his assertion that love *is* the answer, or at least the question.

"Bet you could use a big glass of wine." He grinned at her as he took her coat.

She smiled back. "I've been fantasizing about it since you called."

God, he just couldn't have looked any better. Contrasting this night with last, she couldn't imagine how on earth she'd thought she could marry someone who didn't at least make her feel like this when she saw him.

She remembered her sister saying, months ago, about her husband of fourteen years, *My heart can flutter when he walks in a room.* Well, Laurel's heart was fluttering now, and it wasn't a new sensation when it came to Joe.

Joe led her toward the back of the restaurant, near the fireplace, and gestured with one hand toward a table for four. On one side of it sat a tiny, birdlike woman with gray hair in a bun that sat directly on top of her head. Like the handle on one of those tops you push up and down to make spin. For a second she pictured the tiny woman spinning until she became a blur of fire-engine red, the color of her dress.

Was this Joe's mother? His grandmother? And if she were, how could she be the answer to Laurel's column-writing problem?

Then it struck her. If this was his mother, could he be—could it possibly mean . . . ? But she couldn't believe it. There was no way Joe would follow Dr. Nadalov's advice on getting the families together to arrange a marriage. And he certainly wasn't going to arrange a marriage with *her*.

Was he?

"Laurel," Joe said as they reached the side of the table.

The tiny woman stood up. She came to about Laurel's shoulder.

"This is Myra Kornbluff," Joe continued. "Mrs. Kornbluff, Laurel Kane."

Myra Kornbluff turned sharp gray eyes on Laurel, gave her a bright smile and held out her hand. Laurel took it. She had a surprisingly tight, bony grip.

"Nice to meet you." Laurel glanced at Joe questioningly. Not a relative, she surmised, disappointment settling like a cannonball in her chest. So who the hell was she?

"Very interesting to meet you," Myra Kornbluff said, just a little too loudly, and studied Laurel with an unusual, if good-natured, intensity. "You were right," she said to Joe, "she is very pretty."

Joe smiled proudly, lifting his brows at Laurel, as if to say, *See? I say nice things about you.*

"Let's have a seat." Joe pulled out the chair next to his for Laurel.

She gave him another questioning look as he sat down beside her.

"Mrs. Kornbluff," Joe said slowly, a glint in his eyes as he looked at Laurel, "is a *yenta.*"

"A yenta!" she and Mrs. Kornbluff said at the same time.

"No, no, no." Myra Kornbluff swatted at Joe's hand with her napkin. Several people at neighboring tables glanced their way. "A *yenta* is a blabbermouth. The word you mean is *shadchan,*" she said in what sounded to Laurel like Yiddish.

Laurel's eyes went from Mrs. Kornbluff to Joe and back again. "I—I'm sorry. I'm afraid I don't know what a sh—uh—what that is."

Joe and Mrs. Kornbluff already had glasses of red wine. Laurel would have given her eyeteeth for some at that moment.

"She's a matchmaker."

Laurel's eyes shot to Joe.

"Not a matchmaker." Mrs. Kornbluff scowled, a sight Laurel was sure had frightened many a child. "A *marriage broker.* Sweetheart . . ." She leaned over the starched white tablecloth and patted one of Laurel's hands with a wiry one of her own. "I'm here to help you."

At that point Laurel's certainty that she was in for heartbreak set like cement. Just as she was getting off the arranged-marriage boat, Joe was getting aboard. At least, as far as arranging a marriage *for her*.

Laurel busied herself unrolling the silverware from her napkin and placing it on the table.

"Help me?" She lay the napkin on her lap and smoothed it out.

"Yes, dear. Joe here has told me about your . . . problem." She lifted her hands with a slight shrug as if to say, *For lack of a better word*. "But I must make clear that I am not really a *shadchan*," Mrs. Kornbluff continued, humbly. "No, I cannot claim that esteemed title for myself. The *shadchan* is for Orthodox Jews. I . . . well," she held one hand out to her side and tipped her head toward it, "I have branched out."

"Branched out," Laurel said.

"Yes, I make matches for anyone, for everyone!" She laughed, a tad maniacally.

Laurel shot Joe a look, but he was watching Mrs. Kornbluff, rapt.

"I have clients from all walks of life." Mrs. Kornbluff spread her arms. "Rich, poor, young, old. Jewish, Christian, Muslim, atheist. Whatever you want, I got it. But the *shadchan*, they are different."

Without either Joe or Laurel asking how, she launched into a long explanation of Torah law and Jewish custom, then told them all about the Book of Genesis, about Abraham and his servant Eliezer—the first matchmaker ever—who arranged the marriage of Isaac and Rebecca.

"A match made in heaven," Joe offered after a brief silence at the end of this story.

Laurel had nothing at all to say. All she could think was that Joe had found her a matchmaker—a marriage broker. Joe wanted her to succeed in arranging her own marriage.

"*Exactly!*" Mrs. Kornbluff jabbed a knobby finger into the tablecloth. Laurel jumped. "All matches are made in heaven. This is why professional *shadchanim* must be very smart, very perceptive." She used the same knobby finger to tap her own temple, narrowing her eyes and nodding sagely.

Then she sat up straight. "But no, I am not, as I said, a *shadchan*. I am just a humble marriage broker. But still, this requires much psychological acuity." She gave them the narrow-eyed nod again.

Laurel fought a sinking sensation and reached for her purse, which she'd hung over the back of the chair. From it, she pulled her pen and pad of paper. She tried valiantly not to look at Joe, but he elbowed her in the side as Mrs. Kornbluff waved her empty wineglass at the waiter.

"Is this great?" he asked.

"Yes," she said, trying to infuse the word with enthusiasm. "Great."

He looked at her oddly.

"What we first need to do," Mrs. Kornbluff said, turning back to them, "is *talk* to each other. I need to do an in-depth analysis of what each of you is looking for. I need to get an idea of your personalities, your personal needs, what you are looking for in a mate."

Laurel was thrust back into her date the previous night and felt herself spiraling out of control. She couldn't do it again. She couldn't.

The waiter saved her, arriving at the table with a brisk "Another glass of wine for you, ma'am?"

"That's right," Mrs. Kornbluff handed him her empty glass. "And bring some bread. We haven't had any bread yet!"

"And a glass of wine for me," Laurel said desperately. He began to list the varieties they had but she picked the first one he mentioned. "That one, yes, sounds great."

"For you, sir?" he asked Joe. "Another?"

Joe shook his head and the waiter bowed, stepping from the table.

"Mrs. Kornbluff," Laurel said, "do you mind if I ask you a few questions first?"

Mrs. Kornbluff sat back. She looked tiny and powerful in her red dress, with her sharp smile. "Of course not. People always have questions. I can tell you the whole process, exactly what I do, what you are to do, how everything works out in the end. And for the rest of your life! Hunky-dory!" She looked as pleased with this expression as if she'd made it up.

Laurel thought about being hunky-dory for the rest of her life.

"Did Joe tell you about the column I'm writing?" Laurel asked. "That I'm doing this to use for the content of that column in the weekly newspaper *DC Scene?*"

Mrs. Kornbluff's shrewd eyes moved from Laurel to Joe. "Yes, he told me about your article. I've seen that paper around. It reaches a lot of people, yes?"

"Well, yes, in certain segments of the population. So you're all right with me using your name and quoting you about your services?"

"Of course!" Mrs. Kornbluff smiled, her arms raised over her head. Everything about her seemed designed to belie her tiny stature. Her voice was big, her manner decisive, her gestures exaggerated. "That is what you call good PR for me, right? Advertising! I will find you the best man of your life, your true soul mate, and you will write about it. This will bring me a *lot* of business. Because you would be surprised, many people do not know I am out here."

Judging from the frequent looks they were getting from other diners, Laurel almost found that hard to believe. Except, of course, she herself hadn't thought of this. It had taken Joe. And where on earth had Joe found her?

"Well, that is surprising." Laurel couldn't help exchanging a glance with Joe, then wished she hadn't. Seeing his mirth-filled face had laughter bubbling up beneath her breastbone, that insane, uncontrollable kind of laughter that only pops up in math class and at funerals. "So tell me, Mrs. Kornbluff, just what are the services a marriage broker provides?"

"It is like I said. I make matches for everyone." She leaned forward again, as if she were trying to get close to them to be discreet, but her volume made her words no secret to the rest of the room. "I am like a shoe store. You, Laurel Kane, you are one shoe—maybe an Oxford, size seven, I think—so I find the other shoe, also an Oxford, also size seven. You see? I have eighty, ninety thousand to choose from!"

Laurel smiled as she wrote this down.

"That's a lot of shoes." Joe's laughter was barely controlled, Laurel could tell just from the sound of his voice.

"You bet it is." Mrs. Kornbluff nodded fiercely. "I work seven days a week. I never take vacation. Never get weekends off. Weekends are my busiest time! You should come to my office. I have my wall, my picture wall, *full* of pictures of happy couples I have made. If I am successful with you, I'll put your picture up too!"

"So, what's the process?" Laurel asked.

Their wine arrived and both Laurel and Mrs. Kornbluff took the moment to take a long swallow.

Mrs. Kornbluff set her glass down and leaned forward. "I interview you. Find out what you want. Do my own psychological assessment, if you will." She cackled merrily. "Then I do an intensive search. I'm talking *an intensive search*. Then I screen all the potential husbands, find the ones most compatible with you and your needs, and there you are!"

"Hunky-dory," Laurel said.

Mrs. Kornbluff grinned. "Hunky-dory."

"Do you think we should have told her we weren't serious about marrying whoever she finds for us?" Laurel asked later that evening, after they'd dropped a very tipsy Myra Kornbluff off at her ancient apartment building on upper Connecticut.

Joe could tell that Laurel had been surprised when he'd submitted to Mrs. Kornbluff's "interview," comprising a variety of questions, a number of which seemed unrelated to the project at hand.

What kind of cereal you like in the morning? You a cereal man? Toast? Eggs? Beer? What?

You're, what, thirty-nine? Forty? You ever have one of those little pigs as a child? What're they called? Guineas? Guineas pigs?

Can you read that sign from here? What's it say?

Joe turned his face to Laurel. Her features were shadowed in the dim light of the Explorer. He'd had the feeling all night that he had somehow displeased her with this idea, but he wasn't sure how. That was one reason he'd decided to go along with the interview.

"Aren't we serious about this?" he asked. Had the experience with Peter Lowery been so bad that she'd changed her philosophy? A tickle of hope twitched within him.

Laurel shifted in her seat so she better faced him. "Well, you. I mean, you. You don't want to get married, right? I mean, not this way."

He shrugged and kept driving, past the Uptown Theatre, the Four Provinces, stopping at the light before Rock Creek Park. He hadn't been thinking about himself much at all. He figured he'd go out with whomever Kornbluff found for him, but it was Laurel he'd be watching.

"Are you telling me," she said finally, "that you're considering Dr. Nadalov's approach? You're thinking this Kornbluff woman might find you someone . . . ?" She trailed off, rolling a hand in front of her as if searching for an appropriate word.

He waited a minute. When she didn't continue, he said, eyeing her, "I'm keeping an open mind."

The look she sent him could only be described as alarmed. He smiled to himself.

"What are you smirking about?" she asked.

He dropped the smile. "Nothing. Just wondering what old Myra has in store for us."

She scrunched back around in her seat so she was facing forward again, and huddled down into her coat.

They drove in silence. Around Dupont Circle and down Massachusetts Avenue toward her place on the Hill.

He thought about the last time he'd dropped her off, about how he'd gone in, about how he'd stayed. She'd been amazing that night. So uninhibited that he'd thought, for a fleeting time, that she might actually be changing her mind about him.

Certainly he'd changed *his* mind about *her.* For the first time he'd thought she was reachable.

That what he'd always hoped was the charade of her wanting an arranged marriage had actually shown itself to be just that.

For the first time since he'd met her, it had been just the two of them in that room together. No Dr. Nadalov, no boss waiting for a column, no imaginary man she thought she needed instead of him. Just the two of them. Just the two of them together, with him feeling things he'd never felt before. For the first time he wondered if there might actually be something to the idea of a soul mate.

But he'd stopped by the next night and there she'd been, all ready to go back to Short Stops. He'd had the unpleasant sensation of being slapped in the face.

It wasn't that he'd kidded himself that she'd changed her mind, that he would show up that following night and she would fall into his arms. But he'd thought her attitude might be changing. That he'd had a shot at . . . something.

But she had nothing on him when it came to keeping a sexual relationship sexual. He knew that now.

And he wasn't sure what he wanted to do about it.

He pulled up in front of her house and parked. The street was strangely empty, perhaps because it was Saturday night, perhaps because it was Valentine's weekend and everyone had gone out. In any case, he got a spot right in front of her place.

He put the SUV in park and cut the engine.

"When do you think we'll hear from her?" Laurel asked. She was looking straight ahead, down the street.

"What did she say? A week?" He shook his head. "I can't remember."

"Something like that." Laurel nodded.

"Are you ready for this?" He shifted so he was leaning back against his door. "I mean, after last night?"

She laughed tentatively. "I don't know. Last night . . . I guess it really shook me up."

He sat silently a minute, glad that she'd confided in him. "Laurel," he said softly. He wanted to reach out to her, touch her. Take her hand. "You—"

"I don't think I thanked you for that, for last night." She turned to him.

"You did."

"No, I mean appropriately." She took a deep breath in and for a second he thought she might cry. "God knows what you saved me from last night, Joe. That guy was nuts. Really nuts. Maybe seriously unbalanced. What would have happened if you hadn't shown up?"

She shook her head, obviously horrified at the thought.

"I mean," she continued, "he was already a little out of control. I was starting to get nervous right when you showed up and he—he'd . . ."

Joe's body tensed. "He'd *what*?"

If the man had touched her he'd kill him. He'd track him down and wring his hairy little neck.

She looked at him again and laughed slightly. "I don't mean that I thought he was dangerous. He was too small for that, for one thing." She laughed again.

"You never know, Laurel. Guys, well, they can be dangerous when they want to be, no matter how little they are." But Joe could've taken him. Joe *would've* taken him, by God. "What did he do?"

She waved a hand. "Oh he just kissed me. But it was . . . awful, somehow. Repulsive. Truly repulsive."

He didn't know why, or how, or what it meant, but that was the moment Joe knew he was in love, truly in love. The thought of her kissing someone else, even a man who *repulsed* her, ate at his insides as if he'd just chugged a glass of battery acid.

And realizing it, he knew he could not just have a sexual relationship with her. He wanted the whole nine yards.

"That's a bad sign," he murmured.

She laughed. "One of many. Apparently." She looked over at him.

She seemed to be waiting for something, and he wondered for a second if he'd missed a question she'd asked. Then he wondered if he should just lay his cards on the table and tell her how he felt.

But he couldn't.

He couldn't because he wouldn't be able to bear it if she said, "Joe, you're a really nice guy, but . . ."

Plus she was all geared up again for this *yenta*

thing. The damn stupid marriage broker that he himself—the colossal idiot—had arranged. What had he been thinking?

That she wouldn't go along with it. That after last night she'd realize the whole idea was a mistake. That—maybe—the person she really wanted was him.

He nearly laughed at himself. He was even more foolishly romantic than she thought.

"So, you going to write about Mrs. Kornbluff?" he asked.

"Yeah. Just the basic premise. Then next week I'll report back on our dates. You think she'll let us have them on the same night at the same place?"

He shrugged. "Not up to her. I don't know why we couldn't make it a double date." After last night, he couldn't stand the thought of her cornered by another, perhaps—*hopefully*— repulsive, man.

Her brows rose. "A double date?" She thought a moment. "A double date. That's a *great* idea."

Yeah, a great idea, he thought darkly. One of many. Apparently.

Seventeen

Laurel was just finishing up the column on Mrs. Kornbluff when Angela appeared in her office doorway. In her hand she held a copy of *Love Is Not the Answer*. One finger held her place near the beginning.

"Hey, Angela, what's up?" Laurel sat back in her chair. "How's Philip?"

Angela's smile said it all. "He's great. He said he never thought he'd meet someone who moved the earth for him at a keg party. Isn't that sweet?"

Laurel smiled. "You've got to like a guy who knows how to express his feelings."

Angela sighed. "I know. He's so good for me. Because I was always sort of . . . closed, before. Do you know what I mean? With my feelings."

Closed? Angela? Laurel had never seen a more open book. But maybe Angela harbored a completely different person under her smiling façade.

"So, if things are going so well with Philip, how come you're reading Dr. Nadalov?"

"Oh!" Angela looked down at the book in her hands and opened it. "I was looking at this for you. I wanted to see what you saw in it, but I found this in the introduction. Have you got a minute?"

"Sure."

Angela cleared her throat as if stepping in front of the whole tenth-grade class to read. " 'Acceptance of the premise and predications of this book might well be contingent upon the reader's prior knowledge and, in many cases, colluding concurrence with the ideas contained herein. Ideas which may strike the uninitiated reader as unusual or problematical might never be successfully assimilated into the recipient's cognition. This book should therefore be considered a tool only for those whose routes lie on this chosen path. Those who have chosen a different path most likely will be inaccessible to the ideas contained herein.' "

Angela looked up.

Laurel closed her mouth, which had dropped open during the reading.

"Isn't he, like, saying you have to believe this stuff already, before reading the book, to believe it at all?" Angela asked.

To her credit, she did not look smug, even

though Dr. Nadalov was essentially saying the book was crap unless you already believed it.

"Where are you reading from?" Laurel asked. She didn't remember that part at all, and she had read the thing cover to cover. Some chapters twice.

Angela looked down. "The introduction."

Laurel leaned back. The *introduction?* How could she have missed that? She hated missing introductions.

"I don't know what I was thinking," Laurel said to Sue the night of her double date with Joe.

She looked stunning. Or at least, as stunning as she could make herself look. She wore the short ankle boots he'd seemed to like and a short flirty dress with a plunging neckline. She'd put on enough makeup so that it *showed*—Sue's instruction—and had brushed her hair into careful, tousled disarray.

She had done all this, without kidding herself, for Joe. This, she'd finally confided to Sue.

"Well, damn, Laurel. Good for you! You finally know what you want."

"I don't know . . ."

"Oh, get off it. You want Joe. And you know it. Why do you have such trouble admitting what you want?"

"I don't have trouble. This is different. This is . . . rife with the possibility of failure. There's a very real chance he's not interested in me."

"Laurel, you've slept with the guy twice now.

Which I *still* can't believe you never *told* me about." She stopped, cleared her throat, and continued, "Which . . . okay, is beside the point, at the moment. But you've slept with the guy twice now, so he's *obviously* interested in you."

Laurel snorted. "Sure, for sex."

She brushed more blush on her cheeks, then wiped some off with a tissue. Then on second thought, brushed more back on. It needed to *show*.

"Maybe not even sex, though, anymore," she added. "He dropped me off the other night and I sat in his car forever, hoping he'd get out and open my door or walk me to my door or something, so maybe one thing could lead to another and . . . well, you know. But no, he was planted in that upholstery as if he were sewn into it."

"Did you ever think maybe he was waiting to be invited in?" Sue's voice was exasperated. "That maybe he was unsure what *you* wanted?"

"Joe is never unsure." That was one thing Laurel was certain of. If Joe wanted something, Joe went after it. He was nothing if not confident.

"Every guy is unsure. Kevin taught me that. They may *seem* like they know they hold all the cards, but every last one of them thinks we do."

Laurel stopped looking at herself in the mirror. She'd gotten to the point where she could only see the makeup, not the face. "Not Joe."

Sue scoffed. "Then I've got to meet this paragon of self-confidence. He sounds insufferable."

"That's just the problem," Laurel said despondently. "He's not. He's completely irresistible."

They were all meeting at Café Quiz. Laurel and her date, Mark Pfieffer. Joe and his date, Danielle Reese.

Danielle. The very name made her wilt. Danielles were pretty and graceful and feminine. Danielles were sophisticated and smart. *Danielle Reese.* She sounded like a model.

Laurel hated her already.

She tried to work up some enthusiasm for Mark Pfieffer but it was hard to do. She'd spoken to him on the phone and he'd sounded nice, but then so had Peter Lowery. Besides, she wasn't sure she had sounded so nice. And what kind of guy was he that he employed someone like Myra Kornbluff to find dates for him? Washington was *teeming* with women, for God's sake. What was the matter with him?

Oh shut up, she told herself. It was all just smoke to cover up the fact that she was afraid that her feelings for Joe were going to show. That seeing him with the gorgeous *Danielle Reese* was going to put her over the edge.

She entered Café Quiz with some trepidation. She didn't see Joe, so she started scanning the crowd for Danielle. There were several tall pretty women at the bar, but they were together. She didn't think anyone would show up for a marriage-brokered date with a group of friends. There was another pretty woman coming out of the restroom—a blonde, Danielle would probably be blonde—and Laurel moved into the bar to get a closer look.

"Laurel?" A male voice beside her made her jump.

She turned to see a nice-looking man in his late forties, in a blue suit with a yellow tie looking at her expectantly.

"Yes." Surprise tinted her voice as she realized she hadn't given one thought to looking for Mark Pfieffer. "You must be Mark."

He smiled, a warm, pleasant smile. No aura of the legally restrained about him. "Nice to meet you."

He actually looked pleased at the sight of her, his eyes surreptitiously scanning her the way hers had scanned him a moment before. She hoped her expression looked as optimistic. On the plus side, he looked much more normal and far more appealing than Peter Lowery had at first sight. He had nicely groomed, distinguishedly graying hair, and a youthful, pleasant face. His eyes were blue, with a look of intelligence in them.

But it was all she could do to stop scanning the room for Joe, and Danielle.

"I've got a couple seats at the bar." Mark extended one hand in that direction. "Do you want to have a drink while we wait for the others?"

"Wonderful," Laurel said.

They chatted for a while and Laurel had no idea what she said. For all she knew she'd agreed to marry him as soon as they finished dinner. The only thing she could concentrate on was the door, and whether or not the next person to come through it would be Joe.

Mark, from what she absorbed in the short moments she could tear her preoccupation from the entryway, was a successful investment banker with a sailboat in Annapolis and a town-house in Old Town Alexandria. He'd even been on a talking heads show on PBS for a while, offering his expertise on investments. Maybe that's why he looked vaguely familiar, she thought, focusing on him completely for the first time since she'd arrived.

"And you're a writer," Mark said, appearing genuinely interested.

"Yes, a staff writer and editor for *DC Scene*. Though someday I'd like to write for something a little more serious, maybe do some feature writing."

"*DC Scene* . . . I've seen that paper around. I'm afraid I've never read one, though." He looked apologetic.

She smiled. "Don't worry about it. Apparently a lot of people haven't. Circulation is a major obsession of the publisher's."

She remembered Rulinda's exultation over the response to Laurel's column. "We've upped the print run twenty percent!" Rulinda had crowed, grabbing Laurel's hands and twirling her around the office once. Which was better than a big sloppy kiss, Laurel had thought.

"My problem is that I'm a slow reader," Mark was saying. "It's all I can do to get through the *Wall Street Journal* and the *Financial Times* every morning."

"Hey there." Joe's voice jerked her to attention and his hand on her shoulder made her nerves sing. It was a companionable touch, just to get her attention, but it shot through her body like a laser.

Laurel turned to see him holding out a hand toward Mark Pfieffer. "Hi. Joe Squires."

Mark stood up, a full head shorter than Joe. "Mark Pfieffer."

It wasn't until Mark turned to Joe's left that Laurel noticed the woman next to him. There, about Laurel's height, with her same coloring, an easy, white smile and an air of confidence Laurel could detect even though the woman hadn't said a word, was Danielle Reese.

The two of them looked great together, Laurel thought. Like movie stars. She was even fairly certain Danielle was wearing Armani. And she knew the shoes were Kate Spade.

Joe made the introductions.

"So, Danielle," Mark said, "what do you do?"

Was it Laurel's imagination or was Mark looking interested in Danielle too? With both the men looking at the other woman, Laurel felt like a piece of gum stuck on her barstool.

"I'm a writer," Danielle said.

Laurel's ears pricked. "Really? What do you write?"

"Laurel's a writer too," Joe explained, tipping his head toward Danielle to speak, in what already looked like familiarity.

"Really?" Danielle was all politeness. "I write for *Time* magazine. Features, mostly, an occasional Op Ed. What sort of writing do you do, Laurel?"

That's why the name had sounded familiar. Danielle Reese wrote for *Time*. Regularly. Laurel had read her stuff dozens of times. Read it and admired it.

Laurel looked at the woman with new eyes and felt as if she was looking at a smarter, more confident, more successful version of herself. Like Danielle was the real person and Laurel just the shadow.

They even sort of looked alike, though Danielle was much, much prettier than she was.

"Me? Oh, I just write a little column." She waved a hand dismissively. Danielle's eyes were still on her expectantly, so she added almost under her breath, "For *DC Scene*."

"For who? I'm sorry," Danielle leaned toward her.

Was she *trying* to humiliate Laurel? Not that it was Danielle Reese's fault that she wrote, as Peter Lowery had so aptly put it, *a two-bit column in a third-rate paper*.

"*DC Scene*," Laurel said, leaning toward Danielle so she didn't have to shout it over the noise in the bar.

Danielle straightened, a smile on her face. "I

love that paper! It's by far the best for local events, and their Bizarre Tales is classic. Everybody talks about it. And—oh my God." Her eyes widened.

Laurel glanced at Joe, who was looking at Danielle with that half-amused, half-admiring look he had. She used to think that look was just for her. Her heart twisted.

"*You're* Laurel Kane," Danielle said, then laughed and put a light hand on Joe's forearm. "I mean, I know you just introduced us." She turned back to Laurel, her hand lingering on Joe's arm. "But you wrote that column on that book. What was it?" She thought earnestly, tapping a finger just above Joe's watch. "Just a couple weeks ago. It was fascinating . . ."

"*Love Is Not the Answer*," Laurel supplied, prying her eyes from Danielle's feminine fingers.

"Right!" She laughed and glanced from Joe to Mark, who were both smiling with her, damn them. "That column is the reason I called Mrs. Kornbluff!"

"You're kidding," Joe said.

Danielle shook her head, her dark curls falling with masterful nonchalance around her shoulders. She finally removed her hand from Joe's arm and put a few locks behind one ear. "I thought it was brilliant." Despite the attention of both her own date and Laurel's, she smiled openly at Laurel. "You're really good, you know."

So she was nice. *Dammit*. So she was pretty

and successful and ridiculously nice. So what? Laurel could hate her anyway.

Could and would.

Joe tried not to glare at Mark Pfieffer but it was hard. The man was clearly full of himself, going on about his *good fortune* in buying this stock at the right time, and the *sheer luck* of buying his house just before the real-estate boom, and the reasons not everyone would want a Jaguar but why it's the right vehicle for him.

Pompous ass.

He was just what Laurel was looking for.

Successful, stable, well-spoken, and clearly taken with Laurel. The man could hardly keep his eyes from the teasing, gaping, all-out sexy neckline of her dress.

Investment bankers, Joe argued to himself, were not so stable. Those guys could lose their shirts in a second, if they weren't smart.

"So diversifying portfolios is what I specialize in," Mark Pfieffer said, as if in answer to Joe's thoughts. "There's no being too careful in this business."

Laurel actually looked interested in his financial philosophizing. She was probably mentally checking off every criterion on her list for the Perfect Mate. Good job—check. Nice car—check. Nice suit—check.

After a brief time, a waiter seated them and gave them menus. There was an awkward moment with the wine list, when both Joe and Mark reached for it, but Joe deferred to him immediately. He was rewarded with Mark ordering a cheap Beaujolais, though he wasn't sure this stinginess was apparent to Laurel. She and Danielle were too engrossed in conversation to notice.

Shortly thereafter, they ordered dinner. Danielle had soup and a large salad, same as Laurel.

Joe and Mark both ordered steak, as if proving their manhood to each other.

Joe looked from Laurel to Danielle, as they talked about writing. It was almost uncanny, how alike they looked, though Laurel was much, much prettier. And that they were both writers was even weirder. Myra Kornbluff either had a finely tuned sense of humor or she really did have some psychological acuity. He remembered the way she'd tapped her temple and nodded knowingly at the two of them.

Mark Pfieffer was telling Laurel about how he liked to go to museums when he found himself with unexpected free time.

"This city is full of them," he said. "And I like the challenge in finding the most obscure, most specialized. For example, did you know that there's a museum of dollhouses? And a postal museum? There's also the National Cryptologic Museum, but I haven't been there yet."

Joe smiled, thinking of Mark Pfieffer wandering through a museum full of dollhouses.

Laurel was nodding. "That's fascinating,

Mark, really fascinating. I had no idea." She turned to Danielle. "And what about you, Danielle? Do you have any hobbies?"

Danielle set her fork down and wiped her lips before answering. "I don't know if you'd call it a hobby, but I'm taking a class in photography. I'd like to be able to add it to my résumé and provide features with my own photographs."

She turned to Joe with a smile. "That's why I asked you earlier if I smelled like chemicals. I just came from the darkroom where I was developing photos I took last month of children in India. You were so sweet." She turned back to Laurel. "He said I smelled like springtime."

Actually, Joe had thought she'd smelled like Irish Spring soap, but he'd amended it at the last minute.

For some reason Laurel looked as if she might cry. "You were just in India?"

"Yes, I was doing a piece on the effect of the conflict with Pakistan on Indian children living along the border, and I took my camera with me. If I can convince my editors I'm good enough to write and provide the photos, it would mean more money for me, but savings for whomever I decide to write for."

"That sounds smart." Laurel pushed some lettuce around on her plate. "I guess you get to do a lot of traveling."

Joe's glance moved to Mark, who was concentrating on his steak, pinning it to the plate with his fork as if it might get away while he sawed at it with his steak knife.

"That's my favorite part of the job," Danielle was saying. "Like, last year I went to Utah to do a piece on mountain biking, and the magazine had to send me and a photographer. If I could do both, I'd be a much more attractive writer to hire."

"Where'd you go? Moab?" Mark took a break from his meat carving long enough to ask.

"Exactly. Have you been?" Danielle looked delighted.

"No, but I've always wanted to go. I've heard it's beautiful out there."

"Oh, it *is*. And the biking is incredible." Off she went on a detailed description of the trip, with Mark asking salient questions and Danielle being thrilled at his familiarity with the topic.

Joe decided that if he had to pick one thing he liked best about Danielle, it was that he didn't have to make any effort at all to entertain her. She did all the entertaining for the entire table.

Of course, she was helped some by Miss Inquisitive. Why Laurel was asking her so many questions he couldn't fathom. Was she feeling shy around her date? It was clear to him that he was just what she was looking for.

Joe watched Laurel across the table. After a second, Laurel turned her gaze to him. He made a slight motion with his head and a second later excused himself to go to the restroom. He only had to wait a minute before Laurel showed up in the back hall too, the exact spot where they'd had one of their earliest conversations, he recalled fondly.

The day he'd first decided Laurel Kane was far more interesting than anyone he'd met in a long time.

And now, here he was, handing her over to another man.

Not, however, without the hope that she might refuse to go . . .

"I have a confession to make," he said when she appeared near the restrooms.

He stood near the phones where he'd been that night months ago, when Miss Vampy Hair—Carla—had come out of the bathroom.

Laurel knew that her irritation at his pursuit of Carla had been due to her budding feelings for Joe. It was so obvious now, in hindsight.

Hell, maybe it had been obvious then too. She'd just been too busy making up reasons why it didn't matter what she felt for him.

She wished she could convince herself of those reasons now.

"A confession?" she asked.

He wore a gentle smile, not his usual teasing one.

"I never slept with Carla." He crossed his arms over his chest and cocked his head.

The statement surprised her. "What?"

"Carla, the girl with the hair?"

"I know who Carla is. You didn't sleep with her?"

He shook his head. "Nope."

She frowned, wondering if he was making this up, but she couldn't think of a reason why he would do that. "Why not?"

He laughed.

She shook her head. "I mean, if you didn't, why did you tell me that you did?"

"Because it seemed to bug you. And for a long time bugging you was really fun for me."

She looked into his gray-green eyes. How could she feel so comfortable with this man, and so threatened by him at the same time?

"Bugging me isn't fun now?" Sadness seemed to tug at her soul. She was going to lose him.

His smiled broadened. "You sound disappointed."

She forced a smile, then dropped her head. "I guess I've liked bugging you too. I'd hate to think it was something we're supposed to give up."

He didn't say anything and she lifted her head up again. His expression had turned serious.

"Something tells me you didn't invite me back here to tell me about Carla." She had an inexplicably bad feeling about this. About the whole evening, really. There he was, with a woman who was everything Laurel *wished* she could be, and all she could think about was how long it had taken her to realize that Joe was the one she wanted. He'd been right there in front of her the whole time. And she'd wasted her time with the Larry Lutzkis and Peter Lowerys of the world.

What an idiot.

"I didn't," Joe agreed. "Listen, I thought maybe I'd suggest going someplace else for dessert. Then you and Mark can go off by yourselves somewhere. If you want," he added in what appeared to be an afterthought.

Laurel's stomach plunged. He was scraping her off. He wanted to be alone with Danielle. He'd been attracted to Laurel once, but now he saw that he could have someone much better.

She'd blown it.

Of course, she knew she'd blown it before; but now, in the face of his obvious attraction to someone else, it was undeniable. If she'd only realized earlier that Joe—*Joe*—was the one, he would never have met Danielle. Now she'd lost him. And she'd be stuck going to doll museums with Mark Pfieffer for the rest of her life.

Or maybe not. He was out there with Danielle now, engrossed in the topic of mountain biking. If she didn't get back soon, she'd have lost him too.

"Uh, sure," she said, averting her eyes from Joe's. She didn't want him to see her heart breaking in her eyes. "Yeah, you and Danielle probably want some time alone too."

He cleared his throat, hesitated a moment, then said, "Sure."

"She seems to really like you." Laurel glanced at him but he was looking at the floor now too.

He chuckled. "I don't know how you can tell. She's spent most of the time talking business with you, and she's out there now yukking it up with your date."

Good God, she realized with horror. It was more serious than she'd thought. She'd never seen Joe without an abundance of self-esteem and now here he was, modestly brushing off her compliment.

"Joe, she can't keep her hands off you. And she looks at you like . . ." *Like she'd like to cover you with whipped cream for dessert,* she thought, but she didn't want to give him any ideas.

He grinned. "Like . . . ?"

Laurel blushed and ran a hand through her hair. So much for carefully tousled. She was now genuinely disarrayed. "Like she's got plans for dessert herself."

Joe laughed. "Why, Laurel. You flatter me."

She couldn't stand his laughter, his obvious good mood. He was attracted to Danielle and Danielle was attracted to him. Good for them.

She just wanted to get the hell out of there and go home, where she could start kicking herself for losing the one man she'd ever really been in love with.

The realization nearly knocked her off her feet.

She was in love with the man. And she knew it because she wanted him to be happy, even if it meant handing him over to another woman. Especially because it meant handing him over to another woman. If she'd had to handpick someone for Joe other than herself, she'd have chosen Danielle Reese, the woman she herself would like to be.

"So okay. I'll just suggest to Mark that we go to my place for dessert. I think I've got some ice cream or something." She shrugged and looked off down the hall. An emergency exit sign lit a door at the end. She fervently wished she could disappear through it and not have to finish out this painful evening.

"Your place?" Joe repeated.

"Yes, I think it would be best if we were alone," she said, not that she actually planned to let him in. Not after what had happened with Peter. But it would be easier to tell him she wasn't interested in pursuing a relationship—or rather, a marriage, since that's what Mrs. Kornbluff had been setting up—in a less public place.

She glanced at Joe. His face was flushed. Excitement at being alone with Danielle?

"Fine, sure," he said. "Danielle and I'll get out of your hair."

Her heart ached—actually *ached*—so badly she brought a fist to the center of her chest. "Great. Okay. I'll talk to you later."

She started to turn.

"Uh, Laurel?"

She turned back. He looked unnerved. Was he *nervous* around Danielle? If so, he was more attracted to the woman than Laurel had even feared.

"When do you want to get together? Uh, to talk about the column, I mean? Tomorrow?"

She imagined having to see him tomorrow, or worse, having to get a phone call saying he and Danielle had decided to spend the day together too.

She shook her head. "Let's make it Sunday, okay?"

His cheeks were definitely red. "Is that enough time for you to write the column? I mean, I could . . . I just thought tomorrow would be better."

"I can write my half tomorrow. Sunday's fine."

"Sunday's fine," he repeated.

They stood in awkward silence a moment more. Did Joe know how hard this was for her? Is that why he looked like he wanted to say more?

"Well," she said finally. "We should get back to the table."

He cleared his throat. "Yeah, right. Back to the table."

Yes, back, Laurel thought, *to the drawing board.*

Eighteen

"Can I tell Myra she can put our picture up?" Mark Pfieffer pulled into an empty spot on her street and turned off the Jag's engine. He turned to face her, one arm resting from the back of his seat to the back of hers, his hand not quite touching her shoulder.

She could see his smile in the light from the streetlamps. Under her hands, Laurel felt the softness of the glove-leather seats and figured it was about par for her course that she realized the flaw in her plan just when it might actually have worked.

"I don't know, Mark," she began and watched his smile fade. "I'm just not sure about . . . this process is . . . I just don't think I can—"

"It's Joe, isn't it?" he interrupted.

From what she could tell in the dark, he didn't appear to be angry. But he wasn't happy either.

She sighed. *Yes, yes, it's Joe. It's all Joe. It's only Joe. Joe is the one.*

But am I the one for him?

"Joe and I are just friends." She felt her cheeks burn. Mark had probably noticed how successful a match Joe and Danielle seemed to be and the last thing she needed tonight was pity.

Mark laughed, and she sensed an edge to it. "Then I'd watch out. You may be friends with him, but from the way he was looking at you I'd say he's after something more."

Her eyes flashed up to his. "Really?" Then, at the hope in her own voice, she said, "I think you might have misinterpreted that. He seemed pretty interested in Danielle to me."

Mark shrugged and looked out his window, quiet.

Laurel felt guilty. What did you owe a date that you'd gotten through a marriage broker? Weren't you supposed to give it more of a chance than this?

But she couldn't do it. Not anymore. She knew who she wanted.

"Listen, Mark, I'm sorry. I probably shouldn't have gone through with the date." She picked her purse up from the floor of the car and looked at him. He still faced out the driver's side window. "Would you like to come in for that ice cream anyway?"

He looked down at his lap. "No. No, that's all right."

She hated this. Had she hurt him? She felt terrible. How bad was this? She kneaded her purse strap in her hands.

"I'll tell Mrs. Kornbluff you were perfect for me. I mean, really, you were. You are," she said, her words coming quickly. "It's just . . . it's just *me*. I'm confused about what I want. I have been for a long time, actually."

She looked down her street, at the line of streetlamps casting pools of light in front of the Victorian townhouses. She remembered the time Joe had sauntered under the streetlamp in front of her apartment the night her mother had shown up. Her heart had leaped at the sight of him, and she'd had to trample it down with words and philosophies and deliberate misconceptions about the kind of man he was.

What a fool she was.

"Mark, you're such a nice guy," she said. "I hope I haven't upset you."

He turned back to her. "No, no. You didn't upset me. I'm just wondering . . ." He had a strange look on his face and his fingers played nervously with the keys hanging from the ignition.

Trepidation ate at her stomach. He was obviously tense, obviously not happy with the way the evening was playing out. She should never have gone through with this date. She hadn't been thinking about anyone but herself, as if she were the only one who'd be involved. She hadn't given a thought to how it might affect the hopes and plans of the man Myra Kornbluff found for her.

"What?" she asked gently. "What were you wondering, Mark?"

He cleared his throat. "Uh, do you happen to have Danielle's phone number?"

Laurel marched into her apartment and slammed the door behind her. She found her tote bag on the floor next to the couch and riffled through it, ripping papers and bending file folders without a thought.

Where is it? she thought savagely. *Where is the damn thing?*

She pawed through the overstuffed bag again, having missed it the first time, and finally found what she was looking for. Her fingers grasped the spine and she yanked the book from the bag, papers scattering on the floor.

"Dr. Nadalov," she said as if she faced the evil man in the flesh. *At last, we meet again.*

She ripped off the dust jacket and tore the good doctor's face in half. Then, casting her gaze around the room, she moved toward the kitchen. Halfway there she doubled back to the cluster of vanilla candles on the table near the wall. A book of matches lay beside them. She snatched it up and headed toward the kitchen again.

She moved to the sink, set the book next to it, heedless of the puddle of water it landed in, and began wadding up the pieces of dust jacket. She put them in the sink, lit a match and touched it to a crinkled corner.

Blue flame curled around the edges of the paper. She lit another match and touched it to the other paper ball, so both of them glowed in the darkness of the kitchen. She stood watching them, thinking she should write a letter to the man, telling him he was full of crap.

You couldn't talk yourself out of believing in love. You couldn't take the single biggest relationship of your life and turn it into nothing but a contract. Feelings were involved, whether you wanted to believe it or not.

And feelings could not be ignored.

She knew. She'd tried.

But then there was that statement Angela had read to her. Nadalov *knew* you couldn't turn off your feelings—that's why he'd written that incomprehensible disclaimer in the introduction.

The burning dust jacket began to blacken and fade, so she opened Dr. Nadalov's book and gleefully ripped out the introduction. She'd never in her life destroyed a book like this, but by tearing the pages in half she felt more powerful than she had in years. She fed the pieces to the embers of what was left of the dust jacket in the stainless-steel sink, feeling gratification as the flames licked the paper and words disappeared, crumbling into meaningless ash.

She was on chapter three, "Exposing the Biological Imperative," when the doorbell rang.

She froze.

Then she glanced at the clock. It was nearly eleven thirty.

Her heart pounded in her chest. Could it be

Joe? She couldn't imagine him leaving Danielle so quickly.

The way her luck was running lately it was probably Peter Lowery.

The very thought had her nerves clenching in anxiety. There'd be no Joe to help her if it was. He was off with the beautiful and perfect Danielle Reese of *Time* magazine. She'd be on her own, as she was probably going to be for the rest of her life.

She crept out of the kitchen, debating whether or not to answer the door. The lights were on in the living room, so someone would know she was home from the curtained windows up at street level.

She walked to the door and pressed her palms against it. Leaning in, she called, "Who is it?"

A second passed. She wasn't sure she'd said it loud enough.

Then, "It's Joe," came through the wood.

Relief cascaded over her.

She fumbled with the locks, then flung the door open. "Joe." The word came out on an exhale of sheer happiness. Her mouth curved into a huge, relieved smile.

Joe, on the other hand, looked abnormally serious. His hands were shoved into his pants pockets and his collar was pulled up against the cold. "Hi."

He made no move to come in, so she asked, "What are you doing here?"

Had Danielle not invited him in? What, was she *crazy?*

"I, uh . . ." For the second time that night, she thought he was blushing. He peered around her into the apartment. "I hope I'm not interrupting anything."

She looked behind her into the empty room, thought of the blackened pages of *Love Is Not the Answer* in the kitchen sink. "No, not at all." She turned back to him. "Oh no, Mark went home."

He exhaled. "Good. I didn't see a Jaguar parked anywhere on the street, so . . ."

She nodded. "It was a nice car," she said, for lack of anything else.

He paused. "Look, I, uh . . ."

"Why don't you come in?" She stepped back from the door.

He paused, then entered the room.

She locked the door behind him. Her heart pounded in her ears. If he was here, that meant he was not at Danielle's. And if he was not at Danielle's, that meant . . . Her heart pounded faster. What did that mean?

"Listen, I don't know why I felt the need to do this right now." Again, for the second time that night he looked uncharacteristically unsure of himself. "I found this at my house a few weeks ago, and I think it belongs to you. I've been meaning to give it back for a while now."

He pulled his hand from his pocket and extended it toward her. Perplexed, she took a step forward and peered into his palm.

Shining in the overhead light was her grandmother's shamrock charm.

She inhaled sharply. "Oh my God, I thought I'd lost it!" She picked the metal up, noting how much shinier it was. "I guess I *did* lose it. Where did you find it?"

"In my front hall. I think that morning you dropped your purse . . ." He let the rest of the sentence hang unsaid.

That was the morning after they'd slept together the first time. The morning she'd thought it had all been a terrible mistake.

The mistake, she now realized, was in not acknowledging that being with him was the best she'd ever felt in her life.

She glanced up at him through her lashes. "I was such a jerk that morning."

He shook his head. "No you weren't."

They were silent a minute, standing awkwardly in the middle of her living room.

"Did you polish this?" She turned the shamrock over in her palm. She didn't remember it ever looking so pretty.

He chuckled. "Yeah. I don't know why. I guess I was curious about it. You know, why you carried it."

She couldn't help the smile that tugged at her lips. "And you thought the answer would come if you polished it?"

His eyes glinted wryly, the first familiar expression he'd worn since he got here. "Maybe I thought I'd get three wishes if I rubbed it."

She laughed. "And did you?"

He shook his head slowly, his expression sobering. His eyes were intent on hers, but she had no idea what he was thinking. Or if he knew what *she* was thinking.

Which was that she'd like to throw herself into his arms and beg him to forget not only Danielle, but what a fool she herself had been all these months.

She dropped her gaze to the shamrock in her hand. "I carry it because it was my grandmother's." She told him the rest of the story.

At the end, he crossed his arms over his chest and asked, "So why did she marry your grandfather?"

Laurel shrugged. "She wanted children. And she knew her lover wasn't coming back. I guess she just decided she wanted to get . . . married." She looked up at Joe.

His eyes were smiling now, his lips just slightly curved. "And how did that work out for her?"

Laurel laughed, never realizing how close her own story might have gotten to her grandmother's until this moment. "Not very well. By the time she died, the way she talked about my grandfather, you'd think she hated him. It was quite sad, really."

She looked again at the charm in her hand, the

familiar shape and weight of it, the unfamiliar shine.

"I don't know why I've kept this." She shook her head. "It really isn't very lucky."

"Maybe not," Joe said.

His voice was quiet and she looked up at him. His light eyes seemed to glow with warmth.

"Maybe you didn't keep it because it was lucky," he added. "Maybe you kept it because it was romantic."

She looked back down at the charm, a laugh escaping her lips before she could stop it. She placed the fingers of her other hand to her lips.

It was true. She'd loved the story. She'd loved the tragic young man. She'd loved the way her grandmother had hung onto this trinket through decades, all because she remembered the love she'd had for that young man.

"Joe . . ." She was about to ask why he wasn't at Danielle's when the fire alarm in the kitchen let off an ear-piercing shriek.

She jerked around, realized immediately what it was, but before she could stop him Joe was running toward the kitchen. She followed him into the room. Low flames shot up from the sink, caressing the edge of the book cover where it lay open on the counter.

Joe flipped on the water, jerked up the sprayer nozzle, and doused the flames.

Laurel, one hand over one ear, yanked the smoke alarm off the wall, then pulled off the cover and removed the battery. They stood in the darkened kitchen in sudden silence. Smoke laced the air.

She turned to face Joe, who was examining the singed book and the sink full of ashes. Chapters one through three, she happened to know. Plus the introduction. He turned his head to read the cover on the unjacketed spine. Then he started to laugh.

He turned the book over, noted the missing pages and looked at the ashes, obviously putting two and two together.

He pivoted to face her, holding what was left of the tome.

Laurel blushed so hot she held her palms to her cheeks.

A quizzical expression crossed his face. "Should I take this to mean that you're renouncing the theories of the good Dr. Nadalov?"

Panic blossomed in Laurel's breast. Maybe it was the combination of the fire alarm and the burning book. Maybe it was the way he was looking at her, questioning and intent. But she was pretty sure it was the fact that she knew she had to tell him how she felt, no matter what the outcome might be.

"Joe . . ." Her voice emerged high and reedy. She cleared her throat. "Joe, can I ask you something?"

His eyes scanned her face. "You know you can."

"Are you . . ." *Just say it, dammit. Quit being*

a coward and go after what you want. She cleared her throat again. "Are you going to see Danielle again?"

He paused for so long she honestly thought she might pass out. Then she realized she'd stopped breathing. Slowly, she made herself inhale.

He shook his head. "No."

Adrenaline surged through her again.

"Why not?" Her voice cracked on the question. She said more firmly, "She was perfect for you."

He lifted a brow. "Was she?"

Laurel couldn't take it anymore. She turned away from him and gripped the counter on the other side of the galley kitchen. "Yes, God, I can't even believe how perfect. You guys even looked good together. She's"—she nearly choked on the words—"she's everything I wish *I* was!"

She heard him move, saw his hand on the counter near hers. "What are you talking about?"

"She's so successful, so outgoing. She writes for *Time*! She does her own photography. She mountain-bikes, for God's sake. She's confident and pretty and—"

"And she's not *you*, Laurel. She'll never be *you*."

She turned to face him, tears welling in her eyes. She tried to blink them away, but one rolled down her cheek. Moving a hand upward to push her hair from her face, she wiped it surreptitiously away.

She swallowed hard. "What do you mean?"

He was standing close now, looking at her so tenderly she knew he was either going to take her in his arms or break her heart.

A small smile touched his lips. He laughed slightly. "She looks a little like you. She does the same thing for a living that you do. She even ordered the same food for dinner you did. But she isn't you."

Despite herself, Laurel sniffed. She brought a hand to her mouth and looked at him standing there, in the dark of her smoky kitchen.

"Joe." Her voice emerged as barely a whisper. "I—I'm in love with you."

He exhaled sharply, his head dropping to his chest. She wasn't sure if that was a good thing or not, and she held the edge of the counter with hands that went white-knuckled.

Slowly, he raised his head and she saw the smile on his face. "Well, it's about damn time."

She laughed tentatively. "What?"

"I've loved you since the day you first read to me from that damn burned book."

Her lips curved and her eyes teared again. "Really?"

He nodded. "Really. But I need to know one thing, Laurel."

She nodded too. "I know. I know, Joe."

"You do?"

"Yes." She nodded, knowing that as well as he knew her, she knew him pretty well too. "You need to know, and I need to tell you, that, well, that I think love *is* the answer."

He laughed and she laughed with him.

"I mean it, though. This is real, Joe," she said, serious again. "And this is going to last."

With that, he took her in his arms and kissed her, his hands holding her head, her arms pulling him tightly to herself.

After a second he shifted back and looked down at her, his eyes glittering in the dim light. "I know the headline for your next column."

She smiled up at him, happier than she'd ever been in her life, here in his embrace. "Oh yeah? What's that?"

He squeezed her a little and grinned. "Plain Jane Marries Regular Joe."

The days may be getting longer, but the nights are definitely getting hotter with these sizzling titles, coming in May from Avon Books.

A DARK CHAMPION by Kinley MacGregor
An Avon Romantic Treasure

Stryder of Blackmoor has never desired the comforts of home and hearth—until he gazed upon the exquisite face of Rowena. He dares not succumb to her sensuous charms, but when treachery and danger threaten, the noble knight must stand as the lady's champion—though it could cost him his honor, his heart . . . and his forbidden dream of happiness.

WHAT MEMORIES REMAIN by Cait London
An Avon Contemporary Romance

Cyd Callahan has no memory of the terrible event of her childhood, and she'd rather the truth remain buried. Ewan Lochlain, however, is determined to unravel the mystery of his parents' deaths—and he's convinced Cyd holds the key. But Ewan realizes too late that his personal investigation may have just cost Cyd her life . . .

ONCE A GENTLEMAN by Candice Hern
An Avon Romance

Nicholas Parrish had no intentions of taking a bride, but when Prudence falls asleep in his townhouse, her irate father demands satisfaction. Being a true gentleman, Nicholas agrees to do the proper thing. But he may need to reconsider his plans for a "marriage in-name-only" when his bride decides to make him fall in love with her!

THE PRINCESS AND THE WOLF by Karen Kay
An Avon Romance

Married by proxy to a European prince she doesn't love, the princess Sierra will not believe her husband died in far-off America—and crosses an ocean to discover the truth. But she will need a scout in this wild land, and puts her life in the hands of High Wolf, the proud Cheyenne brave she once loved . . . and should rightly have wed.

REL 0404

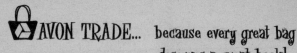